## *What in the world was wrong with her?*

"Good morning, Dan," Brynna managed in a reasonable facsimile of her normal voice. "Aren't you supposed to be on the air?"

"I promised my listeners twenty minutes of commercial-free music," he replied over the phone. "Weren't you listening?" he teased.

Her lips twitched with a smile. "I was listening earlier," she informed him. "But I turned the radio off when I got into the shower."

There was a moment of silence, followed by the rather hoarse query, "Did I interrupt your shower?"

She honestly hadn't meant to be provocative, but his tone told her that her words had conjured up a mental image for him. She swallowed hard. She wasn't used to being part of a man's fantasies. Yet there was something incredibly erotic about being part of Dan's....

Dear Reader,

Welcome to the Silhouette **Special Edition** experience! With your search for consistently satisfying reading in mind, every month the authors and editors of Silhouette **Special Edition** aim to offer you a stimulating blend of deep emotions and high romance.

The name Silhouette **Special Edition** and the distinctive arch on the cover represent a commitment—a commitment to bring you six sensitive, substantial novels each month. In the pages of a Silhouette **Special Edition**, compelling true-to-life characters face riveting emotional issues—and come out winners. Both celebrated authors and newcomers to the series strive for depth and dimension, vividness and warmth, in writing these stories of living and loving in today's world.

The result, we hope, is romance you can believe in. Deeply emotional, richly romantic, infinitely rewarding—that's the Silhouette **Special Edition** experience. Come share it with us—six times a month!

From all the authors and editors of Silhouette **Special Edition**,

Best wishes,

Leslie Kazanjian,
Senior Editor

# GINA FERRIS
## Lady Beware

Silhouette Special Edition

Published by Silhouette Books New York

**America's Publisher of Contemporary Romance**

For my mother-in-law, Edith Wilkins,
who shares my love of both
music—especially "soft
rock"—and reading..

SILHOUETTE BOOKS
300 East 42nd St., New York, N.Y. 10017

Copyright © 1989 by Gina Wilkins

ISBN: 0-373-09549-X

First Silhouette Books printing September 1989

All the characters in this book are fictitious. Any
resemblance to actual persons, living or dead, is
purely coincidental.

®: Trademark used under license and
registered in the United States Patent and
Trademark Office and in other countries.

Printed in the U.S.A.

**Books by Gina Ferris**

Silhouette Special Edition

*Healing Sympathy* #496
*Lady Beware* #549

## GINA FERRIS

has lived her entire life within twenty miles of the Arkansas hospital where she was born and is a confirmed armchair traveler as a result. "I haven't had an exotic life," she admits, "but it has been a happy one, filled with love and encouragement—which is probably the reason I enjoy writing happily-ever-after romances."

Gina met her husband when he sat beside her in her first college class at Arkansas State University, where she was studying journalism. "As foolishly romantic as it may sound," she says, "I knew by the end of that first class that he and I were special together." She began writing fiction when her second daughter was born four years ago and sold her first book a year later, fulfilling a longtime dream. Gina Ferris also writes under the name Gina Wilkins.

IOWA

**MISSOURI**

ILLINOIS

Jefferson City
★

KANSAS

Haskelville
•

Joplin    Springfield
•        •

OKLAHOMA    ARKANSAS

Underlined places are fictitious.

## Chapter One

The eyes met for only a moment and his life changed.

Dan Westbrook stopped in his tracks, gasping for breath, the sweat on his body drying in the breeze off the pond beside which he'd been running. Trying to look as if his halting had nothing to do with the slender blond woman sitting motionless on the park bench, he began some stretching exercises, pulling the weary muscles of his long, tanned legs. A trickle of perspiration ran into his shallow navel, causing him to swipe impatiently at his curl-matted chest. He shook his damp hair out of his eyes and glanced surreptitiously at the woman on the bench.

She was exquisite. Her hair, the delicate shade of white-blond that only nature could produce, tumbled in near-ringlets to her shoulders. Wispy bangs fluttered over her forehead in the breeze. Her skin was ivory pale and smooth, her legs, modestly revealed by the floral skirt she wore with a soft white sweater, long and delicately formed. Despite the nice curves visible to his discerning eyes, she looked as if it wouldn't hurt her to gain a few pounds.

And her eyes. Blue. Wide and clear. And so very sad. The eyes of a woman in pain.

He'd never considered himself an overly compassionate man. He didn't feel the need to give money to every street beggar he passed, or take in each homeless animal. Yet now he found himself fighting the oddest urge to take an unknown woman into his arms and comfort her.

Ridiculous. The woman would probably scream for the police.

Which didn't mean he couldn't speak to her. He was new in town, hadn't met many—make that *any*—eligible women as yet, and this one looked as if she had potential, despite the sad eyes. Could be she needed some cheering up. He knew just the good-time guy to do the job, assuming, of course, that she was unattached. Only one way to find out.

There was a water fountain a few feet to the right of the bench on which she sat. He casually headed toward it, intending to take a drink of water before approaching her equally casually. Which line would it be this time? Did she come here often? Hadn't they met someplace before? He could simply tell her he was new in town, looking for a friend. The old sympathy approach. Without undue conceit, Dan knew he was attractive enough to women to make those lines work. He was also fast enough on his feet to enjoy a few pleasant evenings with a woman and still manage to avoid messy and unwanted entanglements.

But not fast enough on his feet to avoid one small brown-and-black mutt of a dog.

Dan had taken maybe four steps toward the water fountain, his attention focused on the beautiful blonde, when something tangled around his feet. His eyes widened in surprise as he felt himself falling. He hit the ground hard, landing flat on his back. Air left his chest in a painful whoosh.

The next few moments passed in a haze. As he struggled to pull a razor-sharp breath into his deflated lungs, Dan was only dimly aware of the sounds around him. The mutt yapping in his face. A kid's voice griping because Dan had stepped on his dog. And another voice insinuating itself smoothly into the cacophony until finally it became the only one Dan heard. Breathing normally now, he blinked to clear his vision and found himself looking up into bottomless blue eyes a man could drown in, eyes set in the angelically beautiful face of the woman who'd been sitting on the bench.

"Are you all right?" she asked him, obviously not for the first time. Her voice was music.

Dan managed not to wince in chagrin that his smooth, practiced approach had gone so drastically awry. This wasn't exactly the way he'd wanted to get her attention. "Yeah," he answered, trying not to wheeze. "I'm okay."

The boy had managed to get his dog back on its leash, callously deserting the scene. Grateful that the park wasn't crowded enough to have given much attention to his fall, Dan struggled to sit up. The woman gave him a hand. Her skin felt like satin, he noted, even as he grimaced in pain at the movement. He wasn't seriously injured, but he'd have some dandy bruises the next day, he thought in disgust.

"Your shoulder is bleeding," the woman murmured in concern, taking a survey of his injuries. "And so are a couple of places on your back."

Dan glanced behind him. "Just scrapes from the rocks I landed on," he replied carelessly. "I'm sure they're not bad."

"You should put some antiseptic on them."

"Don't worry about it. I'll pick some up on the way back to my hotel," he assured her without really thinking about his words.

"Your hotel?" she repeated.

He nodded. "I just moved here last week. Haven't found a place to live yet."

"You'll never be able to treat those scrapes by yourself. Do you have anyone—" She stopped, her cheeks going a bit pink at the personal nature of the question. "Is there someone who can . . ."

"I don't really know anyone in town yet, other than the few people I've met on the job. But really, don't worry about it. I'll be fine. Thanks for being concerned."

His words seemed to bring her to a decision. She stood, straightening her skirt, and helped him up. "My house is just on the other side of the park. Why don't you follow me there and I'll treat those scrapes for you."

"There's no need for you to go to all that trouble."

She smiled. "Now what kind of a new neighbor would I be if I let those scrapes get infected?" she chided gently. "Welcome to Haskellville, Mr. . . ."

"Dan," he supplied. "And you're . . ."

"Brynna," she returned, following his lead and omitting her last name also. "I walked to the park. Do you have a car with you?"

He shook his head. "I'm staying at the Colonial Inn. Since it's less than a half mile from here, I jogged over." He adjusted his steps to match hers as she began to walk in the direction of her house. "Haskellville is a beautiful town," he commented when she made no effort to continue the conversation.

She seemed pleased by his remark. "It is, isn't it? I've lived here all my life and I still love it."

Dan couldn't imagine spending one's whole life in one town. He'd been bouncing from one state to another practically since birth, having been raised by a career-Navy father. Later, he'd chosen a career in radio and relocated whenever the opportunity to grab a bigger market came along. He smiled at the thought that this last move had been to a market smaller than he'd worked in a long time. Yet he had no intention of leaving Haskellville, Missouri, for many years.

Brynna led him out of the park, turning a corner that opened onto the residential street on which she lived. Dan paused in surprise. It was an older lane, laid with red brick. Huge trees lined the road, the spreading branches almost meeting overhead. He thought they'd be especially beautiful in late summer, when the leaves would be full and dark, providing shade for the street. The neatly landscaped houses were old, but very nice, obviously belonging to people with money. Brynna stopped at the second house on their left. Nice place. Not too big, not too small. Pale yellow with white shutters and trim and a long, inviting porch complete with porch swing. There'd be flowers in a few weeks. Lots of them.

It didn't look like the house of a single woman, Dan thought, suddenly conscious that he was wearing nothing but a pair of skimpy gray shorts and grubby running shoes. Would her husband wonder at her bringing home a bleeding, barely dressed stranger? He wished that he'd politely refused her kind invitation. He hadn't been thinking straight since he'd seen her.

"You know, I'm really not dressed for visiting," he commented as she unlocked the white door with its leaded glass panes. "And these scrapes have almost stopped bleeding. I think I'll just—"

"Don't be silly," she reassured him with a smile that affected him right down to his knees. "There's no one else here, so it doesn't matter what you're wearing. And those scrapes really should be cleaned. You fell hard."

"Your, uh, your husband's not here?" he asked awkwardly.

"I'm not married, Dan. I live here alone." Barely pausing in the floral-papered foyer, she headed straight back through the house, drawing him with her. "I think the kitchen will be best. It's right through here."

Dan gathered fleeting impressions of beautifully decorated rooms with more floral patterns, and then they were stepping through swinging doors into a large, bright kitchen. The room managed to look charmingly old-fashioned and efficiently modern all at once, he thought as Brynna settled him in a chair at the tiny kitchen table and began to rummage in the pantry for her first-aid kit. He hadn't been quite in control of things since he'd fallen over that dog, he mused in rueful amusement. He'd planned a smooth, practiced come-on to a beautiful woman; instead, he'd found himself meekly following her home so she could nurse his ridiculously minor injuries. Nice going, Westbrook.

He managed—barely—to be brave and stoic as she cleaned and treated the raw places on his back and shoulder. He even thanked her afterward without mentioning that they'd felt a lot better before she'd set them on fire with whatever she'd used as antiseptic.

"You're welcome," she said, smiling as if she knew exactly what he was thinking. He was inordinately pleased that the sad look he'd first seen in her eyes was gone now. This woman should never look so sad when she could smile like this.

Putting away her supplies, Brynna glanced over her shoulder. "You must be thirsty. Would you like a glass of iced tea?"

"That sounds great, if you have some made up."

She pulled a heavy glass pitcher out of the refrigerator and began to fill two glasses. "You say you've only been in Haskellville for a week?" she asked as she handed him his glass and slipped into the chair opposite him at the table to sip her own.

He nodded. "Eight days, actually. I'm the new owner of KHVL." He tried, but failed, to keep the pride out of his voice at that announcement. His own radio station—a goal he'd been working on for too many years to remember.

"How nice," she responded immediately. "That's my favorite station."

"It is?"

"Yes. I love the soft-rock-and-oldies format. And the new morning deejay is very good. Dan—" Her eyes widened. "Dan Westbrook. That's you, isn't it?"

This time he made no effort to hide his pleasure. "Yeah. I couldn't give up being on the air just because I've moved into management. I really enjoy morning drive time. You've heard my show?"

"You've been waking me all week," she admitted, again with that touch of pink blush he found so delightful. "My radio goes on at eight."

There was something agreeably intimate about knowing that his voice was the first she heard every morning. Hoping to capitalize on that intimacy, Dan leaned forward and gave her his most winning smile. "I'd like to take you to dinner tonight, Brynna. My way of thanking you for welcoming me so kindly to your town. Can I pick you up at eight?" It was short notice, but he hoped she'd be free on a Thursday evening.

He could almost see the friendly warmth leave her eyes, as if she'd deliberately pulled down shutters and closed him out. "I'm sorry, I already have plans for this evening."

He shouldn't have been quite so disappointed. After all, it wasn't the first time he'd been shot down, though it hadn't happened in a while. "Maybe tomorrow night?" he suggested instead, risking another rejection on the faint hope that she really did have plans and wasn't just making an excuse.

She shook her head, glancing pointedly at her watch. "Thank you, but no."

He took the hint. Draining his glass, he rose to his feet. "I suppose I'd better go. Thanks again for the first aid."

"You're welcome again. I'm sure we'll see each other around. Haskellville is a small town."

"You can bet we will," Dan promised. She didn't respond, though he thought he detected a flicker of wariness in those beautiful blue eyes. Surely she wasn't afraid of him, he wondered; not after she'd brought him into her home and had her hands all over him. Hadn't he been a perfect gentleman?

He was still moping over her firm rejection as he jogged halfheartedly back to his lonely, no-frills hotel room. But by the time he arrived his chin was tilted in a cocky gesture of confidence. It just wasn't in him to give up so easily. Beautiful Brynna was definitely someone whose acquaintance he wanted to pursue. She'd simply have to learn that he wasn't a man who took rejection easily.

Not that he had anything more in mind than an amusing and mutually satisfactory interlude, he told himself as he inserted the key into the door. Despite the odd sense of protectiveness he'd felt upon first seeing Brynna, he wasn't interested in long-term commitments, in serious relationships. He'd learned his lessons too well to repeat that particular mistake. But he and Brynna could have some good times for a while. He'd like to see more of that bewitching smile of hers, get to know that slender, enticing body much more intimately. All he had to do was convince her that he was just the guy to take the sad look out of her eyes and give her a reason to smile.

Chuckling at the arrogance of his thoughts, he headed for the shower, already planning how soon he could see her again.

"Good morning." The male voice was rich and husky, low and intimate. Brynna stirred on her pillow, her eyelashes fluttering against her cheeks as the words slipped softly into her consciousness. "It's eight o'clock. A beautiful morning in early April. Unseasonably warm, cloudless, fragrant. A day to be savored, treasured. A day to be happy."

Brynna's lashes lifted slowly and she focused blearily on the clock radio beside her bed. Happy? She remembered being happy. How she wanted to be again!

"I've got a special song to play this morning, dedicated to the beautiful blue-eyed blonde who welcomed me so kindly to her town yesterday. Every time I hear this song from now on, I'll think of the moment we met."

Brynna blushed, realizing that Dan Westbrook was speaking about her. She steeled herself for a sentimental, seductive love song, only to burst out laughing when the radio began to throb with the opening strains of "Another One Bites the Dust." Hardly the usual type of music for Dan's station, but so appropriate to the way they'd met. The man certainly had a healthy ego if he could laugh so at his own clumsiness.

And he'd made her laugh, as well. When was the last time she'd awakened to laughter, she wondered, her smile fading a bit.

Sighing softly, Brynna tossed back the covers and sat up, pulling her pale violet nightgown taut against her too-slender body. Leaving the radio on, she dragged a hand through her pillow-tangled hair and moved toward the bathroom. She was still humming the song Dan had played for her while she dried her hair some twenty minutes later. As she ran her comb through the cleverly cut top layers and down through the curls that fell around her shoulders, her reflection suddenly claimed her full attention.

She'd lost weight, a fact made evident by the prominence of her finely carved cheekbones and the hollows at the base of her throat. She noted the violet shadows beneath her eyes and the slight downward curve of her full mouth. She looked sad. Was this the way she looked all the time now? She glanced away, troubled by the thought.

This wasn't the way she wanted to look. Nor how she used to look. How many times had she been told that her smile lit up a dark room? How many people had once commented on the happy sparkle in her blue eyes? How many times had her father called her his sunshine?

Her throat tightened. *Oh, Daddy.*

She closed her eyes against the tears. "No," she said out loud. "I won't cry. I've cried enough."

It was time to stop mourning. Time to put her failed marriage and the more recent tragedy behind her and get on with her life. Time to be happy again.

On a new surge of determination, she marched into her bedroom, lifted the receiver of her extension phone, and punched a familiar number. "Mitzi? Hi, it's Brynna."

"Well, hi." Brynna's cousin-by-marriage sounded pleased to hear from her. They'd been friends for years, but had drawn especially close since the loss of Brynna's parents six months earlier. "How are you, Bryn?"

"Better," Brynna answered confidently. "Much better."

Surprised, but pleased, Mitzi responded immediately to the renewed optimism in her friend's voice. "Oh, I'm so happy to hear that."

"Mitzi, I want to help with the Festival. I'd like my old job back, organizing Show-Down. Has anyone else volunteered yet?"

"Angie Howerton said she'd do it only if nobody else would, but she's not too thrilled about it. I've made a few arrangements on my own already, but it desperately needs an organizer. Bryn, are you sure?"

"Yes. I'm sure. I need this, Mitzi."

"You're right. You do. So, get busy, kid. You've got a zillion-and-a-half things to do in the next three months."

Brynna laughed at Mitzi's enthusiasm—and the sound was welcome, even to her own ears. It had been too long since she'd felt like laughing. *Thanks, Dan,* she thought suddenly, picturing the entirely too handsome man who'd literally tumbled into her life.

She and Mitzi agreed to meet for lunch and discuss the plans for the Summer Festival held every July for the past thirty-odd years, sponsored by the Haskellville Women's Club. Brynna's mother, Alice Haskell, had been the organizer of the annual function for each of the past fifteen years. This year, Mitzi Haskell, wife of Brynna's cousin Perry, would have that responsibility.

"And now one of my favorite songs," Dan's voice announced from the bedside table as Brynna rummaged in her closet for something to wear. "Here Comes the Sun." Again, Brynna had the unsettling sensation that he was speaking directly to her.

As she dressed, she found herself singing along with the cheerfully optimistic Beatles tune. It happened to be one of her favorite songs.

It really was a beautiful day. Brynna hummed with the radio in her car as she drove to the country club where she'd agreed to meet Mitzi for lunch. Dan Westbrook was still on the air. His show lasted from 7:00 a.m. until noon and he'd chosen to play upbeat, cheerful songs that morning. The Fifth Dimension was singing, "Up, Up and Away" as Brynna drove past the lovely little park where she'd sat lost in bittersweet memories the evening before.

Suddenly another image crossed her mind. A man running in the park, tall, shirtless, his well-built legs exposed by gray shorts. Nicely developed chest accentuated with damp, dark whorls of hair. A thick head of hair that had looked black because of perspiration, but had dried a rich brown. Nice tan, strongly carved nose and chin. One long, sexy dimple down his right cheek. Penetrating eyes of a dark blue, almost navy. A grin that entreated her to smile in return.

Dan Westbrook. Just the thought of him made her shiver. It hadn't been easy turning down his invitation to dinner, but she'd been afraid to accept. It had been hard enough for her to treat the scrapes and bruises on his broad, solid back without making a complete fool of herself by stopping to stare and admire. Dan Westbrook was the very picture of a virile, sexual male. Something about him made her nervous, too much aware of him as a man, and of herself as a vulnerable woman. Much too vulnerable just now. She had to remember that.

She turned her small, American-made car into the parking lot of the Haskellville Country Club and spotted Mitzi just going inside. She pulled into a parking space, her mouth crooking into a smile as Dan Westbrook's voice came on again after a soft drink commercial. "It's twelve noon and time for me to sign off. This has been an entire morning of happy music dedicated to the pretty lady with the sad blue eyes. I hope you're feeling better today. And now with the news, here's—"

Brynna turned the key in the ignition, killing the car engine and, with it, the radio. Dan Westbrook wasn't a man who'd be easy to resist.

"So, who are we going to get as the Master of Ceremonies for Show-Down?" Mitzi asked, her red hair ablaze in the club's bright overhead lighting. She propped her gaminely pointed chin in one hand as she nibbled a pencil eraser and pored over a steno pad covered with her looping scrawl. Her half-eaten salad was pushed to one side and forgotten.

Brynna hadn't even thought about it, but barely hesitated before suggesting, "How about Dan Westbrook?"

Mitzi looked up, a puzzled frown forming a light crease between her uptilted green eyes. "Who?"

"Dan Westbrook, the new morning man at KHVL. I know you don't listen to that station, but he's very clever and amusing. I think he'd be very good as our emcee."

"I suppose you could talk to him and find out if he'd be willing," Mitzi agreed cautiously, "but we usually choose someone better known. Someone who's a draw, himself."

Knowing that thirty-three-year-old Mitzi was anxious about her first time as coordinator of the Summer Festival, Brynna understood her friend's hesitation. "I know, but I think by the end of July Dan Westbrook will be well-known around here, Mitzi. I read an article about him when he first took over at KHVL. It said he was quite popular in the larger markets he played. And—I've met him," she admitted.

Mitzi looked sharply at her friend, as if reading something into Brynna's words that Brynna had intended to keep to herself. "Have you? When was this?"

"Yesterday, in the park behind my house. A small dog got away from its owner and ran right under his feet, causing him to fall and scrape himself up pretty badly. I—uh—took him home with me and treated his injuries." Maybe she'd been a bit too honest, Brynna felt when Mitzi smiled broadly. Mitzi had been trying to get Brynna back into the social scene ever since Brynna's divorce almost a year earlier.

"Is he attractive?" Mitzi asked avidly.

Brynna shrugged with an attempt at nonchalance. "Yes, I suppose you'd say he's attractive. And he seemed very nice."

"He does sound like a definite possibility," Mitzi agreed, though Brynna had to wonder if her friend was still talking about the festival. "Why don't you talk to him about it?"

"Yes, I'll do that." What had she gotten herself into? Brynna wondered in near exasperation. Hadn't she already decided to stay away from Dan Westbrook? Still, this *was* business, of sorts. She'd coordinated the popular talent competition that closed out the Summer Festival several times, so she knew she'd be very busy during the upcoming weeks. She welcomed the diversion.

"I've already talked to several members of the Women's Club, and everyone's just thrilled that you're doing Show-Down again, especially Angie. You always do such a good job. We're also pleased that you—well, that you've decided to get involved in things again," Mitzi said delicately, choosing her words with care.

"You mean you're glad that I've stopped licking my wounds and have rejoined the living," she clarified bluntly, knowing how uncharacteristic her antisocial behavior of the past six months had been.

Mitzi, looking distressed, shook her curly head. "No, I *didn't* mean that! You had a perfect right to take some time to yourself after—" She couldn't finish the sentence.

Brynna could, to the relief of them both. "After Mother and Daddy were killed," she said clearly. "I really *am* learning to deal with it, Mitz. It's still horribly painful, of course, but I'm adjusting. I have to."

"Yes, you do," Mitzi agreed compassionately. "We all do."

Brynna took a deep breath and dropped her eyes for only a moment before meeting Mitzi's again. "How's Perry holding up?"

Mitzi ran her fingers through her mop of curls in a characteristically frazzled gesture, her mouth turning downward. "It's not easy," she admitted. "He always knew that he'd take over as CEO of Haskell Manufacturing, of course, but he certainly didn't expect it to be so soon—or so tragically. It's a big job for him to try to fill Uncle Bryan's shoes. Your father was such a brilliant businessman."

Brynna nodded, swallowing the all-too-familiar lump that immediately formed in her throat. "Yes, he was. But so is Perry," she said firmly. "He'll do a fine job. I know he will. I'm not at all worried about my stocks in the family company," she added with a weak smile, trying to ease the sadness that lurked beneath their conversation.

Brynna could have taken over the company herself, had she wanted to, but she'd decided years ago that she had no interest in the corporate world. She'd chosen marriage and her own career, leaving the business world to her father and her cousin. She'd never regretted that decision, didn't regret it now. If only she could recapture the joy she'd once known in her own work.

Mitzi closed her steno pad. "I'll give Perry your vote of confidence. He'll appreciate it." She hesitated a moment before asking, "What about your writing, Brynna? Have you written anything lately?"

"No. I just can't seem to get interested in it again."

"It's such a shame. Your books are delightful. Margie's been begging for another Lexi Beamer book, though I've forbidden her to bug you about it. All her friends adore your books."

"I'm going to try," Brynna promised herself, as well as her friend. "Soon."

"Good. Now, as much as I've enjoyed this lunch with you, I have to go. It'll be time for Nathan to get out of preschool soon."

"Mitzi," Brynna said impulsively, reaching out to take her friend's hand as she rose from the table. "Thanks for being so wonderful during the past few months. I don't know what I would have done without you and Perry."

"We love you, Bryn." Mitzi leaned over to kiss Brynna's cheek, her green eyes suspiciously bright as she forced herself to smile naturally. "Come over for dinner tonight, okay? The kids would love to see you."

"Could we make it tomorrow night?"

"Sure. See you then."

They walked out of the club together, speaking to people they knew, stopping for a quick hug before going to their separate cars. Brynna was already making plans for Show-Down as she drove home, grateful that she had something now to keep her occupied.

## Chapter Two

Dan smiled down at the woman who opened the door. Brynna Haskell—for he now knew that was her last name—was even lovelier than he remembered, and he'd pictured her all too often in the week since they'd met in the park. He hadn't believed his luck when she'd called and reminded him of their meeting—as if he could have forgotten. When she'd asked him to come by to discuss an upcoming civic event he'd jumped eagerly at the opportunity to see her again.

Standing this close to her, he noted again how small she was, probably no more than five, four, compared to his own six feet. Seeing that she was nicely dressed in a simply cut blue shirtwaist dress that emphasized her blue eyes, he was glad he'd stopped by his new apartment to change. Beige slacks and a crisp, green-striped shirt were much better than the running shorts he'd come calling in last time. He was glad to see her smiling this time, though he fancied there was still a trace of sadness in those memorable eyes. "Hi."

"Hi," she replied in the softly musical voice he remembered so clearly. "Please come in."

Brynna led him into the living room—or perhaps parlor would better suit the delicately old-fashioned room, he thought—and invited him to be seated in one of the two matching floral wing chairs that faced the gold chintz sofa. Fresh flowers nodded from crystal vases on the spinet piano against one wall and were arranged in a brass bowl on the butler's table in front of the sofa. Dan thought her monthly florist bill would probably equal the amount he spent on food, but chose not to dwell on that. If he started comparing incomes, he would probably begin to feel inferior. After all, every penny he had just now was tied up in the radio station. He would draw only enough salary to get by on until he pulled the station out of the low-ratings slump it had fallen into under the old management.

Brynna perched on the couch and straightened the skirt of her dress primly over her knees, trying to decide what to ask first. On the telephone, she'd told him only that she wanted to talk to him about participating in the annual talent show. He'd expressed an interest, and she'd invited him over—somewhat shyly—to discuss it in more detail. She'd forgotten how very handsome he was, she thought, her throat tightening. How strongly she reacted to him.

The long slash of a dimple on his right cheek deepened as he smiled at her. "Tell me about the Haskellville Summer Festival," he encouraged her, seeming to sense that she was at a loss for words.

Latching on to the subject with grateful enthusiasm, Brynna gave him a brief history of the day-long event, traditionally held the last Saturday in July. "Twelve weeks from tomorrow," she added with a rueful smile. "I counted."

He returned the smile and waited for her to continue.

"The day begins with a parade down Main Street, and ends with Show-Down. During the day, there are lots of things going on in the square at City Hall. Bands playing in the gazebo, square dancing in the parking lot, arts and crafts booths, concessions, games for the children. This year there will be a pet show with awards for the prettiest pet, the most unusual pet, and so on. We'll have demonstrations from local dance and karate schools, an antique car show at the Main Street Shopping Center, sidewalk sales. It's lots of fun."

Dan was familiar with small-town festivals. He'd lived in lots of small towns as he'd drifted from one radio station to another during the past few years. "Sounds like fun," he agreed. "Tell me about Show-Down. How long has that been going on?"

"Almost as many years as the Festival," she answered. "You know how people love to show off their talent. We get acts from all around the area. It's quite popular. Sells out every year. The proceeds are donated to the Needy Families Fund. At one time we let anyone who wanted to compete do so, but we've had so many acts apply in the past five years or so that we hold auditions now with a panel of judges. We accept the top twenty-four acts for competition, twelve in the children's category and twelve in the adult division."

"Twenty-four acts?"

"Yes. The show takes almost four hours, with intermission, entertainment and judging, though we limit each act to four minutes. No one complains. The people around here love the show, long as it is."

"And what would I do as emcee of this show, assuming I were chosen?" Dan asked, eyes lingering on her smile. It really was beautiful, revealing even white teeth between very kissable lips. He wondered how long it would be before he'd have the chance to taste those lips.

"You would welcome the guests, introduce the judges and each contestant, entertain the crowd between acts with clean, family-oriented jokes." Brynna was beginning to relax now as she launched into the discussion of the program she knew so well. "You mentioned on the phone that you'd done similar work in the past."

"Frequently," he assured her.

"I've been listening to you in the mornings. You're very entertaining. I think you'd be a wonderful emcee for Show-Down."

Pleased, he rubbed his thumb along the strong line of his chin. "Thanks. Did you happen to catch my show last Friday?"

Friday. The day she'd had lunch with Mitzi. The day she'd decided to get on with her life. "Yes, I heard part of it," she admitted.

"I was talking about you, you know." Dan watched closely for her reaction.

Brynna twisted her hands in her lap. "Yes, I know. You made me laugh when you played 'Another One Bites the Dust.'"

"I'm glad. You looked so sad in the park. I was hoping the upbeat songs would cheer you up."

Taken aback by the suddenly personal nature of their conversation, and vividly aware of him once more as a disturbingly attractive man rather than a potential emcee for her show, Brynna took a deep breath and tried to sound casual. "Um—thank you, they did.

"About Show-Down, Mr. Westbrook," she added immediately, hoping the formal address would restore a more businesslike atmosphere. "Are you interested?"

"Oh, I'm interested."

Something in his voice made her wonder just what he was interested in. Oh, dear, she thought. He hadn't pressed when she'd turned down his dinner invitations last week. She'd thought that meant he'd asked more out of appreciation for her first aid than because of a more basic attraction. Maybe she'd been wrong.

Again, she tried for a strictly professional tone. "As coordinator of Show-Down, the final decision of emcee is mine. So, since you've already indicated that the fee I stated over the telephone is acceptable, I'd like to consider it official."

"Fine with me. I'll give you plenty of free promotion on the air, of course, since it's a civic event. I'd also like to donate my fee to the charity, though I'd prefer it if you didn't make that public."

"That's very generous of you, Mr. Westbrook—"

"Dan," he corrected her firmly. "And I insist. I won't make money from a charity event like this. Besides, you must realize that the publicity will be good for my station."

She did realize that, of course, but she suspected that Dan Westbrook was a very nice man to whom such generous gestures came naturally, regardless of the benefits. "The emcee is usually on the committee that auditions acts and chooses the twenty-four contestants," she informed him. "I'll also be on the committee, of course, along with three or four others. The auditions were done live in the past, but for the last two years we've asked for audio or video tapes and we make our selections from the tapes. It involves several long hours of weeding through many amateur efforts to choose," she admitted with a grimace. "Still interested?"

He chuckled. "Sure. It'll be fun."

She looked skeptical. "We'll see if you still call it 'fun' after you've sat through over a hundred bad tapes."

He laughed, and the sound warmed her. He had a very nice laugh in addition to that very nice radio announcer's voice, she thought approvingly. There was entirely too much about Dan Westbrook that she liked. She was glad he hadn't said anything else that could be construed as indicating an interest in her.

But the thought had come too soon.

Stretching his legs in front of him, Dan gave her a look that only a fool could interpret as anything but pure masculine interest and asked, "What are the chances of you being free to have dinner with me tonight, Brynna Haskell?"

Brynna stared at the depressingly few green words on the computer screen and ran both hands through her hair in a gesture that was both weary and despairing. Something was wrong, but she didn't know what. Lexi and her friends had become adolescent automatons, completely lacking whatever spark she'd originally instilled in them to make them so real for her faithful young readers. She'd been trying for the past four months to work on this one book, and she had gotten exactly nowhere. Brynna's fingers tightened in her soft tresses. What if she were never able to write again? What if she'd lost that, too?

The doorbell's chime interceded before a full-scale anxiety attack could develop. Pressing the button that would store what little she'd written, Brynna pushed herself away from the computer, smoothing her pink sweater over the waistband of her gray slacks as she headed for the door. She wasn't expecting anyone, but she'd welcome whichever of her friends had decided to drop in at 6:00 p.m. on this particular Friday. Lord knew she needed the diversion.

With only mild curiosity, she flicked the lace curtain back from the diamond-shaped window in the front door. Dan Westbrook! She certainly wasn't expecting him!

She hadn't seen him since their meeting about Show-Down, though she hadn't been able to put him completely out of her mind. He hadn't allowed her to do so. Every morning he woke her at eight o'clock with a special song and a personal message that only she could know was meant for her. She'd found it mildly amusing at first, a rather original campaign to get her to change her mind about going out with him. He'd taken her continued refusal of his dinner invitations easily enough, but she was beginning to realize that he wasn't a man who was easily discouraged.

The next morning he'd awakened her with, "I have a special song this morning for a new friend I'd like to get to know better. Good morning, friend." And he'd played "I'd Like to Get to Know You" by Spanky and Our Gang.

He'd sent a similar message every morning since. And her amusement had slowly transformed itself into a very feminine awareness—a realization that Dan Westbrook was seriously interested in her, and was clearly declaring his intention to do something about it. Though some secret part of her was rather pleased by the flattering attention, another part of her was definitely nervous. Dan was too attractive, too disturbing, too—too— Well, whatever he was, she wasn't sure she was up to his challenge just yet. Maybe in a few months, when she was back to her old poised, imperturbable self—not that she'd ever had experience with a man quite like this one.

But for now the man was standing on her doorstep, waiting for her to open the door. She turned the knob. "Dan. I wasn't expecting you."

He smiled mischievously, a little-boy smile totally at odds with the full-grown male sparkle in his wickedly expressive eyes. "I know. I won't ask to come in. I just wanted to drop something off. You *do* have a VCR, don't you?"

"Yes." She said the word questioningly.

He held out a videocassette tape. "I'd like you to take a look at this when you have time. It's not necessary for you to watch all of it—just fifteen or twenty minutes."

"What is it?"

"It's a teenage beauty pageant a friend and I emceed together last year. His name's Chet Traylor and he's starting as afternoon deejay at KHVL next week. It's just a suggestion, but if this show of yours is four hours long, you might want to consider having us as a team, just to liven things up."

Brynna hesitated. "We've never had more than one emcee before."

"Maybe it's time for something different." Dan's grin deepened his tantalizing single dimple. Pushing his hands into the pockets of his thin leather jacket he backed away from the door. "Let me know if you're interested and I'll talk to Chet. I know he'd be glad to do it, and he'll want the same terms I do—fee to be donated to the Needy Families Fund."

"Wait," Brynna said impulsively, calling herself a fool even as she spoke. "Would you like to come in? We could have a glass of tea and look at this together."

Though his smile indicated that her invitation pleased him, he shook his head regretfully. "Thanks, but I can't stay. I have to meet someone. I'll call you to find out what you thought of the tape, okay?"

"Yes, of course." Brynna wondered if he were meeting a woman, and bit the inside of her lip in dismay at her immediate and totally unjustified flash of envy. As he walked away, her eyes drifted down to the lean hips outlined by his close-fitting jeans. *Lord, he's got a nice—*

*Brynna!* she chided herself. *What's gotten into you?*

Hoping he hadn't noticed that she'd been standing in the doorway watching him, she quickly closed the door and pressed her forehead against it. She really wasn't up to dealing with this just now. With so many other problems to worry about, what was she doing allowing herself to become infatuated with an attractive radio announcer?

Infatuated? Okay, she mused, chewing on the end of one rounded fingernail, perhaps she was a bit infatuated with him. It was perfectly understandable. After all, he was nice looking, charming, flatteringly attentive. A man very different from those she'd dated before, from the one she'd married. She was at a particularly low point in her life, susceptible, vulnerable. She would have to be very careful not to interpret her attraction to him as anything more than that.

She looked down at the tape in her hand, then walked briskly toward the den, where she turned on the VCR and sat down to watch.

"Well, Dan, you getting settled okay?" the older man asked as they waited for the waitress to bring their steaks.

"Yeah. I'm damned glad to get out of that motel room. Thanks for recommending the apartments, Mason. The place I rented is exactly what I wanted."

Mason Everett, the stocky, balding local attorney Dan chose to represent his interests during the negotiations on the radio station, had become a friend during the past few months, though twenty years separated them. Widowed,

Mason had been delighted to discover that Dan played a wicked game of chess. They had already spent two long, pleasant evenings bent over Mason's exquisite ivory chess set in his den, snifters of expensive brandy at their elbows. They planned to end this evening the same way. "How are things going at the station, Dan?"

"Things will be better when I can afford two more announcers," Dan admitted. "But before I can do that, there has to be a bigger audience to draw bigger advertising. I'm really depending on Chet to help out there."

"If your friend does for the afternoon ratings what you've done for the morning ratings, you're well on your way to having the number-one radio station in the area," Mason predicted, his gray eyes gleaming from beneath thick gray eyebrows. "That billboard on Main Street was a stroke of genius. I hear we've come close to having a few fender benders because teenage girls slam on the brakes to get a better look."

Feeling his cheeks warm, Dan frowned into his coffee cup. "That was the advertising department's idea," he muttered. "I let Gloria, our top salesperson, talk me into it. I feel like a fool every time I drive down Main Street, which happens to be every day, since my apartment is two blocks down from that stupid sign."

Mason laughed. "You were a popular deejay in Chicago. Surely you had your picture flashed around there."

"Well, yeah, but not quite so—"

"Provocatively?" Mason suggested.

Dan's answer was drowned inside his coffee cup, sounding suspiciously like a growl to the amused older man. By the time he'd drained the cup and a flirtatious waitress—who recognized Dan from the billboard—had deposited their dinners in front of them, Dan had regained his equilibrium. He allowed Mason to get a good start on his steak before bringing up the Summer Festival. Only after he'd discussed his role in the Festival did he mention Brynna. "Do you know her?" he asked casually.

Mason nodded. "Of course. Known her since she was born. Held her on my knee plenty of times."

Dan's own knees tingled as he imagined Brynna perched there. He cleared his throat abruptly. "Tell me about her."

Mason's thick brows shot swiftly upward. "Anything in particular?"

Dan shrugged with a studied nonchalance that didn't even fool himself. "Anything at all."

"She's a very attractive woman."

Dan's lips crooked into a sheepish grin. "Now tell me something I hadn't already found out for myself."

Mason laughed and cut another piece off his steak. "I'm not sure what to tell you. She's a lovely woman, gracious and thoughtful and kind. Talented, too. My granddaughter loves her books."

"Books?" Dan's head lifted sharply.

"Yeah. She's a writer. Writes books for girls. She's done a series about a little girl whose name I can't remember right now, but they've been very popular."

"Does she write under her own name or a pen name?"

"Her own. Brynna Haskell. She'd already married by the time she wrote the first one, but she chose to use her maiden name for publication. Good thing, I guess, since she went back to that name after her divorce a year ago."

"She's divorced?"

"Mmm."

Dan found that very interesting. He'd wondered about her occasional displays of shyness with him, the rather flustered way she reacted when he tried to assert his interest in her. He was pleased to know that she was more experienced than she'd seemed at first, less likely to expect from him more than he was willing to give. A woman so recently divorced would probably be no more interested in another lasting entanglement than Dan was, which suited him just fine.

Mason eyed him sharply. "Thinking about taking her out?"

Dan grinned at the somewhat protective tone of the older man's question. "Yeah. Maybe."

Mason nodded. "That's good. She needs to get back into a social life. Poor kid's had such a rough time lately."

Dan thought immediately of the first time he'd seen her, when she'd looked so very sad. "She's not still grieving over the end of her marriage, is she?" he asked, wondering if that was the reason Brynna repeatedly turned down his invitations. Was she still in love with her ex-husband? If so, what had gone wrong with the marriage?

"Oh, no, she's over that," Mason answered confidently. "But she *is* still grieving for her parents. She was awfully close to her mother and dad. More so than most young women her age, I think."

"She lost her parents?" Dan asked in instant sympathy.

Mason nodded sadly. "Bryan Haskell was my best friend. He was fifty-six years old; Alice was only fifty-four. They died six months ago in an automobile accident."

"Oh. I heard shortly after I arrived that two members of the Haskell family had recently died. I hadn't realized they were Brynna's parents. She must have been devastated."

"She was. I was worried about her for the first couple of months. She looked like she just wanted to shrivel up and die with them. I saw her last night, though, and she looks better than she has since the tragedy."

"Does she have any brothers or sisters?"

"No. She was the only child Alice could have. Maybe that's why the three of them were so close. I know her parents were very supportive of Brynna during her divorce, and she probably feels pretty much alone right now, despite her many friends and her cousins.''

Dan could clearly picture her sitting on that park bench. Yes, she had looked so alone. He remembered his impulse to take her in his arms and comfort her. He still wanted to do so. Even more now that he'd actually met her. Strange thoughts for a man who had no intention of allowing a woman to become too important in his life.

While they finished dinner, Dan continued to think about Brynna. Perfectly understandable, he assured himself. She was pretty, sexy, nice. He was new in town, hadn't dated in a while, was susceptible to a lovely face and a pair of sad blue eyes. He'd do well to keep his attraction to her in perspective. He hadn't had his heart kicked around since he was an angry, too-emotional, twenty-three-year-old rebel, and he intended to keep that vulnerable organ well guarded, whatever the outcome of his single-minded pursuit of one Brynna Haskell.

''Brynna, this is wonderful! We *must* have these two at Show-Down!'' Mitzi's voice was thrilled as she stared at the television screen in front of her on which two very funny men swapped witty repartee and self-consciously pretty teenagers vied for a rhinestone crown in an extravagantly produced pageant. One of the announcers was Chet Traylor, a short, pleasantly homely man in his early thirties with a wicked sense of humor. The other was Dan Westbrook, handsome, good-natured straight man to Traylor's outrageous jokes.

Brynna was as pleased as her friend. ''Now you know why I had to rush over here with this tape as soon as I finished watching it. Isn't it great?''

"Terrific. Don't you think so, Perry?" Mitzi asked her husband, who was sitting beside Brynna on the couch. Brynna wondered if she only imagined that Mitzi's voice changed when she spoke to her husband, became more strained, as if wondering how he would respond to a simple question.

One hand wearily massaging the back of his neck beneath the collar of his slightly rumpled white shirt, Perry nodded. "They're good together. I think they'll be a big hit at Show-Down."

Brynna covered Perry's free hand with her own, smiling at him. He looked so tired, she thought sympathetically, thinking that his weariness made him look older than his thirty-four years. The past months had been hard on Perry, who'd adored the uncle whose place he was now having to take at Haskell Manufacturing. Perry's own father— Bryan's brother—had died of a heart attack when Perry was only eleven. Bryan had served as a surrogate father after that, grooming Perry to take over the family business since Brynna showed no interest in doing so. Brynna had always regarded Perry as an older brother. She felt guilty that she'd been so wrapped up in her own problems during the past months that she hadn't realized what a hard time he was having.

Perry twisted his hand under Brynna's until their fingers locked in a warm, supportive clasp, but before he could speak they were interrupted by twelve-year-old Margie. "Dan Westbrook is *such* a babe! All the kids at school want a copy of that billboard to hang in their bedrooms. He's almost enough to make us want to listen to that old stuff he plays on his radio station."

Brynna looked questioningly at her carrot-topped twelve-year-old cousin, reclining on the floor in fashionably colorful fleece separates. "What billboard?"

"You haven't seen it? It's really radical. Jessica Nelson's older sister Jennifer—she's sixteen—is in *lo-o-o-v-e* with it. And Dan Westbrook was deejay at the school dance last Friday night and Jennifer said all the girls went nuts over him. She said he smiled at her once and she thought she was going to faint. And *Jessica* said—"

"Margie," Mitzi interrupted gently, "Brynna only asked what billboard." She turned amused green eyes toward Brynna. "I take it you haven't driven down Main Street in the past couple of days?"

"No, I don't think I have. I've been writing—or trying to write—and I've hardly been out of the house."

"Well, your Dan Westbrook has his gorgeous face—and body—plastered all over the billboard down by Arthur's Barber Shop. I can understand why all the kids are swooning over it. First time I saw it, even my thirty-three-year-old heart kicked into high gear. Nice-looking billboard." She smiled coyly at her husband, obviously expecting a protest.

Brynna smiled at Perry, expecting him to teasingly object to his wife's words, as he would have in the past. But he sat gazing at nothing, lost in his own thoughts. She wasn't sure he'd heard a word they'd said since he last made a contribution to the conversation. She frowned a bit and turned to Mitzi, whose own smile had faded. "Sounds like an interesting billboard," she agreed.

"You should drive by and see it," Mitzi suggested, making an effort to hold on to her cheerfulness.

"Maybe I will," Brynna murmured, trying to hide the sudden disquiet she felt. Something was wrong between Mitzi and Perry. The thought of problems in the marriage she'd always considered so perfect made her heart twist. Even during her own marriage to Russ, she'd always envied Mitzi and Perry the almost palpable love and intimacy they shared. The kind of love Brynna had longed for but never quite found with Russ. She hoped fervently that whatever problems Mitzi and Perry had could be worked out.

And then the peace of the room was shattered when nine-year-old Bryan and five-year-old Nathan erupted through the doorway. "Mom! Nathan won't let me alone! I'm trying to play with my Gore Monsters and he keeps—"

"Was not! I was just—"

"—and then he turned off my stereo and—"

"—and he called me bugface and—"

Mitzi quickly, and with the ease of frequent practice, settled the dispute between her sons while Margie groaned and rolled her eyes, flopping back down on the carpet to watch the rest of the tape still playing on the TV.

## Chapter Three

Even as she turned the corner that would put her on Main Street, Brynna told herself that she was only going to look at the billboard out of mild curiosity. After all, she *was* in charge of Show-Down. This type of publicity was very good for her project.

The sign was illuminated by a row of upward-pointing lights. Brynna parked in the deserted lot of Arthur's Barber Shop and gasped, her heart beating a strange rhythm in her chest. It was, as Mitzi had said, one nice-looking billboard.

Big block letters across the top said, "Start Your Day the Easy Way with Dan Westbrook and KHVL." Below that a larger-than-life-sized Dan smiled down at her, his sexy dimple deeply carved, his indigo eyes crinkled in lazy amusement. He was sitting at the console of the radio station, long, denim-covered legs stretched in front of him, booted feet crossed at the ankles and propped on the edge of the desk.

He wore a headset mike and held a coffee cup loosely in one hand. His light blue shirt was unbuttoned halfway down to reveal a wide vee of the hair-smattered chest Brynna remembered so clearly from the first time she'd seen him. Both the thin shirt and the washed-soft jeans emphasized the lean, well-muscled body beneath. She recalled having her hands on that body the first time they'd met, finding it all too easy to remember what he looked like beneath that blue shirt. She swallowed hard.

No wonder Jessica Nelson's older sister had felt faint when Dan Westbrook smiled at her. Brynna Haskell was considerably older and more sophisticated and she had experienced much the same reaction, on more than one occasion.

She jumped when someone tapped on the window beside her, only then aware that she was sitting in a dark, empty parking lot at ten o'clock at night. There wasn't a great deal of crime in Haskellville, but—

She wasn't sure she was relieved when she turned abruptly to find Dan Westbrook—the real Dan Westbrook—smiling at her through the glass. He'd caught her staring at the billboard of him. How embarrassing!

"Hi," he greeted her when she cranked down the window.

"Hi," she returned, trying to think of something else to say.

"I was just driving by on my way home, and I thought this was the car I'd seen in your driveway." He crossed his arms on the door and leaned in the open window. "Whatcha' doing?"

He asked so casually that she answered with easy candor. "Staring at your billboard. My young cousin told me about it, so I thought I'd take a look on the way home."

Looking a bit sheepish, he grimaced. "Believe me, it wasn't my idea."

She laughed at his expression. "It's a very good picture," she surprised herself by teasing him. "My cousin tells me that all the teenage girls love it. Jessica Nelson's sister almost swooned."

She thought his cheeks reddened, though she couldn't be sure in the dim light provided by the street lamps. "I guess I deserve that for allowing this billboard," he almost groaned. "I suggested using the faces of some of the artists whose music we play, but the advertising department decided I should be introduced to the community, instead."

"I think it's great. The more popular you become, the more people you'll draw to Show-Down."

"Speaking of Show-Down, did you get a chance to look at that tape?"

"Yes, and it was wonderful! I showed it to Mitzi—she's my cousin's wife and the coordinator of the Summer Festival."

"Yes, you mentioned her to me. Did she like it?"

"She loved it. If your friend Chet agrees, we'd be delighted to have you as cohosts of our show."

"I can assure you he'll agree. Chet's a real ham. Loves to get up in front of an audience."

Brynna smiled knowingly. "I don't think he's the only one."

Dan laughed and shrugged. "Okay, so I'm not exactly the shy type. I like the personal appearances as much as Chet does."

"I also want to talk to you about doing an intermission act. That Smothers Brothers takeoff you and Chet did on the tape was wonderful." Showing considerable talent with both guitars and singing, the two men had done a wickedly funny impersonation of the Smothers Brothers—Dan as the straight, exasperated Dick, and Chet as the rather dense, but lovable Tommy. Brynna had laughed until her sides hurt as Chet whined the old line "Mom always liked you best."

"We could talk about it now, over a drink somewhere," Dan suggested tentatively. "We could go to my place," he added even more tentatively. "I have a nice white wine chilling in the refrigerator."

Her throat tightened as she realized in amazement that she was actually tempted to accept. She couldn't, of course. She didn't even know this man—not really. And she'd already decided that she must keep her attraction to him under control, something she could hardly do if she went to his apartment at this time of night. But still she was tempted. "Thank you, Dan, but I can't tonight. I really should go home."

He accepted her refusal without protest. "Perhaps we could meet for lunch next week. Chet will be in town then, and he'd join us. You could ask Mitzi, as well."

Yes, she could handle that. After all, that was business. And two others would be there to diffuse the tension that seemed to develop at odd times between them. "Yes, that will be fine. Why don't you call me and we'll name a time and place."

"Fine." Still he didn't immediately move away from her window. "I had dinner with a friend of yours tonight. Mason Everett."

Brynna smiled, wondering why the news absolutely delighted her. Of course she'd assumed Dan was having dinner with a woman that evening, but finding out otherwise shouldn't have made any difference to her, at all. It wasn't as if she wanted to date him herself. Was it? No, of course not, she told herself firmly, even as she spoke with continued casualness to the man leaning into her window, so enticingly close to her shoulder. "Mason's a very good friend. He's also my attorney."

"I know. He told me. And he told me about your parents. I'm very sorry, Brynna."

Her smile vanished. "Thank you," she managed, willing herself not to respond emotionally to the warm sympathy in his rich voice.

"I remember how badly it hurt when my own dad died, when I was twenty-one," Dan added rather awkwardly, as if he wanted to offer comfort but didn't quite know how. "It took me a while to get over it. I still miss him and it's been thirteen years."

She nodded understanding. "Is your mother still living?" she asked quietly, realizing that she knew little about Dan, though she had the strangest sense of having known him for much longer than a couple of weeks.

His face went suddenly blank, automatically wiped of all expression. Brynna was startled by the abruptness of it. His voice was equally expressionless when he responded to her question. "I lost my mother when I was twenty-three," he told her.

"I'm sorry," she murmured, wondering at the change she sensed in him. It seemed that she'd inadvertently broached a subject that Dan considered off-limits.

He didn't actually shake his head, but she watched as he almost visibly threw off the dark mood that had threatened and forced a smile. "Guess you're ready to get home. I'll call you next week about lunch."

"All right. Good night, Dan."

"Good night, Brynna." The words were a caress. She was still blushing from the intimacy of his tone when he leaned further into the window and dropped a light kiss on her lips, slightly parted in surprise.

"Don't expect an apology for that," he told her when he pulled back, his smile dangerous. And then he was gone, crossing in long, graceful strides to the Trans Am a few yards away. Staring after him, Brynna remembered that she'd never heard the car pull into the lot. She'd been that intent on the billboard picture.

He'd kissed her! Nervously licking tingling lips, she started her car and threw it into gear, suddenly anxious to get home.

"It's a rainy Friday morning in Haskellville. Good day to stay in bed, curled up beneath the sheets and dreaming of the best things in life. And while I'm on the subject, here's Hall and Oates with a song that describes what's on the top of *my* list—"

Brynna groaned and buried her face in the pillow as "Kiss on My List" began to play from the bedside radio. Dan Westbrook was driving her crazy! If she had any gumption at all, she'd start listening to another radio station in the mornings. Instead, she continued to wake to his voice—even found herself waking before the radio automatically switched on, then lying in quiet anticipation to see what song he'd play for her next. What in the world was wrong with her?

Even if she could have succeeded in erasing his brief kiss from her memory, as she'd tried so hard to do, Dan would have sabotaged her efforts by reminding her of it every morning. Each wake-up song he'd played for her had made some reference to a kiss. He had no intention of allowing her to forget it. Dan Westbrook was one determined man.

She thought of him as she brushed her teeth, showered, and dried her hair. Today was the day she'd promised to have lunch with Dan and his friend Chet. He should be calling at any time to set the time and place. Her throat tightened at the thought. She could only be grateful again that Chet was joining them. She reminded herself sternly that her fascination with Dan was nothing more than infatuation, brought on by loneliness. To base a relationship on that would be sheer folly.

Or did he even want a relationship? As far as she knew, he was pursuing her only out of masculine ego, challenged by her continued refusal to go out with him. A man like that wouldn't be accustomed to being turned down.

And still her heart pounded foolishly when the phone rang. Then did a series of gymnastic flips when his mellifluous voice greeted her with a deep, "Good morning, Brynna."

"Good morning, Dan," she managed in a reasonable facsimile of her normal voice. "Aren't you supposed to be on the air?"

"I promised my listeners twenty minutes of commercial-free music," he replied. "I'm disappointed that you didn't know that. Weren't you listening?" he teased.

Her lips twitched with a smile. "I was listening earlier," she informed him. "But I turned the radio off when I got into the shower."

There was a moment of silence, then a rather hoarse, "Did I interrupt your shower?"

She honestly hadn't meant to be provocative, but his tone told her that her words had conjured up some mental images for him. She swallowed hard. She wasn't used to being part of a man's fantasies. There was something incredibly erotic about being part of Dan's.

She closed her eyes tightly, telling her overactive imagination to behave itself. "No, you didn't interrupt me. What time do you want to meet for lunch?" she asked, anxious to change the subject.

"My show's over at twelve, so why don't we make it twelve-thirty at Ellie's? I've already talked to Chet and he's available when we are."

"Okay, I'll call Mitzi. See you then." She loosened her grip on the receiver.

"Brynna," he said swiftly, knowing that she was about to hang up.

"Yes?"

He hesitated as if he didn't really know what to say. "I— uh—how are you?"

*How are you?* If she didn't know better, she would think she made him as nervous as he made her. Which was ridiculous. Wasn't it? "I'm fine, Dan."

She could almost see him wince over the telephone. "Dumb question, huh? It's just that now that I have you on the telephone I'm reluctant to let you go."

"Why?"

"Brynna." His voice was gently chiding. "You know why."

Yes, she knew. She knew that for some strange reason he was as affected by the chemistry between them as she. And he was not going to allow her to ignore it. Oh, *why* couldn't he just let it go? Surely he could see that she wasn't ready for this. If he was simply interested in a new conquest, there were plenty of available women around, all of whom would probably love to have a chance at the handsome new bachelor in town. Instead, he seemed to be spending his evenings attending school dances and dining with Mason Everett, of all people.

And as much as she tried to tell herself that she wished he'd find another woman to chase after, she still remembered the relief she'd felt last week when she found out his dinner engagement had been with Mason. Talk about mixed emotions! "Dan—"

"I'll let you go now," he interrupted. "Do me a favor, though, will you?"

"What?" she asked warily.

"Turn on your radio." And then he hung up.

Brynna replaced her own receiver, her eyes going to the radio beside her bed. She really shouldn't turn it on, she told herself. He'd just make her more confused. She wouldn't turn it on. She walked out of the bedroom, only to find herself pausing before the expensive stereo system in her den. "Brynna, you are such an idiot," she muttered even as her finger pressed the power button.

She didn't move as a rapid-mouthed announcer urged her to buy a used car and a stuttering computer told her to try Coke. And then Dan's voice came on. "You're listening to KHVL, easy music for a rainy day. It's nine-fifteen, fifty-three degrees outside, and the weather service is predicting that the rain will continue into the evening. We have music by Elton John and Barbra Streisand ahead, but first, here's an oldie from Eddie Holman for a special friend."

"Oh, damn," Brynna whispered, covering her face with her hands as Holman's high, quavering voice sang to his "Lonely Girl," imploring her to let him make her broken heart like new. Brynna had never been courted with music before. She was finding it very hard to resist.

She really should start listening to another radio station. But she knew even as the thought crossed her mind that she wouldn't.

Brynna dashed under the awning of Ellie's, shook the water from her blue-and-white floral umbrella and snapped it shut. Raindrops sparkled around the hem of her khaki London Fog raincoat and spotted her nylon-covered ankles beneath. Her gray flats were wet and cold from an unfortunate step into a deep puddle. She'd faced the elements and now it was time to face Dan. Given a choice, she wasn't sure which was more unnerving.

She turned to smile at Mitzi, who was just ducking under the awning, shaking raindrops from her curly red hair in a manner that reminded Brynna of Margie's poodle. "See? You should have shared my umbrella."

"You may be right," Mitzi agreed, lowering her wet purse to her side. "My purse doesn't provide much cover. What are we doing out on a day like this?"

"I was just asking myself the same question." Brynna pushed open the wood-and-stained-glass door and stepped inside the quaintly decorated restaurant with its glossy wood floors and round wood tables with bentwood chairs. Brynna spared only a glance for the familiar decor, her gaze going instead to the dark-haired man who'd risen to his feet across the room. Dan.

Had she been less preoccupied, she would have noted the speculative look she received from Mitzi when Dan stepped forward to take her hand, his smile warm and welcoming and meant entirely for her. Or the lifted eyebrows of Dan's friend Chet when Dan murmured a greeting and Brynna answered with a hint of a blush. Or even the gentle laughter on the faces of their friends when the introductions were behind them and they were seated—only for Brynna to discover that Dan still held her hand tightly in his.

Her flush deepening, Brynna extricated her fingers and tried very hard to concentrate on something other than Dan. She failed miserably, her eyes turning inexorably back in his direction.

Later, she could not have said exactly what she ate for lunch—or even *if* she ate. She could not have given the details of the rather casual business meeting that took place, though she knew decisions had been made about the Show-Down program. There was a great deal of laughter on Mitzi's part at Dan and Chet's shenanigans. But all Brynna *could* have described later was Dan. How he looked when he grimaced at Chet's teasing, the way his eyes crinkled in the corners when he laughed, the way his throat worked when he swallowed. The way her knees weakened when his eyes met hers and he smiled a very private, intimate smile for her.

"Wow." Mitzi said, not taking her eyes from the road in front of her.

Brynna glanced at her friend from the passenger seat in Mitzi's car. "Wow what?" she asked, distracted from the deep reverie that had lingered after lunch ended.

"Wow as in that is one fine-looking man. In person, as well as on a billboard."

"Oh." Brynna looked quickly down at her folded hands. "You mean Dan."

"Yes, I mean Dan. Chet's nice, but he's hardly a wow."

Brynna felt the searching look that preceded Mitzi's next observation. "He's interested in you, you know. *Very* interested."

Denying it would only be foolish. Of course she knew. The problem was what to do about it. "I know. He's asked me out."

"And?"

"And *I* turned him down."

"You're kidding."

Brynna glanced resentfully at Mitzi. "No, I'm not kidding. Mitzi, I'm not ready to start dating yet. I'm especially not ready to start dating a 'wow.' "

"Come off it, Bryn, you've been divorced for almost a year and we both know the marriage was over long before that. You're not still carrying a torch for Russ. I know you've been in mourning, but it would be good for you to get out again. Your folks wouldn't want you to live the rest of your life in seclusion."

"I have no intention of living the rest of my life in seclusion," Brynna returned with a calmness she didn't quite feel. "And you're absolutely right. I never loved Russ as a wife should love her husband. Which only goes to show that I'm not a very good judge of my emotions even at the best of times."

Puzzled, Mitzi tilted her head. "What's that supposed to mean?"

"Mitzi, I married Russ because all my friends were getting married and I was too old to keep living with my parents. He was ready to be married—or thought he was—and so was I. He was handsome and charming and pleasant company and I thought we had enough in common to build a marriage around. I was wrong, of course. I allowed myself to be persuaded by well-meaning matchmakers because I was vulnerable at that point."

"That's understandable. Many young people marry for much the same reasons, only to find out later that they should have waited."

"True. But now I'm twenty-seven years old, and I'm still vulnerable. And it would be all too easy for me to fall again for someone handsome and charming and pleasant, only to discover later that I'd made another terrible mistake. I can't afford to do that again, Mitzi."

"What absolute rot!" Mitzi's voice was warm with indignation. "I've never heard anything so asinine in my life. You, Brynna Haskell, are one of the most levelheaded, intelligent people I know. Yet you make yourself sound like some kind of silly space cadet, ripe for the picking by any good-looking hustler who happens along. We both know you're too sharp for that."

"Am I?" Brynna asked wistfully. "That's exactly the way I feel right now. I hardly know Dan Westbrook and I've been acting like—like one of Margie's moonstruck friends! I'd hardly call that levelheaded and intelligent!"

"I'd call it inevitable!" Mitzi returned forcefully. "He just happens to be a really nice guy who's obviously attracted to you, as well."

"How do you know he's a really nice guy? How would either of us know? We don't even know him. He could be an ax murderer, for all we know."

"Brynna," Mitzi chided in tones of pure disgust.

Brynna flushed a bit, but lifted her chin in defiance. "I know it sounds silly, but still—you've been as taken in by his charm and pretty face as I have. And you're a happily married woman. I'm the one who'd be taking the risk, allowing myself to become involved with someone I hardly know."

"So get to know him," Mitzi argued logically. "But you can't do that unless you spend some time with him. You don't have to throw yourself into an affair. Just go out with him, see if he's as nice as he seems. What could be the harm in that?"

The harm could be finding herself in an affair with Dan Westbrook before she'd had time to learn *anything*, Brynna thought. Look at the way she'd responded to him at Ellie's—she'd done everything but melt at his feet when he looked at her. His touch affected her as no man's had before. "He excites me," she heard herself saying aloud, then felt her cheeks go scarlet.

Mitzi only laughed. "Glad to hear it, kid. Shows you're still among the living."

"You don't understand," Brynna murmured haltingly. She'd always been uncomfortable talking about intimate matters, even with her mother. Were she not so very close to Mitzi, so sure her friend would understand, she'd never be able to speak so frankly to her. "This isn't like me. When Russ and I split, he finally admitted that my lack of passion was one of the reasons he was unhappy with our marriage."

"Bull. You're a warm, loving woman, Brynna. If there was any lack of passion in your marriage, it was because you were with the wrong partner."

"You really think so?" Brynna asked doubtfully. She'd never wanted to consider herself a cold woman, but her experience had been limited to the vaguely unsatisfying embraces she'd shared with Russ. She'd been fond of Russ, was still fond of Russ, but there had definitely been something missing in her feelings for him. Could it be that with another man . . . ? Her thoughts turned briefly to Dan but she forced him out of her mind. That was no way to keep herself out of an impetuous affair!

Mitzi parked her car in the driveway of Brynna's house and turned an affectionate, sympathetic look on her friend. "I really think so," she affirmed. "I also think you're underestimating yourself, Bryn. Give yourself a little credit, will you? Trust your instincts. I'm sure they're good ones. Everyone is entitled to at least one mistake in her life. Remind me sometime to tell you about the loser I was involved with before Perry and I met at college."

Brynna's brow lifted with interest. "Okay, I will." Perry had brought Mitzi home to Haskellville as his wife after meeting her at the college they both attended in the East. Brynna hadn't known Mitzi before the marriage, though she felt now as if she'd known her all her life. She'd only been fourteen when Mitzi and Perry married. "Would you like to come in, Mitzi?"

"No, thanks. I've got a whole list of things to do this afternoon. I enjoyed the lunch, though. This is going to be the best Show-Down ever. Oh, and Bryn?" she added as Brynna climbed out of the low sports car.

"Yes?"

"Think about what I said, will you? Dan Westbrook might be exactly what you need to put that happy light back in your eyes. You won't know until you give it a chance."

"I'll think about what you said," Brynna promised.

How could she help thinking about Dan when he invaded her every waking thought against her will? Not to mention her dreams.

"Man, oh, man. I can't *wait* to tell Delia about this!" Chet announced with a hearty laugh, leaning back in his chair in Dan's office and looking smug.

"What can't you wait to tell your wife?" Dan asked absently, glancing up from the mail he'd just opened.

His homely, pleasant face beaming, Chet winked one brown eye and grinned mischievously at his longtime friend. "I can't wait to tell Delia that the great stone heart has finally cracked! That the invincible has fallen. That the gates have been stormed."

"*What* are you talking about?" Dan demanded. "Honestly, Chet, sometimes—"

"I'm talking about you, buddy. You and a pretty, well-bred blonde with big, eloquent blue eyes and a voice like birds singing. Brynna Haskell, in case your tiny little mind didn't recognize the description."

"Talk about tiny little minds," Dan muttered. "There's nothing going on between me and Brynna Haskell. Not yet, anyway," he added with a grin.

"Can't say you're not trying," Chet answered cheerily. "You did everything but sit up and beg for her attention over lunch. Never thought I'd see the day. Wait'll Dee hears!"

"You're an idiot." Dan ripped open another envelope and perused the contents in disgruntled haste.

Unoffended, Chet continued. "You're actually going to sit there and tell me that this one's not special?"

"Look, I'll admit I'm interested in her. What's so strange about that? She's attractive and single. *I'm* single."

"Glad you didn't try to tell me *you're* attractive."

Ignoring Chet's remark, Dan looked steadily at the letter in his hand. "I still don't see anything all that funny."

"Hey, man, I've seen you interested in pretty women before, but I've never seen you look at anyone that way. I think this is more than just interest. I think you've fallen hard. It's not like I don't know the feeling, you know. That's exactly the way I used to look at Delia. Still look at her that way most of the time, I'd imagine."

"You, of all people, know exactly how I feel about permanent entanglements. Brynna's great-looking and she and I could have some good times for a while, but that's all there would be to it. She's not the only attractive single woman in Haskellville, you know."

"Sure," Chet murmured, obviously not at all convinced.

"Let's talk about the programming for afternoon drive time," Dan suggested curtly, drawing a notepad in front of him.

"Coward," Chet muttered, but he let it go at that.

Chet's words stayed with Dan all afternoon. He was still thinking of them when he went home to his sparsely furnished apartment. Was he allowing himself to become too obsessed with Brynna Haskell? He barely knew the woman, after all. He'd spent more time in fantasies about her than in her presence. And that wasn't like him. The signals he received from her were mixed. Though he sensed she was attracted to him, he could tell she was fighting that attraction. She gave him no encouragement. And yet he continued to pursue.

He took a deep breath and popped the top on a can of beer. Chet was wrong, of course. Dan's attraction to Brynna was nothing more than physical. And she was extraordinarily beautiful. He couldn't even look at her without wanting to know what it was like to touch that porcelain skin, kiss those pouty lips, run his hands over her soft curves. He shifted in his chair, growing uncomfortably aroused just at the images forming in his mind.

"Whoa, son," he warned himself aloud, his fingers tightening around the cold can. "You haven't even been out with her yet." Time to get his feet back on the ground, look at the situation with clear, cold logic. She was beautiful, he hadn't been with a woman in a while—too long, apparently. It was only natural that he'd want her.

He needed to relax. When the time came, he decided, he'd lay it on the line to Brynna. Tell her that he wanted her, that they could be great together while it lasted, but that it wouldn't last forever. If she agreed, he'd take full advantage of her consent. If she wanted more—well, as he'd told Chet, there were other women in Haskellville. He'd even met a couple of them during the past few weeks who'd subtly indicated they wouldn't mind getting to know him better.

Unfortunately, it was still Brynna Haskell whose image made him toss and turn in his bed at night, still Brynna who appeared at odd, inconvenient moments in his thoughts. "Sex," he told himself aloud, trying to believe that was all it was.

## Chapter Four

Brynna eyed the ringing telephone with nervous anticipation. Some instinct told her exactly whose voice would greet her when she answered it. "Hello?"

"Brynna," said the very voice she'd expected. "It's Dan. Have dinner with me."

"Umm—" She stalled, startled by the abrupt invitation. He'd said nothing about dinner when they'd parted after lunch. "Tonight?" It was already close to six.

"Yes."

"Rather short notice, isn't it?"

"Yes." He offered no apology.

She took a deep breath. "Okay."

He hesitated for a moment. "Was that a yes?"

"Yes."

"Okay, then. I'll—uh—I'll see you in an hour?"

"All right. I'll be ready."

"Fine."

"Fine."

Brynna hung up the phone. Had she really just accepted a last-minute date with Dan Westbrook? Had she lost her mind? He'd caught her off guard, she rationalized. Hadn't given her a chance to think.

Suddenly she was laughing. She'd never know what to expect next from Dan. Maybe that's what she liked so much about him. Still smiling, she rushed to dress. She had only an hour to get ready. Something told her he wouldn't be late.

"Oh, that was smooth, Westbrook," Dan groaned, cradling his own receiver. "Real smooth." What had happened to all his practiced lines, his easy conversation? His intelligence? He'd sounded like a jerk.

But—she'd said yes. He'd fully expected her to turn him down, give some excuse or another as she had the other times he'd asked her. She'd totally dumbfounded him by accepting. No argument, no excuses, very little hesitation.

He laughed. He didn't know why he was so surprised. Nothing about this crazy pursuit had been predictable thus far. Why'd he expected it to start being so now?

He looked down at his jeans and sweatshirt. Oh, hell, if he was going to pick her up in an hour, he'd better get on the ball. He bolted for the shower, telling himself even as he did so that he was acting like a kid getting ready for a date with the prom queen.

He wasn't so sure that he liked the feeling.

Brynna enjoyed her dinner with Dan. The awkwardness she'd expected never developed. Dan told her about radio, making her laugh often with anecdotes from his years in the business. She talked about her writing, even admitting that she was having difficulty with her latest book, for the first time since she'd begun her career.

"Maybe you don't want to write the Lexi Beamer books anymore," he suggested after listening attentively to her problem.

She grimaced. "That's exactly the conclusion I've come to. But I've built a readership with Lexi."

"That doesn't mean your readers won't accept a new character from you," he pointed out. "Do you still want to write children's books?"

"I can't imagine writing anything else. I love the age group of my readers."

"Then write for them. But write what you want to write."

Brynna looked thoughtfully across the table. "You're right, of course. I've known for months, I think, that I was simply burned out on the Lexi Beamer books, but I've never really put it into words until tonight. I suppose there have been so many changes in my life during the past year that I resisted making another one."

Dan didn't follow up on her remark about the changes in her life, making her wonder how much he knew about her. Haskellville was such a small town that everyone knew everything about everybody—and he *was* a friend of Mason's. Not that Brynna had anything to hide.

At one point she tried to ask about Dan's family, but he changed the subject without much effort to be subtle about it. He mentioned his father occasionally, and with a great deal of affection, but he might as well never have had a mother for all he said about her. Brynna remembered the way he'd withdrawn into himself the night she asked about his mother. He was obviously carrying some deep wounds from that relationship. Thinking wistfully of her close and loving relationship with her own mother, she felt sorry for Dan.

Brynna was well aware of the attention she and Dan received during the evening. The restaurant they'd chosen was popular in the area, and Brynna knew many of the other diners. She knew there would be some speculation about her being out with this attractive man. Somewhat to her own surprise, she realized that it was the first date she'd had since her divorce. Meaning it had been over five years since she'd been out with any man other than Russ! Good thing she hadn't thought of that earlier. She'd have been a nervous wreck.

Dan drove her home after dinner. Brynna drew a deep breath as he pulled into her driveway. Now was the tricky part. She wouldn't invite him in. She'd proven something to herself by going out with him, discovering that she could, indeed, still enjoy a man's company. It was more than time for her to resume a social life, but she intended to keep this date no more than that. An experiment, of sorts, on her part. That was all it was, a successful experiment. She'd have had a nice time with any personable, charmingly attractive man. There was nothing special about her reactions to Dan Westbrook.

She had her door key ready when Dan walked her to the door. Twisting the key in the lock, she turned with a polite smile to her intently watching escort. "Thank you for dinner, Dan. I had a lovely time."

Something in his eyes told her that he realized the evening was at an end. His smile was sadly accepting. "So did I. Let's do it again. Soon."

She kept her answer deliberately vague. "Yes, we'll do that. Good night."

She was in his arms before she'd even realized he intended to kiss her.

"Good night, Brynna," he murmured even as his head lowered to hers.

It should have been an ordinary good-night kiss, the type that follows most dates between mere acquaintances. She should have pulled back the moment it became apparent that this was no ordinary kiss. But "should haves" had no chance against the explosion of sensations that rocked through her the moment his lips touched hers. She couldn't think, couldn't remember that she was trying to keep her attraction to this man in perspective. Couldn't do anything except cling to the lapels of his jacket and lose herself in the depths of that kiss.

Sensations overwhelmed her. She knew she responded to Dan as to no one in her past, but she hadn't realized how truly cataclysmic her responses could be. The moment her body touched his, she began to tremble, her reactions so intense they frightened her.

By the time the kiss drew to an end, he'd discovered and explored every centimeter of her mouth. She thought she felt his hands tremble on her back as he finally lifted his head, but she was shaking so hard she couldn't be sure. Dan looked as dazed as she felt when she stared mutely up at him. And then she cravenly turned and almost bolted into her house, closing the door firmly behind her.

It was a long time before her hands stopped shaking. She acknowledged now that her attraction to Dan was much more serious than she'd allowed herself to realize. She'd tried to tell herself that it had simply been too long since she'd been with a man, that she would have reacted as strongly to any handsome, charming date. She was wrong. She couldn't imagine anyone else leaving her in this state with nothing more than a kiss.

"I can't do this," she moaned, hiding her face in her hands as she sat curled on her couch. She couldn't allow herself to become involved with Dan. Her life was in too much of a mess right now to take on a challenge of that magnitude. Her career was in shambles, she was still trying to adjust to being single again, just coming to terms with the deaths of her parents. She couldn't even consider entering a new relationship at this time, particularly with Dan. She was too vulnerable to him, too uncertain, too unpredictable in her reactions to him.

The ironic part was, she thought as she finally composed herself enough to change into her nightgown, that Dan had never indicated that he wanted more from her than a few dates. He was obviously attracted to her, but something about his attitude told her that he had no more intention of starting something serious than she did. He'd admitted that he was new in town, hadn't yet met many single women. If only Brynna could trust herself to spend a few pleasant evenings with him without making a complete idiot of herself by falling head over heels in love. But how could she trust herself when only a kiss could set her quivering with hunger for him?

Moaning over her own imprudence, she splashed cold water on her face, carefully avoiding the reflection of the dreamy-eyed flushed woman in the mirror, whose kiss-darkened lips still trembled, still longed for more.

And it had only been a kiss.

Dammit, it had only been a kiss! Dan slammed his fist into his pillow and threw himself onto his side, unable to sleep and furious with the source of his restlessness. He ached all over, tense with frustrated sexual arousal, and all he had done was kiss her good-night. He couldn't remember ever being affected that way by a kiss, even when he'd been a randy teenager and any contact with the other sex was enough to turn him on. He was a thirty-five-year-old adult now, an experienced male, and it was utterly asinine for him to work himself into this state with nothing more than a routine dinner date and one admittedly fantastic kiss.

Brynna Haskell was dangerous. Something about her got to him in a way no other woman had in years. Even with Melanie, he couldn't remember reacting quite so strongly, quite so soon. Maybe it was Brynna's sad eyes, maybe the powerful sexual attraction he felt for her. Whatever it was, he didn't need it right now. Hadn't he learned anything in the past twelve years? If his mother and Melanie had taught him nothing else, he should have learned that a man had to guard himself against letting any woman get too close, particularly a woman at a low point in her life. Too often, he'd discovered, those women turned to some sympathetic man, leaned on him, used him to rebuild their own shaken confidence. And then, just about the time he grew accustomed to being the center of their lives, they decided they were strong enough to move on, leaving the poor fool lonely and devastated.

Oh, no, it wasn't going to happen to this man again. Not to Dan Westbrook. Poor little rich Brynna could cry on some other man's shoulder over her problems. One of her own social circle, perhaps, who might hold her attention longer than the owner of a small radio station who'd never come close to earning the kind of money her father had left her. Her husband had been one of her set, and he'd managed to hold on to her only for a couple of years. Even if Dan were interested in a long-term relationship—which he was *not*, he assured himself firmly—Brynna Haskell was hardly the type of woman he'd be looking for.

But, damn, what a kiss! Even though Brynna had seemed strangely flustered by the embrace—surely she'd expected him to kiss her good-night—the kiss had escalated into an expression of desire that had left his body still thrumming with hunger for her. Incredible.

Reminding himself that he had to get up early for work, he threw an arm over his eyes and tried to put one sexy, blue-eyed blonde completely out of his mind.

He failed miserably.

Sipping her tea, Brynna reread what she'd just typed into her computer. Reaching the bottom of the screen, she nodded, satisfied with the progress of the work she'd done that morning. Dan had been right. New characters, a slightly different focus to her story line, were making all the difference in her work. Perhaps the traumatic changes that had taken place in her personal life since she'd started writing had also affected the stories that had always swirled around in her head.

It had been just over a week since her date with Dan. During that time, he'd called her three times to ask her out, but she'd had a convenient excuse each time. He'd accepted her prevarications patiently enough, but he hadn't stopped calling. Nor did she expect him to do so. He'd made his interest in her quite clear.

And still she trembled whenever she thought back to that kiss. The force of her response continued to unnerve her. She'd never known such feelings, not even in her marriage to Russ, a marriage that, admittedly, had not been particularly passionate. Having never experienced these emotions before, she simply didn't know how to interpret them. Was she reacting only to the physical chemistry between herself and Dan? Or, more frightening still, was she allowing herself to fall for him, a man she knew nothing about, a man whose reticence about his past made her wonder what secrets he was hiding? Not wise, Brynna. Not wise at all, she thought soberly.

Chewing idly on a ragged fingernail, Brynna wondered how she would ever be certain of her emotions when she couldn't even understand her response to a simple good-night kiss. She almost laughed, though, at the absurdity of referring to that kiss as "simple."

"I suppose I could fire a gun into the air, if only I happened to have one with me," a woman's voice observed close to Brynna's ear, making Brynna jump and almost spill her iced tea.

"Mitzi!" she exclaimed. "How long have you been standing there?"

"Nearly five minutes," Mitzi replied with a grin. "I knocked on the kitchen door, but when you didn't answer I came on in. I figured you were probably immersed in your work, as usual. I tried saying your name and loudly clearing my throat, but you were somewhere in another dimension. And you had the most fascinating expressions crossing your face. Were your thoughts fit for mixed company?"

Brynna chuckled and waved Mitzi to a nearby chair. "I was working out a new plot," she replied, resisting the impulse to cross her fingers at the half-truth. After all, she *had* been working on a new plot a few minutes earlier. She didn't have to mention that her latest and most disturbing thoughts had concerned one Dan Westbrook.

"How's it going?" Mitzi asked as she settled into the chair Brynna had indicated.

"Not bad. I'm pleased with it so far. I'm going to try an all new character, totally different style. What do you think?"

"I think whatever you write will be wonderful. You seem to just know by instinct what young girls want to read."

"And *you're* prejudiced." Brynna lifted her tea glass. "There's more in the kitchen. Want some?"

"No, thanks. I just stopped by to drop off your first batch of audition tapes." With the toe of her sneaker, Mitzi nudged the package she'd placed at her feet when she sat down.

"How many?"

"Ten."

"Wow. And the deadline's still a month away."

"Umm. These are the people who've had tapes ready for months, just waiting for the announcement that it was time to send them in. At least we know Show-Down is still a popular event."

Brynna looked thoughtfully at the other woman, noting the purplish smudges under Mitzi's green eyes. "You look tired, Mitz. Are you okay?"

Mitzi shrugged. "Sure. I've just had a busy couple of weeks, what with the kids and the Festival and the volunteer work at the hospital and all."

Brynna frowned. The hospital had been another of her mother's pet projects. She wondered if Mitzi was going a bit overboard trying to fill Alice's place in the community. "I didn't know you were volunteering at the hospital now."

"Umm. Leslie called a couple of weeks ago and said they were desperate for help. I couldn't turn her down."

"Mitzi—"

"Now, Brynna, don't start mothering. I promise I won't overdo it."

Brynna sighed, but allowed the subject to drop. "How's Perry?"

Mitzi's expressive faced closed down at the mention of her husband. "I guess he's okay. We're—he's—"

"You're having problems, aren't you?" Brynna asked carefully.

Mitzi winced. "I should have known we couldn't hide it from you. Yeah, we've been quarreling a lot lately, but I'm sure it's just a bad time for both of us. We'll work it out."

"Oh, Mitzi, I hope so. You and Perry have always been so happy."

Tossing her head, Mitzi scowled. "I know, but I can't be the only one to work at keeping things that way. He has to work at it, too, and lately he—well, he doesn't have time for anything but the company. Sometimes I think he forgets all about me and the kids when he's not around us."

"You know that's not true."

"Do I?" Mitzi muttered resentfully, as she pushed herself to her feet. "I've got about a zillion things to do this afternoon. And you've got better things to do than listen to my complaints, I'm sure. Can't wait to read that new book, Bryn."

"Mitzi," Brynna said as she stood, "if you ever need to talk, you know I'm here, don't you? Anytime, day or night."

Mitzi impulsively hugged her friend. "I know. Thanks. But don't worry about Perry and me, all right? You just take care of yourself. And, speaking of which, have you been out with Dan again?" Mitzi had heard about the date, of course, through the awesomely efficient Haskellville grapevine, though Brynna had been frustratingly reticent about her evening with Dan.

Brynna shook her head, trying to ignore the little frisson of awareness that coursed through her at the mention of Dan's name. "No, only that once."

Mitzi looked disappointed. "Maybe you didn't give him enough encouragement. Why don't you—?"

"Mitzi." Brynna tugged one of Mitzi's copper curls, deciding not to disclose that Dan had asked again, and she had been the one to hold back. "Butt out."

Mitzi laughed. "Okay, I get the message. But if you ever need any advice—"

"'Bye, Mitz."

"See you later, Bryn."

Carrying her empty tea glass, Brynna wandered toward the kitchen. She paused in front of the stereo system in the den, reaching out without thinking to push the power button. The afternoon deejay was chattering brightly about the weather. Again, she thought of Dan.

He hadn't stopped sending her those veiled messages in the morning. And she still found that unusual manner of pursuit much too intriguing, waking each day with a sense of anticipation, eager to hear the song he'd chosen just for her.

He was smooth, she thought in reluctant admiration. Much too smooth. She was completely out of her league with him.

"Darn it, Brynna, stop it!" she said aloud, her voice irritated.

Dan closed the thick file, slipped his pen into his shirt pocket and leaned back into his chair with an exhalation of weary relief. "That wraps it up, then. Sounds good. Thanks for the assistance, buddy."

"Anytime," Chet returned, opening a can of beer and passing it to Dan. He then reached for one for himself, shifting more comfortably into the chair at the round oak dining table. "Ain't it fun being the boss?"

Dan groaned. "Yeah, fun. How come I was so all-fired eager to buy my own station?"

Chet grinned. "I tried to tell you."

"Yeah, I know. But would I listen? No-o-o-o."

Chet laughed, then shook his shaggy brown head. "Don't worry about it, buddy, you're doing fine. Just be careful you don't overwork yourself."

"You must have forgotten who you're talking to. When was I ever in danger of overworking?" Dan asked lazily, leaning back in the chair and sipping his beer.

"Yeah, well, you can pretend, but we both know you're a perfectionist when it comes to your job—particularly now that you're the boss. So, what do you do for relaxation these days? Got a date tonight?"

"Mmm. Mason and I have a hot chess game planned after dinner."

Chet groaned. "Another chess game with the old attorney? Come on, Westbrook."

"Give me a break. I like Mason. I enjoy his company."

"Women, Westbrook. I'm talking women. Remember them?"

"If it makes you feel any better, I have a date this weekend."

"Now, that's more like it. Brynna Haskell?"

Frowning, Dan shook his head. Brynna had turned him down yet again for a weekend date, claiming that she had been invited to a dinner party with friends. He'd believed her, but it was becoming clear enough that she was avoiding him. He hadn't given up on her, but he'd rather defiantly made a date with another attractive, seemingly interesting woman, perhaps as a balm to his increasingly bruised ego. Or maybe to prove to himself that he could handle his intense attraction to Brynna. "No. Someone I met at the supermarket. Her name's Casey."

"At the supermarket, huh? Sounds more like the old Dan Westbrook. I was beginning to wonder if you'd taken a vow of celibacy—or if you'd decided there was only one woman in Haskellville you wanted to date."

Dan muttered something unintelligible into his beer.

"So what's with you and Brynna, anyway?" Chet probed rashly. "Did you discover that she wasn't quite as fascinating as you thought?"

Exasperated with his friend's unsubtle snooping, Dan tried to decide how to reply without admitting the real problem. Finally, he answered in his most nonchalant tone. "Brynna's okay. I just don't want to tie myself down to anyone in particular. You know that."

"She's just okay, huh?" Chet's laughing brown eyes clearly indicated he didn't buy Dan's prevarications for a minute.

Dan's can hit the table with a thud. "Thanks again for the help with this paperwork, Chet. Guess I'd better be going."

"Why don't you hang around for a while? Dee'll be home from her shopping soon. She'll want to see you."

"Tell her I'll see her later. I've got things to do this afternoon before I meet Mason for dinner."

"Dee wants to have you over for dinner next week. Her first dinner party in our new home. What do you say?"

"Just let me know when. You know I'd never miss one of Delia's great meals."

"I'll tell her. See you tomorrow, Dan."

"Yeah. See ya', Chet."

Dan wandered restlessly around his small apartment, wasting time until his dinner appointment with Mason. He thought of the coming weekend and tried to work up some enthusiasm for his date with the attractive Casey, but his thoughts kept turning from the dark-eyed brunette to a certain blue-eyed blonde. The problem was that Chet was right, he reflected glumly. There *was* only one woman in

Haskellville he really wanted to date. For now, he qualified.

Muttering a curse, he shoved himself off the couch and headed for the shower.

## Chapter Five

Brynna woke before her alarm went off on Wednesday, two weeks and four days after her date with Dan. He was on her mind even as the last remnants of sleep cleared away. She'd be seeing him at a late-afternoon meeting of the Women's Club, which all participants of the Summer Festival had been requested to attend. Already her palms were damp at the thought of seeing him. "Idiot," she muttered, rolling onto her back and staring at the ceiling as if there were explanations of her uncharacteristic behavior printed there.

The radio clicked on beside her.

"It's eight o'clock, clear, sunny and warm. This is Dan Westbrook and KHVL with all your favorite music. But, first, a song for a special blue-eyed friend. Good morning."

Brynna's throat tightened as We Five began to sing "You Were on My Mind." Had she really been on his mind when he'd awakened that morning, as he had been on hers?

She found herself smiling as she headed for the shower, though she would have been hard-pressed to fully describe her feelings.

Her telephone rang later that morning as she sat at her computer determinedly thinking about nothing but the story taking shape on screen. Expecting the caller to be Mitzi, she snatched the receiver up in the second ring, her eyes and half her concentration still on the story. "Hello."

"Good morning, Brynna."

That quickly, she forgot all about her work. "Hello, Dan," she said, her voice rather husky.

"Are you working?"

"Yes. I've started a new book with new characters. It's going very well, so far."

"I'm glad. I'd like to read it when you're finished."

She smiled. "It's written for young girls, you know. Probably not your usual reading material."

"I'd still like to read it." He paused for a moment, then continued briskly, "I won't keep you from your work, but I thought I'd ask if I could pick you up for the meeting this afternoon."

She pulled her lower lip between her teeth before answering hesitantly, "Thank you, Dan, but I wasn't planning on going straight from here to the meeting. I have a few errands to run first."

"All right," he agreed equably. "I'll see you there, then. Save me a seat, okay?"

"Umm—sure."

"Guess I'd better go. Stan's almost finished with the news report. See you this afternoon."

It took Brynna several minutes to get her mind off Dan's phone call and settle down to work. Even then she found herself hitting strange keys in the middle of sentences. And wearing an utterly fatuous smile.

Turning off the engine of her car, Brynna fixed her eyes on the large, modern brick and glass building ahead of her. She hadn't visited the offices of Haskell Manufacturing since her father died. After seven months, it was time for her to do so.

She pushed open the entrance door to the building and stepped inside, where she was met with surprised smiles. Returning the warm greetings, she made her way down a long hallway to the office of the CEO, the office that had been her father's.

Perry's secretary, a middle-aged woman with motherly eyes and the brisk efficiency of a state-of-the-art computer, looked up at Brynna's entrance. "Miss Haskell! How nice to see you."

"Thank you, Jane. Is Perry in?"

"Why, yes, he is. And he's alone just now. Go right on in; he'll be delighted to see you." Jane knew it wasn't necessary to formally announce Brynna to her cousin, any more than she would have needed to do so with Mitzi.

Brynna had expected to find changes in the office—had even hoped for those changes. She was stunned to enter the office and find everything exactly the same. If Perry had even moved a chair since he'd moved into his late uncle's position, Brynna couldn't tell it. She frowned a bit as she met her cousin's startled eyes.

Perry rose immediately from the desk at which he'd been poring over a deep stack of papers. "Brynna! This is a nice surprise." Circling the desk, he stopped in front of her to press a kiss to her cheek. "What's up, sweetheart?"

"I was in the neighborhood and thought I'd stop by and sweet-talk you into taking me to lunch. What do you say?"

Perry winced apologetically. "I'd love to, Bryn, but I can't today. I'm going to have to skip lunch to get ready for a one o'clock meeting."

Brynna studied the changes seven months had made on her cousin's handsome face, the hollows in his cheeks, smudges under his eyes, lines that hadn't been there before. "How much weight have you lost lately, Perry?"

He shrugged, evading her eyes. "A few pounds. Nothing I didn't need to lose."

"Perry, you're working too hard. Mitzi says—"

"Mitzi doesn't have time to notice *what* I'm doing." Perry dismissed his wife's opinion irritably. "She's too busy trying to run the Haskellville social scene single-handedly."

"Perry." Brynna lifted a hand to his cheek, her eyes engaging his. "I love you. Don't expect me to stand by quietly while you ruin your health and your marriage."

Covering her hand with his, Perry sighed. "Brynna, I'm not ruining anything. I promise. I just need some time to get things back in order around here. Then Mitzi and I can talk about whatever problems we've been having."

"Your family comes first. Whatever comes up here has to take second place to your wife and children, Perry. Surely you know it was always that way with Dad."

The harried, pressured look that crossed her cousin's face at the mention of his uncle broke Brynna's heart. Perry was trying so hard to fill Bryan's shoes—too hard, in Brynna's opinion. Didn't Perry understand that he'd never be Bryan, that he shouldn't even try? He had his own talents, his own strengths, different but completely equal to his late uncle's. She wished she knew how to convince him of that, but suspected he'd have to learn it on his own. "Please don't hesitate to call me if you ever need to talk," she begged him.

"I won't. Thanks, Bryn. I love you, too, you know."

"I know." She stepped away from him. "I'll let you get back to work now."

"I'm glad you came by. Really. Next time I promise I'll make time for lunch with you."

"Next time I'll call first," she assured him, adding gently, "I think it's time for some remodeling around here, don't you? This office has looked the same for the past ten years."

Perry shrugged and shoved his hands into the pockets of his gray slacks. "I'm comfortable with it this way."

"All right. But think about it, okay? It's your office now and it should look like it. Personally, I think it's well filled."

Seemingly pleased with the compliment, he smiled warmly, though she noted the weariness that still shadowed his blue eyes. "Thanks, sweetheart."

It hadn't been as hard as she'd expected, Brynna reflected, driving away from the building. She hadn't been haunted by painful memories of her father when she'd entered his office. Perhaps because she was so deeply concerned about the man who occupied that office now. She had the nagging feeling that she should have tried harder to convince Perry to take better care of himself. But Perry was an adult and she really had very little right to interfere in his life. She'd done all she could. She only hoped she had made some impression on him.

Dan combed his hair with his fingers, straightened the collar of his white shirt and brushed absently at a speck of lint on his dark slacks. His actions drew a low laugh from the man walking at his side. "Primping, Dan?" Chet taunted. "Want to tell me again that Brynna Haskell's nothing special?"

Pushing open the door to the Chamber of Commerce building, where the Women's Club was holding its meeting, Dan glared at the other man. "You know, Traylor, there are times when I don't even like you. This is one of them."

Undaunted, Chet laughed again. "Sorry, boss," he murmured without evidence of regret.

Muttering beneath his breath, Dan entered the conference room, his eyes automatically scanning the milling, chattering crowd inside. He wouldn't have admitted to Chet that he was looking for Brynna, but his search ended the moment he caught sight of the slender blonde standing with Mitzi and the mayor.

Nothing had changed. Two weeks and four days and a pleasant, if platonic evening in the company of another woman had made not the slightest difference in Dan's reaction to Brynna. He still felt as if someone had knocked the breath from him the moment she caught sight of him and sent a bright, welcoming smile across the room.

As if her smile were a magnet pulling him across the room, he moved toward her, absently returning the greetings of the few people there he knew. He didn't stop until he stood beside her. "Hi."

"Hi. Dan, have you met our mayor, John Beatty?"

"Yes, we've met. Nice to see you again, mayor." Dan extended a hand to the man he'd met twice before. Mayor Beatty was a pleasant-featured man in his early thirties, towering a good two inches over Dan's own six-two. Dan had liked the mayor from the first time he'd met him, which didn't lessen his urge to rearrange Beatty's face. Brynna had smiled at the man with too much easy affection. Dammit.

Mitzi stepped behind the podium at the front of the room and spoke into the microphone. "If everyone will take their seats now, we can get started."

Dan made sure he was seated next to Brynna. Chet slipped into the empty seat on his other side, still wearing his most provoking grin. Dan ignored him. "You look lovely today," he murmured to Brynna as Mitzi performed the routine duties in presiding over the meeting.

Brynna flushed and smoothed the skirt of her floral-print silk dress over her knees, not meeting Dan's eyes. "Thank you," she whispered.

"You're welcome," he returned, his low voice amused. She shot him a sideways glance, her eyes sparkling with her smile, before directing her attention to the front of the room.

Dan made a halfhearted effort at concentrating on the proceedings of the meeting for perhaps ten minutes, as various Summer Festival project chairmen gave their reports. But then he leaned close to Brynna again. "I've missed you," he told her, surprising even himself.

Surprised, she caught her lower lip between her teeth, making him long to erase the resulting teeth marks with a long, hard kiss. She didn't answer him, but turned her eyes slowly back toward the front of the room.

Dan shifted casually in his seat until his thigh pressed discreetly against Brynna's in the close quarters. No one around them would have been aware of the move, but Dan relished the feeling. Brynna didn't move away, though he knew she was as distracted by the contact as he.

"You smell so good," he murmured into her ear a few minutes later. "Like flowers and sunshine."

"Dan," she whispered in a thin voice, keeping her face firmly turned away. "Stop it."

"I'm not sure I can," he muttered, as much to himself as to her.

Brynna jumped when Mitzi called her name for a second time, asking for a report on Show-Down. Dan watched her compose herself before she stood and gave a quick summary of the steps already taken and the number of entries already received. She concluded by introducing Dan and Chet as masters of ceremony. He smiled at her as she sat back down. "You did that very well."

Her answering smile was brilliant. Between her teeth, she murmured, "I'm going to strangle you when this is over."

He laughed softly, pleased that she wasn't totally unaffected by him. He'd hate to think he was the only one caught in the web of attraction.

The meeting ended soon afterward. Standing when the others did, Dan caught Brynna's wrist in his hand, making sure she didn't slip away. "Chet and his wife, Delia, have invited me to dinner tonight and Delia told me to feel free to bring a guest. You'd like her. How about it?" It wasn't the smoothest invitation he'd ever offered, but then Brynna seemed to do that to him. He waited expectantly for her reply.

Overhearing, Chet seconded the invitation. "Please come, Brynna. Dee doesn't know many women in Haskellville, yet. She'd be really pleased for you to join us."

The rueful glance Brynna shot Dan let him know that she couldn't resist the double invitation. "I'd be delighted, if you don't mind that I can't stay very late. I have an early appointment in the morning."

Assuring her that would be fine, Chet smiled broadly. "Dee's going to be tickled to meet you. She's heard a lot about you." He, too, glanced meaningfully at Dan. Anything Delia had heard about Brynna hadn't come from Dan.

"I'll pick you up in an hour, okay?" Dan asked Brynna.

Even as he made the arrangements he wondered if he'd made a mistake asking her to join him at the Traylors' house that evening. Chet was already convinced that Dan had met his match in Brynna, and Delia probably thought so too, based on whatever Chet had told her. Dan wasn't sure he was up to an entire evening of not-so-subtle matchmaking. Especially when he seemed to have no willpower whatever against this particular woman.

Brynna liked Delia Traylor on sight. A year or two younger than Brynna, she was cheerful, artlessly outspoken and hopelessly naive. Her attractive, gamine face was highlighted by enormous gray eyes and a delightfully crooked, seemingly permanent grin and framed by a short, shaggy mop of hair that had been bleached golden blonde. She stood maybe five-three, Brynna estimated, and would normally have been petitely built. At present, she was large with pregnancy.

"It's so nice to meet you," Delia gushed with obvious sincerity. "I haven't had a chance to meet many women my own age, yet. I'm glad you could come tonight."

Brynna murmured an appropriate response as she glanced around the room. Simply furnished, the Traylors' small frame house still seemed to reflect the cheerful, enthusiastic personalities of its owners. Brynna felt immediately comfortable there, as if the house, itself, were welcoming her as warmly as her hosts. "When is your baby due?" she asked Delia.

"The end of August. *If* I survive that long."

Chet affectionately ruffled his wife's already disarrayed hair. "Dee's not long on patience," he explained.

"And you are?" Dan asked meaningfully, making Delia laugh and explain to Brynna that Chet was the most impatient person she'd ever known.

An hour later the four of them were chatting like old friends as they made a considerable dent in the mountain of fried chicken, creamed potatoes and vegetables that Delia served. Though Delia modestly explained that she wasn't much of a cook, Brynna enjoyed every bite of the meal, and said so. She couldn't remember laughing so much in a very long time. At one point during the evening she surprised even herself by telling a joke that had the others rolling with laughter. She was suddenly very glad that Dan had asked her. She'd needed this.

Dan stayed close by Brynna's side during the evening, encouraging her to have a good time, making sure that she was included in the conversations between the three friends who'd known each other for so long. She was very much aware of him, of the frequent glances that caught and held between them, the shared smiles, the mingled laughter. His recurrent touches that were no more than fleeting caresses, yet left her aching for more. That more cautious, more sensible side of her tried to protest that she was headed for deep trouble with Dan, but she boldly ignored the warnings. She was having much too pleasant an evening to worry about the future.

They lingered for a long time over dessert, but eventually it was time to leave the table. Brynna immediately offered to help Delia with the dishes. Banishing the men to the living room, and meeting with only token resistance, the two women began the routine of cleaning up, chatting easily as they worked. "You should come to the next meeting of the Women's Club," Brynna told Delia. "It's a wonderful way to meet people here in town."

Delia grimaced, running a hand through her shaggy hair. "I'm not really the Women's Club type," she admitted. "I don't suppose you belong to a bowling team?"

Brynna laughed. "This isn't one of those snobby, exclusive groups you're imagining," she assured Delia. "Many of us have jobs, which is the reason we meet late in the afternoon, so people can come straight from work and still have the evening free to spend with their families. We work in the community—and I mean we work, not just spreading money around. We roll up our sleeves and build playground equipment, hold bake sales and fund-raisers to provide food and clothing for the underprivileged, offer community education programs such as CPR and childcare. Believe me, Delia, you'd fit in.''

Looking intrigued, Delia conceded that the Women's Club sounded like an organization she might enjoy and promised to attend the next meeting before making up her mind.

''I like you, Brynna,'' she commented with the artless candor that Brynna had already learned to associate with her.

''Thank you, Delia. I like you, too.''

''I knew you'd be okay when Chet told me how Danny acted around you. Chet thinks it's really funny that Danny's finally found someone who's knocked him for a loop.''

Brynna's cheeks flamed. ''I—uh—''

''I think it's great, myself. I've wished and wished that Danny would find someone special, you know? He needs someone. All men do,'' she added with a chuckle. ''But Danny—'' She shook her head in fond exasperation. ''The man's as slippery as an eel when it comes to getting involved with a woman. Darn that ex-fiancé of his. She really burned him.''

''Dan was—engaged?'' Brynna asked hesitantly, not wanting to gossip, but intrigued by this conversation about the man who'd made such an impact on her.

''Yeah, a long time ago. We didn't know him then, but Danny told Chet about it once. The woman sounded like a bitch—a faithless one, at that. I think she really hurt him. I don't think he's really trusted a woman since.''

"He should know better than to judge all women by the actions of one," Brynna commented, frowning.

"That's what I've told him about a million times," Delia agreed. "He always assures me that he wouldn't dream of doing that, but—" she shrugged expressively "—he's still single."

"Mmm," Brynna murmured noncommittally.

"So why don't you try to do something about that?" Delia challenged with a cocky grin.

Brynna flushed scarlet. "Delia—"

"Do something about what?" Dan's voice asked from the doorway. Brynna froze in dismay, praying he hadn't heard Delia's ridiculous words.

"Nothing you'd be interested in," Delia shot back with an impish smile at Brynna. "What do you need, Danny?"

Seemingly resigned to the nickname that only Delia would ever call him by, Dan patted her on the shoulder before draping a careless arm around Brynna. "I came to see what was keeping you two so long. Figured Brynna might need rescuing."

"Well, I like that!" Delia protested with mock indignance. "I'll have you know that Brynna and I have been having a very nice time getting to know each other. Haven't we, Brynna?"

"Yes, we have," Brynna agreed, grateful that Delia hadn't told Dan exactly what they'd been talking about. She was having a hard enough time dealing with the feel of his arm around her waist. It really shouldn't be causing this silly tendency to forget to breathe. Nor the sudden weakening of her knees. One would think she'd never been this close to a man before.

Of course, Dan Westbrook wasn't the average man. Something about him brought out the strangest urges in her. Like this impulse to turn in his arms and rest her cheek on his shoulder. Or to pull his head down to hers and . . .

"Brynna?" Dan interrupted her fantasy, sounding as if it wasn't the first time he'd said her name.

"Yes?"

"I asked if you're ready to go. It's getting late and you said you had an early appointment."

"Yes, I do."

Chet and Delia saw them to the door, urging Brynna to come back for another visit. Brynna promised to call Delia before the next Women's Club meeting. And then she and Dan were alone in his car.

"I had a very nice time tonight," she said when the silence between them stretched a bit too long for comfort. "I really like your friends."

"They're nice people."

"They seem to have a very good marriage."

"Yeah, well, every once in a while a guy lucks out," Dan muttered, his eyes trained on the road ahead. "Chet did."

"It doesn't sound like you have a very high opinion of marriage in general," Brynna remarked tentatively.

His look was unreadable. "You should know how rarely it works out."

There didn't seem much to say in response to that. She was stung by the barely veiled reference to her failed marriage and turned her attention to the passing street signs.

Dan seemed to regret his curtness as they pulled into her driveway. "You promised me a full schedule of events and participants for the Summer Festival to use for promotion," he reminded her. "Do you happen to have one with you? I could start tomorrow."

Brynna nodded, reaching for her door handle. "They're inside. Come in and I'll get you one."

Brynna walked straight to the desk in her study upon entering her house, all too aware that Dan was following her closely. She hadn't realized quite how close until she turned, schedule in hand, to find him only inches away, so close she could feel the heat of his body. Her breath caught painfully in her throat as their eyes locked.

Very slowly, Dan reached out to stroke her cheek with one callused finger. "You are a beautiful woman, Brynna Haskell."

She cleared her throat, already beginning to tremble. "Dan, I don't think this is a good idea."

"I," he told her quietly, "think it's an excellent idea."

And then he lowered his head to hers.

## Chapter Six

Dan felt Brynna stiffen as he took her into his arms. His lips brushed hers once, then again, coaxing a response. "I've wanted to kiss you again for the past two weeks," he murmured, his hands spreading across her slender back. "Let me kiss you, Brynna."

Her hands lay tensely on his chest. He could feel them trembling. "Dan, I—"

"Just a kiss, honey. I won't push for anything else." Again he wondered at her nervousness with him. The woman had been married, for heaven's sake. What had that husband of hers done to her? "Relax, Brynna," he whispered against her lips. "Relax and kiss me back."

Even as his mouth settled on hers, Dan told himself he only wanted to find out if this kiss could possibly be as powerful as the one that had haunted him for more than two weeks. He almost hoped it would not be.

He hoped in vain. Whatever insanity had gripped him the last time he'd kissed her returned full force when Brynna's lips opened hesitantly beneath his. He groaned, a sound of mingled despair and desire, and thrust into her mouth, hungrily reclaiming the territory he'd explored so briefly before.

Brynna's initial stiffness began to melt in the heat of the kiss. Her hands moved up slowly to his shoulders, where her fingers flexed unconsciously in a catlike, kneading motion that made him shiver. Pulling her soft, slender form more firmly against him, Dan ran his open palms down her back to the slight curve of her hips where he paused to flex his fingers into resilient flesh, cautiously testing her response. Brynna moaned low in her throat and stirred restlessly against him, beginning to tense again.

The movement almost shattered his fragile control. He wanted nothing more than to sweep her into his arms, carry her to the nearest soft surface and bury himself in her feminine warmth. He'd wanted her from the first time he'd seen her. The time he'd spent with her since that first day had only served to whet his hunger for her. He wondered dazedly if he'd ever wanted another woman this much.

Sex, he told himself as he'd tried to do before. Nothing more than sex. And still he kept the kiss gentle, persuasive, wanting to give her nothing but pleasure.

Widening his stance, he pressed more insistently against her hips, bringing her firmly against his hardening maleness. She had to know how much he wanted her, he reasoned, had to understand just what she did to him with no more than her kiss. He almost groaned when she didn't pull away. She wanted him, too. Whatever she might say, however hard she may fight it, she wanted him. The knowledge made him harden even more.

Her breasts were firm and soft against his chest. He needed to know how they'd feel in his hand. He thought she would fill his palm beautifully. Sliding a hand between them, he cupped one swelling mound. He'd been right. The fit was perfect. Tearing his mouth from hers, he strung kisses down her flushed cheek to her throat, tasting her skin as he worked his way downward. Brynna arched, eyes closed, head thrown back, giving him better access to her curves.

"Oh, God, Brynna, I want you so much," he muttered, his mouth hovering just over the tip of one fabric-covered breast.

His voice seemed to startle her out of the sensual haze she'd almost slipped into. She pushed frantically against him. "No! No, we have to stop. Dan, please."

He swallowed a curse and reluctantly allowed her to step away from him. Her cheeks were stained with scarlet passion, her blue eyes blazing hot with the desire he'd roused in her. White-blond curls tumbled artlessly around her flushed, damp face. It was all he could do to keep from reaching out to pull her back into his arms. She was so damned beautiful—especially now, with that cool, carefully cultivated poise of hers so thoroughly shattered.

"I want you," he told her again, his voice rougher than he'd intended.

"I—" She swallowed and twisted her hands in front of her. "I don't want this, Dan."

"You want me."

Her eyes widened at his blunt statement. "I'm—attracted to you," she said carefully. "I think that's obvious enough. But that doesn't mean I'm going to bed with you."

"Brynna—" he began, speaking in a low, seductive tone, one hand reaching for her. He could change her mind, he thought confidently. All he had to do was kiss her again and she'd have to admit that she wanted him as much as he wanted her.

"No." There was no hesitation in the firmly spoken word. His hand fell to his side.

Brynna took a deep breath, tossed her hair back and faced him squarely. "Dan, I like you," she began. "You're very nice and I enjoy being with you. But I'm not interested in a more serious relationship right now. I don't want to get involved with you."

He almost choked. What the hell was she doing giving him *his* speech? He knew what was coming. The old sure-we're-good-together-but-let's-not-read-too-much-into-it routine. How many times had he used the same approach? *We can have a great time for a while, but don't expect it to last.* How many women had he said that to?

He certainly couldn't remember any woman turning the speech on him. He didn't like it.

Annoyance made him short with her. "I never said anything about getting involved. Not the way you mean it anyway."

She nodded understandingly. "I know. You'd like an affair—maybe even a one-night fling. But that kind of thing's all wrong for me. I can't take sex that casually. And I don't trust myself to know what I'm feeling when I'm with you."

"You want me," he said again, less confidently this time, uncertain what she'd meant by that last statement but not so sure he wanted to pursue it closely.

She hesitated, then shrugged delicately. "I've been divorced for a year and you're a very attractive man. I suppose it was only natural that I got a bit carried away when you kissed me. I'm sorry if you thought I was asking for more."

He'd been annoyed. Now he was furious. *Carried away?* he repeated in silent wrath. She was claiming that she would have reacted that way to the kiss of any man who was reasonably good-looking and mildly entertaining? She actually believed kisses like that came along all the time? He brutally fought down the temptation to demonstrate that there had been more between them than the momentary response of a woman who'd been too long without a man.

"Fine," he said, his lips feeling unusually stiff. "If you want to tell yourself that's all it was, then fine. I have no intention of standing here arguing with you."

She eyed him warily, as if she'd just realized how thoroughly angry he was. "I think you'd better go now. As I said, I have an early appointment tomorrow."

He nodded stiffly. "Right. I'll be seeing you."

"Good night. And thank you for asking me tonight. I really did have a very nice time."

His muttered response was unintelligible.

Much later that night Dan finally realized he was acting like an idiot. Dammit, he wasn't looking for a serious relationship, so why act like an outraged suitor? What a jerk.

Yet he still utterly hated the idea that she thought she would have melted in the embrace of any other man in the same way she had in his. Someday he was going to prove her wrong. Someday soon.

"This next song is for a lady who doesn't know just how persistent some men can be." Dan's voice announced cheerfully. Brynna glared at the radio as it began to play "We Can Work It Out" by the Beatles.

Dan was so sure they'd have an affair. She'd seen it in his eyes when she'd sent him away the night before. He'd listened to her careful speech with visible anger that she was proving resistant to his lethal charm, then finally left with the smug certainty that he could make her change her mind. Arrogant man.

She only hoped she'd have the willpower to prove him wrong. Despite her fear of the power of her response to him, it was all too easy to get carried away when he held her, kissed her. And she wasn't even a particularly passionate woman, she thought with a mental wail.

Throwing back the comforter, she defiantly snapped off the radio and shoved herself out of bed. She really was going to start waking to another radio station, or maybe just to the buzz of the alarm.

Even as she made the decision she knew she wouldn't follow through on it.

Despite her resolutions, Brynna still found herself three days later walking hand in hand with Dan through the park where they'd met six weeks earlier. The picnic had been Dan's idea. It had taken him all of five minutes on the phone to talk her into it.

So much for willpower.

There had been a bit of awkwardness between them when he'd first picked her up. Neither of them could seem to forget about the kiss they'd shared the previous time they'd been together. Brynna had caught Dan staring at her mouth almost as many times as she'd found herself staring at his. Yet both of them had managed to carry on a pleasant, impersonal conversation during lunch. Lulled into a sense of security by the nonthreatening camaraderie he established between them, Brynna allowed herself to relax.

It had seemed quite natural when he'd reached out to twine his fingers with hers. They hadn't spoken so far during the walk, but the smiles they'd shared had been warm and friendly. Nothing more, she assured herself.

"Tell me about your ex-husband."

Startled by his request, Brynna turned to find him staring idly at a group of children playing kickball, his expression unreadable. "What do you want to know?" she asked curiously.

"Did you love him?"

Though she wondered at the suddenly personal nature of his question, particularly after their carefully innocuous conversation during lunch, Brynna never considered not answering. "I loved him. I still do, in some ways."

His hand twitched around hers, though his voice held little inflection when he spoke again. "Then what went wrong? Why aren't you still married?"

"These are awfully personal questions, Dan." Brynna pointed out gently.

"I know. You don't have to answer, of course. Just tell me to butt out."

She pulled her hand out of his and pushed both of hers into the pockets of her full cotton skirt. "I'd like to know why you asked. Why the sudden curiosity about my marriage?"

Dan shrugged. "I want to know more about you. Your marriage seems to be a fairly important part of your past."

She nodded a slow acknowledgement of his reasoning, though she wondered if he would be willing to talk about his long-ago engagement if she asked. She wouldn't ask, of course. Dan always made it quite clear that he didn't want to talk about his past, other than in a general, impersonal manner.

"Russ and I were very good friends," she said finally. "We had fun together. We laughed at the same jokes, enjoyed the same music and movies, never ran out of things to say to each other. Both of us thought those things made an excellent basis for a marriage."

"And they didn't?"

She shook her head. "No. There were a few things we forgot to take into account."

"Such as?"

Her cheeks warming, she carefully avoided looking at him. "Such as passion. Our love life wasn't really—exciting. We were friends, not lovers, and Russ, especially, began to want more."

"Was he unfaithful?"

Brynna couldn't believe they were actually having this conversation, that she was speaking so frankly to Dan when she'd hardly told anyone else about the end of her marriage. It seemed easy to talk to him, for some reason. Maybe it was just that she wanted to talk about it now, to put it behind her once and for all. "No, he was never unfaithful. Russ didn't believe in adultery, any more than I did. When he finally admitted to himself that he wanted more, he came to me very honestly, and we talked.

"There were other problems, of course, by that time. I was ready for children; he wasn't. He was terribly unhappy teaching college and living in Haskellville when he desperately wanted to be out on exotic digs—he's an archaeologist. He tried to settle down, but he's a nomad, a wanderer. He was being smothered here, though he'll always consider this his home, his refuge between adventures. I would have been miserable without roots, drifting from one primitive location to another, as he's been doing since our divorce. We both knew it was time to end it. It was all very amicable."

"And very sad," Dan observed quietly.

"And very sad," she agreed. "We were both hurt by our mistake of confusing deep friendship for real love."

"Is that the reason you're so cautious about forming new relationships?" Dan asked, finally getting down to the purpose of all his questioning.

"Yes," she answered honestly. "I don't want to make the same mistakes again."

"You don't think you learned anything from your mistakes?"

She pushed a blowing strand of hair out of her face and shrugged. "I hope I have. I know I've learned to be more careful."

"By never getting involved again? Don't you think that's going to extremes?"

She sighed and turned to lean against a thick tree trunk, facing him without blinking. "Dan, I didn't say I never want to get involved again. I enjoyed many things about being married, and I'm not opposed to the idea of marrying again someday. But next time I want to be absolutely sure I know what I'm doing."

Talk of marriage seemed to make him very uncomfortable. He tugged at the collar of his knit shirt. "So what are you going to do until you meet someone you finally decide is worth taking a risk on again? What's wrong with spending some of that time enjoying yourself without worrying about future complications?"

She smiled at his lack of subtlety. "You mean, why not indulge in a few light, undemanding affairs until Mr. Right comes along?"

"I didn't say that exactly," he hedged.

"Mmm. But it's what you meant. That's your philosophy, isn't it?"

"I'm not looking for permanence at all," Dan returned instantly.

"Just the affairs?"

He blew out a deep breath, exasperation written on his attractive face. "I'm not *looking* for either. But I'm not running like you are. When I meet someone I enjoy being with, someone I desire, I let nature take its course. I'm honest from the beginning about my feelings. I always make it very clear that I'm not looking for marriage or even long-term relationships. The women I've known over the past few years have understood that from the beginning. We've had some good times, then parted without hard feelings."

"All very civilized, very sophisticated. No guilt, no regrets."

"Right."

Her smile twisted as she resisted the urge to add that it was also very cowardly. Dan was so careful to appear cool, but the truth was he was every bit as scared of making mistakes as Brynna. It was perfectly obvious that he'd been terribly hurt in the past and she knew he was leery of being hurt again. Did he think she didn't realize that? Men, she thought in exasperation. "How convenient for you. You've been very fortunate to find such understanding, undemanding women."

"Stop laughing at me."

She tried unsuccessfully to swallow a chuckle. "I'm sorry. Sometimes it's very hard for women not to laugh at the games men play."

"Only a woman could interpret total honesty as a game."

"Honesty, as *you* see it. Why don't you just go ahead and get to the point of this conversation, Dan? You've asked about my past, made your own feelings about marriage and commitment quite clear, and now you obviously have something else to say. So say it and get it over with."

"You know, you can be very irritating," Dan told her, though his mouth twitched with the beginnings of a reluctant smile.

"So I've been told," she agreed equably.

He placed his hands on the tree on either side of her head, effectively trapping her within his arms. "The point is," he said, his voice low and seductively deep, "that I want you. You're driving me crazy with wanting you. And, since neither of us is in danger of expecting too much from the other now that we've been perfectly honest with each other, I don't see why we can't just go ahead and enjoy each other without worrying about how long it's going to last." He lowered his head and nuzzled her cheek with his lips, waiting for her answer.

Brynna rested her hands on his chest, her breath growing slightly ragged in reaction to his nearness. His mouth strayed closer to hers, making her lips quiver for his kiss. Forgetting about the others enjoying the pretty little park on this beautiful Saturday afternoon in June, she hesitantly turned her head until her lips found his.

Dan kissed her deeply and, though she sensed the male satisfaction in him, she ignored it for the moment, allowing herself to fully enjoy the embrace. This man knew how to kiss, she thought with very feminine appreciation, parting her lips further for him. She was suddenly very brave, she thought with rueful self-mockery, knowing that the public park gave her courage she wouldn't have had had they been alone.

Dan's own breath was uneven when he finally pulled back, his eyes blazing as he smiled down at her. "Wow."

"Mmm," she murmured, returning the smile.

"Lady, you are one hell of a kisser," he told her warmly, unknowingly echoing her own thoughts.

"Why, thank you, sir," she returned, teasingly fluttering her eyelashes, knowing he mistakenly believed she'd just agreed to an affair and that he wasn't going to be at all happy when he found out he was wrong. But there was a rather intoxicating sense of power in testing her feminine wiles on this man, particularly since she still felt safe in their surroundings.

"We are going to be fantastic in bed," he continued, still in that rather smug tone. "Tonight we'll—"

"No."

He blinked at the gentle, unequivocal interruption. "What?"

"I said no. I'm not going to bed with you, Dan."

He shoved himself away from the tree, his hands going into his pockets as if to keep them from wrapping around her throat. "You're *trying* to drive me crazy, right? This is some kind of twisted game of yours."

"No game, Dan. I'm just not going to bed with you. I enjoy being with you, but I'll understand if you decide you're not getting equal pleasure as things are with me. I'm sure there are several lovely, modern women in the area who'll be quite happy to comply with your neat little rules. I'm not one of them."

His face darkened. "Then you *do* want a commitment from me."

She moaned in sheer exasperation at the deliberate obtuseness of the male mind. "Dan, I don't want *anything* from you. Including a casual affair. All I want is to get my life back into order, get my career reestablished, start enjoying myself again. I want to spend time with the friends I've neglected during the past months, make new friends such as you, and Chet and Delia and have a good time with Show-Down. That's what I need now. Fun. My work. Friends. I've been terribly unhappy for the past few months since I lost my parents, and now it's time to be happy again. I simply can't handle the demands of an affair."

He was still for a long time, no longer looking angry but thoughtful. Finally he sighed, pushing a hand through his breeze-tossed dark hair. "I won't pretend to like what you're saying, but I do understand, I guess. I'm sorry if you've felt that I was pressuring you into a physical relationship. And I'm sorry if I was causing you stress just when you're starting to enjoy yourself again. I want you to be happy, Brynna. You deserve it.''

She was touched by the sincerity in his words. ''Thank you, Dan.''

His smile didn't quite reach his eyes. ''So you just want to be friends, huh?''

''Yes. Just friends.'' For now, she added silently, wondering if there'd ever come a time when she'd be ready for more. If any man could change her mind about having an affair, she was pretty sure Dan would be the one. Not that she had any intention of saying that aloud after finally convincing him that she wanted their relationship to stay platonic.

He sighed again. ''Okay. Friends. How about taking in a movie with me tonight?''

She regarded him with undisguised skepticism. ''You still want to go out with me?''

''Brynna, I am perfectly capable of controlling my baser instincts,'' he answered with cool dignity. ''And I have been known to have a few very good friends who were women. Just friends. I'm not exactly a raving sex maniac.''

She laughed. ''I'm sorry. I didn't mean to insult you.''

He nodded, satisfied that he'd made his point. ''Let's go. I need to run by the station for a while before I pick you up tonight.''

Absurdly happy with the outcome of their confrontation, she matched her steps to his. He slipped a casual arm around her shoulders. ''I give it a week,'' he remarked idly without turning to look at her.

''Give what a week?'' she asked, her own arm going irresistibly around his lean waist.

"Until you beg me to make love to you. I suppose I can wait that long." Reaching his car, he dropped his arm and opened her door for her, smiling challengingly down at her.

Resisting the urge to kick him hard, she lifted her chin in defiance and slid into the car, refusing to comment on his remark. And hoping fervently that she'd be able to prove him wrong.

Brynna looked in dismay at the stack of tapes Mitzi had just dumped into her hands. "Lord, I can't believe the response we're having already this year. They're coming in from all over the state."

"The coverage we received in the state-wide media last year really attracted attention," Mitzi agreed. "This should be the biggest Summer Festival we've ever had. And it doesn't hurt that we have that talent agent from Chicago as a Show-Down judge this year. All these hopeful performers are just sure this will be their big break."

Brynna piled the tapes on a table and waved her friend into a chair. "Sit down. You've been so busy lately that we've hardly had time to see each other. Boys, there are cookies in the kitchen. Help yourselves," she added to Bryan and Nathan, who'd accompanied their mother on the delivery errand.

"Is it okay, Mom?" Bryan asked Mitzi eagerly.

"Sure. But don't make a mess in Brynna's kitchen, okay? Nathan, let Bryan get yours for you," she added, dropping into an armchair. "School's only been out a few weeks and I'm already wishing for fall," she confided to Brynna. "Bryan, especially, is getting restless."

"He'll settle into a routine soon," Brynna assured her. "Probably just before school starts back."

Mitzi grimaced and nodded agreement. "Have you seen Dan lately?" she asked unexpectedly, changing the subject.

"We had a picnic last Saturday, and then went to a movie later that evening." And she'd managed not to strangle him over his glib confidence that it was only a matter of time until they became lovers.

"Yes, I heard."

Brynna groaned. "Who was the informer this time?"

"Bill Satterfield. I saw him this morning. He said he ran into you at the movie theater."

A young attorney who'd been in partnership with Mason for a little over two years, Bill had been divorced not long after Brynna. "Yes, I did see him. He was with his oldest son, Billy."

"He asked about you. I think he was trying to find out if you're back in circulation or whether there's anything serious between you and Dan. I think he'd like to ask you out."

"What did you tell him?"

"That he should give you a call."

"Thanks a lot."

"Well, why not? Bill's cute, nice, single. You'd probably have a good time with him." Mitzi paused meaningfully, eyeing her friend with mischievous eyes. "Unless, of course, it *is* serious between you and Dan."

"Dan and I are just friends," Brynna returned.

"Mmm. His choice or yours?"

"Mine," Brynna admitted, "but he doesn't want a long-term involvement, anyway. Only an affair—and you know I'm not interested in that."

"If all you want is an occasional date without worrying about the long term, then you should go out with Bill. He's not ready to get into another relationship yet, either. He's just looking for some pleasant feminine companionship right now." She grinned. "I think he's tired of going out with his kids."

"*If* he calls, I'll decide then," Brynna promised.

"He'll call."

"Maybe."

Mitzi turned a frown of intense concentration on a chipped fingernail. Her voice was suspiciously casual when she asked, "Does Dan still excite you?"

"Mitzi—"

"Just curious. I think it's really cute the way he plays special songs for you every morning."

Brynna choked and Mitzi laughed gleefully. "You know about that? How? You don't even listen to that station!"

"I do now—ever since we decided to let him emcee Show-Down. And I know he's talking to you because you're the only blue-eyed blonde I've personally seen him panting after."

"Dan Westbrook," Brynna pronounced sternly, "is a conceited, smug, arrogant playboy."

"And he makes your knees melt," Mitzi added humorously.

"And he makes my knees melt," Brynna repeated with a deep sigh. "Maybe I *should* go out with some other men. Maybe the problem is that Dan's the only interesting male I've been with since Russ and I split up."

"Or maybe the problem is that you and Dan Westbrook are a great couple who happen to belong together," Mitzi proposed, more seriously this time. "It happens, you know. And the sparks between the two of you are pretty obvious."

Brynna shook her head vigorously. "No. He's not interested in a commitment and I don't trust my feelings for him. We're completely wrong for each other."

"Keep telling yourself that, Bryn. You might even start to believe it eventually."

Before Brynna could continue the argument, they were interrupted by Mitzi's sons returning noisily to the living room, their mouths still bearing the evidence of the chocolate cookies they'd consumed. Mitzi left soon afterward, leaving Brynna more confused than ever about her feeling for Dan Westbrook.

## Chapter Seven

Dan, you have to stop sending me these messages every morning. People are starting to catch on."

Dan grinned at the stern tone that didn't quite hide her pleasure, even through the phone line. "Hey, I'm being discreet. These are very innocuous songs," he protested.

"This morning you played 'Do You Think I'm Sexy?' by Rod Stewart. That is not a discreet, innocuous song. Neither was the next one you played."

"'I'm Going to Kiss You All Over'? Don't you like that one?"

"Dan—"

"Brynna, I'm just a deejay playing popular adult contemporary songs. Both of those happen to fit into that category."

"Tell me, Dan, do you take requests?" she asked mildly.

He grinned warily. "Sure. Do you have a song you want to hear?"

"Mmm. And I'd like to dedicate it to you."

"Okay, let me have it. What is it?"

"'You're So Vain' by Carly Simon. Would you play that for me, please?"

"Sure," he returned immediately. "And I'll follow it up with 'Seduce Me Tonight.'"

"Fine. And then you play 'Only in Your Dreams' by Debbie Gibson."

"That's 'Only in *My* Dreams'," he corrected her.

"That's what I said. Only in your dreams, buster."

He laughed. "Let's call it a draw, shall we? Don't you want to know why I called?"

She took a deep, audible breath and evidently decided to allow him to change the subject. "Okay, why did you call?"

Leaning back in his chair, he crossed his sneaker-clad feet on the edge of his desk, absently twining the phone cord around one finger. "I called to invite you to that country club thing this weekend. Mason's gotten me a membership and it'll be my first social outing there. Will you go with me?"

Brynna paused for so long it made Dan uncomfortable. Why was she hesitating? he wondered. Hadn't he been a perfect gentleman on their last few dates, despite his warnings that their relationship wouldn't always remain platonic? Granted, it had been longer than the week he'd originally given her. They'd been out several times in the almost-three weeks since that picnic when they'd each made their positions about commitment clear. And each date had ended with powerful good-night kisses that made it equally clear that no amount of willpower was going to hold them back much longer. Was she going to take the cowardly way out and refuse to see him?

He wasn't prepared for the answer she gave. "Thank you for asking, but I already have a date for the Independence Day dance."

His feet fell heavily to the floor. "You have a date?" he repeated blankly. "With a man?"

"It's not with a German shepherd," she laughed.

"Who?"

"Dan," she protested.

"Who is it, Brynna?"

"Bill Satterfield," she finally answered in resignation.

He pictured the attorney, a quiet, affable man in his late thirties. "Mason's partner?"

"Yes."

"I thought he was married."

"He's divorced."

"How long have you been seeing him?"

"Dan, would you stop it? This will be my first time out with him, for heaven's sake. It's not as if you and I have any kind of commitment. We're just friends, remember? I certainly don't expect you to stop seeing other women just because you and I have dinner together occasionally."

He thought her voice sounded a bit hollow, but he could have been mistaken. He was still thoroughly rattled to have her turn him down because she was going out with another man. He'd gotten used to having her free. Gotten accustomed to the idea that he was the only man she was seeing. "You're right, of course," he told her coolly. "You're quite free to date anyone you like. I hope you have a good time."

"Thank you. I guess I'll—see you there?"

"Yes, I'm sure I can find someone else to take."

"I'm sure you can," she replied quietly and, again, her voice sounded rather odd.

"I've gotta get back to work. Talk to you later, okay?"

"Sure. 'Bye, Dan."

He hung up without answering and slammed his fist into the wall beside his desk.

"Bill Satterfield," he muttered, nursing his bruised knuckles in his other hand. An attorney with money, breeding, class. Just the kind of guy he'd expect Brynna Haskell of Haskellville to date. Bill Satterfield wouldn't push her into an affair. He'd probably say please before he even kissed her. Was that what she wanted? Would she find that attitude so refreshingly unthreatening that she'd allow Bill to charm her right into a serious relationship, maybe even a second marriage for both of them?

Dan stopped himself and ran a hand through his hair in disgust. He was being ridiculous. All Brynna was doing was going out with another guy and here he was imagining her married to the jerk. As she'd said, it wasn't as if they had any kind of commitment, and that was his choice as much as hers. So he had no reason at all to feel—

Jealous. The word hit him right in the gut. He was jealous. No wonder he hadn't immediately recognized the emotion. He couldn't even remember the last time he'd felt it. Obviously, he wasn't quite as detached about Brynna Haskell as he'd hoped. Maybe it was just as well he'd be seeing someone else this weekend. It would be only the second time since he'd moved to Haskellville, he realized uncomfortably. He needed to get his perspective back, remind himself of all the reasons he didn't want to get involved with any one woman.

And he still hated the idea of Brynna spending an evening with Bill Satterfield—or any other man. Damn.

Brynna pushed the back onto a diamond drop earring and studied her appearance in the mirror. Not bad. Sleekly upswept hairdo, dramatic evening makeup, diamonds glittering at ears and throat, strapless evening gown in a rich shade of royal blue. She tried to tell herself that she was really looking forward to the dance that evening. If only she were.

She tried to convince herself that Bill Satterfield was charming, amusing and nice to be with, but she expected to have a miserable evening.

She'd made a terrible mistake accepting this date when she knew full well she'd spend the entire evening wishing she were with Dan. Though she'd tried to believe that seeing other men would help her overcome her infatuation with Dan, she was afraid it was already too late for that. She seemed to be obsessed with the man, and she honestly didn't know what she was going to do about it.

He hadn't liked finding out that she had a date with another man. In fact, he'd been unreasonably displeased considering that he was the one who had such a phobia about commitment. He hadn't called since she'd turned down his invitation, nor had he sent any special messages over the air. Unless he had some particular reason for playing a lot of songs lately about fickle women, beginning with "Runaround Sue" the morning after she'd declined his invitation.

She wondered who he'd bring to the dance, and was nearly overcome by the wave of sheer jealousy that rushed through her at the mere thought of Dan with another woman.

"Oh, Brynna, you are really in trouble this time," she muttered, hiding her skillfully made-up face in suddenly trembling hands.

By tradition the women of Haskellville attended the Independence Day dance in red, white or blue gowns while the men wore dark evening clothes. This year was no different. The first person Brynna saw when she and Bill entered the country club was Mitzi, wearing a sparkling white confection with a red sash and shoes. Mitzi fluttered like a hyperactive butterfly around the large, crowded room while Perry stood more quietly in one corner, looking very handsome in his evening clothes and talking to a couple of executives from Haskell Manufacturing. Brynna was accustomed to seeing Perry at Mitzi's side at such functions. She wondered sadly if they were still having problems with their marriage.

"Hi, Brynna. Ooh, that's a gorgeous dress!"

Brynna turned with a smile at the sound of Delia's voice. "Thank you, Delia. You look lovely, yourself." Delia wore a flowing maternity dress of red, white and blue print, her shaggy bleached hair decorated with a matching clip-on ornament. Chet stood behind his wife, his smile looking a bit strained as he eyed Brynna's date. "Delia, Chet, have you met Bill Satterfield?" Rapidly making the introductions, Brynna ignored Chet's look of disapproval.

They chatted briefly with the other couple until greetings from other friends interrupted. Promising to find Delia later, Brynna drifted on at Bill's side.

"Would you like to dance?" Bill asked with characteristic solicitousness.

"Yes, that would be nice." Forcing herself to stop searching the floor for one particular dark-haired man, Brynna tried to concentrate exclusively on her date as she turned into his arms on the dance floor. Bill held her quite correctly, firmly enough to lead, yet loosely enough for propriety. Brynna thought fleetingly that Dan would probably hold her plastered to his chest.

Maybe he wasn't coming to the dance, she thought with feeble optimism.

The next turn she and Bill took brought Dan into her field of vision. She stumbled slightly, causing Bill's arms to tighten as he steadied her. She wondered why being held so close to this man didn't evoke the same wild, terrifyingly delicious responses she felt whenever she was close to Dan.

"Are you all right?" Bill asked in concern.

"Yes, fine," she assured him with a forced smile. "I've gotten out of the habit of wearing such high heels, I suppose."

"Did I remember to tell you how beautiful you look tonight?" he asked, his own smile warm.

"Yes, but thank you again," she replied, wishing she were anywhere but here, listening to the compliments of one man while her heart broke at the sight of another at the side of a curvaceous black-haired beauty Brynna had never seen before. Who was she? she wondered, her eyes drifting inexorably back to the woman at Dan's side. She was impossibly gorgeous in her flame-red dress. Where had he found her? Did *she* go berserk every time Dan touched her? Did *she* find his rules about no-strings affairs perfectly acceptable? It was all Brynna could do not to moan aloud.

Did she have to dance so close to him? Dan asked himself, staring moodily at the couple on the dance floor as he pretended to listen to something Chet was telling him. Brynna looked so cool, so beautiful in her evening finery. Satterfield looked like someone out of *Gentlemen's Quarterly.* And they were dancing too close.

So how come she wasn't pulling back from that other guy in a panic the way she did every time he got that close?

Maybe he should have just skipped this stupid dance all together. But, no. He wouldn't give Brynna that satisfaction.

He turned abruptly to his date. "Would you like to dance, Karen?"

* * *

It was a long evening. Brynna smiled until her cheeks ached, made endless trivial conversation with people she'd known all her life, pretended to enjoy herself and tried desperately to keep her eyes off Dan and his beautiful date. She wasn't always successful. More than once during the evening she looked for him only to find him looking back from across the room. The first time their gazes met he nodded in greeting. After that he kept his expression shuttered.

Claiming exhaustion at one point during the evening, Brynna found a quiet seat in a corner while Bill headed for the refreshment table to get them something cool to drink. Relieved at the opportunity to stop pretending, if only for a moment, Brynna reached upward to discreetly massage the tense muscles at the back of her neck.

"Can't remember the last time I've been so amused," a familiar male voice spoke from just behind her.

Brynna turned to find Mason sitting in a chair nearby, grinning at her with the ease of a man who'd once bounced her on his knee. "Hi, Mason. What do you find so amusing?"

"You," he returned succinctly, scooting his chair closer to her. "And the two boys knocking themselves out for your attention tonight."

"What two boys?"

"Bill and Dan."

Her cheeks warming, Brynna frowned, checking her old friend. "Don't be ridiculous. Dan and I haven't even spoken this evening."

Mason chuckled. "I've been watching for quite some time. Watching you watching Dan, watching him watching you, watching Bill trying to ignore the fact that you and Dan are watching each other. I'm fond of both of them, Brynna, but something tells me Dan's the one who'll win

out in the end. He isn't the kind to give up when he wants
something badly enough."

"Mason, please. You're imagining things."

"Mmm," he muttered. "So you say."

"Mother always said you were a terrible tease," Brynna
scolded him fondly.

"Yes, she did, didn't she?" He didn't look at all repen-
tant.

"And you're completely off base about this evening,"
she continued stubbornly. "Dan's hardly interested in
watching me when he has such a beautiful date to hold his
attention."

Looking over her shoulder, Mason grinned in visible delight. "Try telling him that," he advised, just before a
warm, large hand fell firmly onto Brynna's bare shoulder.

She looked up into Dan's unsmiling face. "Dance with
me," he said, and his words were not a request.

Her heart fluttering dementedly, she looked around for
her date. "Bill—" she began, only to be interrupted by
Mason.

"I'll talk to Bill until you get back," the older man
promised, his gray eyes sparkling. "You kids go ahead and
dance."

Sighing her surrender, Brynna allowed Dan to lead her
silently to the dance floor. She discovered immediately that
she'd been right in her speculation about the way he'd hold
her. A gust of air couldn't have passed between them when
he took her into his arms. She wondered if he could feel the
pounding of her heart.

"Are you having a good time?" he asked her, his voice
rather rough, as if he, too, were affected by their close-
ness.

She tried to smile, tried to lie and tell him she was having a wonderful time. Their eyes met. Her smile faded.

"Not particularly," she heard herself answering. "Are you?"

"No," he replied bluntly.

Brynna turned her eyes downward, fiercely studying his tie. "She's very beautiful."

"Yes. So are you."

"I've never seen her before," Brynna commented, ignoring the latter part of his response with some effort. "Is she from Haskellville?"

"No, she's from Springfield. She's in sales. She calls on the station a couple of times a month."

"Oh." Brynna looked quickly around the room. "Where is she now?"

"Getting some fresh air with Delia."

His hand was warm against the skin above the low-cut back of her dress. Heat radiated from that point to somewhere deep within her. His thighs brushed against hers as they danced. Her breasts brushed his chest. She was finding it very hard to breathe, to concentrate on the beat of the sensuous song playing in the background. She tried to find something to say, anything to dispel the sexual tension hovering around them. She couldn't think of anything.

"Brynna, look at me," Dan ordered softly.

Knowing she shouldn't, she obeyed, her gaze meeting his almost fearfully. He stared hungrily down at her. "It's not going to work, you know," he told her, his voice suddenly very gentle.

"What's—" She cleared her throat. "What's not going to work?"

"You're not going to be able to deny the attraction between us for much longer. You've tried everything, including hiding behind another man, and you know it's not working."

She swallowed hard. "Dan, please. Not here. Not now."

"When, Brynna? How much longer do you expect me to wait?"

"I've never asked you to wait. I've told you I'm not going to have an affair with you. Why can't you just accept that and stop pushing me? Why don't you concentrate on some woman who isn't just trying to get her life back together?"

"Is that really what you want me to do? Leave you alone and find someone else?"

This time she was able to voice the lie. "Yes," she said, her eyes meeting his with no effort to hide the pleading in them. "Your date tonight looks like a woman who knows what she wants. A woman who isn't afraid to take chances. I'm sure she's more your type than I am."

He stepped back as the music stopped. "I guess you've made yourself clear enough this time. I'll take you back to your nice, unthreatening date." He made no effort to hide his sarcasm, though he probably wasn't aware that he failed to conceal his hurt.

She hadn't meant to hurt him. She hadn't even known that she could.

Dan nodded curtly to Bill as he left Brynna with him. He spoke only briefly to Mason before rejoining his friends. Brynna watched him walk away, the threat of tears behind her eyes. Tears she refused to shed. Pushing them resolutely away, she smiled at Bill as she accepted the drink he'd fetched for her. "Thank you, this looks wonderful. The fireworks display starts soon, you know. I've heard this year's display will be the best ever."

Bill's answering smile looked natural enough as he replied. Still, Brynna had the distinct impression that he'd just conceded defeat in a contest she hadn't realized he'd entered. Avoiding Mason's gently mocking eyes, she led Bill over to a table of mutual acquaintances, hoping that lively conversation would allow her to stop thinking about her confrontation with Dan.

The fireworks were all that had been promised. Everyone gathered outside the clubhouse at the appropriate time to watch the display over the golf course. Even Brynna found herself captivated by the cascades of sparkling, dancing light and explosions of dramatic colors. One burst of silver and gold was so beautiful it was almost painful. Her throat tight, she looked away for a moment, only to find her eyes locked with Dan's as the reflection of the incongruously cheerful colors splashed across his stern face.

He very deliberately turned away.

Grateful for the darkness surrounding her, Brynna blinked back tears and turned her eyes skyward again, hoping she'd have herself more firmly under control by the time the fireworks ended. She had to maintain control for the rest of the evening. At least until she was alone.

"I had a very nice time tonight, Brynna. Thank you for going with me."

Brynna looked at the very nice, sadly unexciting man on her doorstep. "Thank you for asking me, Bill."

"We'll have to do it again sometime," he said politely.

Knowing he wouldn't ask again, Brynna agreed with equal courtesy. He hesitated, as if wondering whether to kiss her, then with a regretful smile brushed his mouth against her cheek and walked away.

"Damn," Brynna muttered the moment her door closed behind her. "Damn, damn, damn."

The evening had been a disaster.

She locked her door and wandered dispiritedly into her bedroom, reaching behind her to lower the zipper of the blue gown. She should have worked out her feelings for Dan before going out with anyone else, she thought glumly.

If only she knew *how* to work out those feelings. She couldn't even understand them. Attraction, yes. Fascination, definitely. Love?

No, please, not that.

The dress neatly put away, along with her shoes and jewelry, she shoved her hands through her upswept hair, scattering pins. Wearing nothing but a thin robe, she sat at her dressing table and ruthlessly brushed out her blond curls before taking off her makeup.

Was he kissing her now? Was he running his hands through that glossy black hair, tasting those luscious red lips? Had he told himself that he'd been wasting his energy on Brynna, decided not to miss this opportunity to make up for lost time? Would he spend the night in her bed, waking in the morning sleepy-eyed and satisfied, maybe wanting to make love again in the early morning light?

Pained by her own too-vivid imagination, Brynna buried her face in her hands and drew a deep, unsteady breath. She was going to drive herself crazy this way. She was the one who'd pushed Dan at the other woman. Now here she was aching with jealousy, longing to be the one with whom he woke in the morning. She really had made a mess of things.

Knowing she'd never be able to sleep, she still went through the motions of getting ready for bed, scrubbing her face until her skin glowed red and slipping into a plain cotton gown that fastened with tiny buttons to her throat and fell straight to mid-calf. In the darkness she crawled between the sheets on her big, terribly lonely bed. She wasn't aware that she was crying until one fat tear slid into the corner of her mouth, salty against her quivering lips.

She must have fallen into an uneasy sleep because the heavy pounding on her door brought her upright with a startled gasp of disorientation. Pushing her hair out of her face, she blinked her luminous clock into focus. 2:00 a.m. Who in the world? she wondered as the knocking started again.

Climbing out of the bed, she wrapped herself in her robe and hurried into the living room. "Who is it?" she called out, staring suspiciously at the front door.

"It's Dan. Open the door, Brynna."

She froze. Dan? Why was he here?

"*Now* Brynna," he ordered impatiently and she knew he wasn't going away until he'd said whatever he'd come to say.

She unlocked the door. He stood on the porch, glaring at her in what appeared to be fury. He'd changed into jeans and a short-sleeved sweatshirt since she'd seen him last. Did that mean he'd been home? He hadn't stayed with the brunette? "What do you want?" she asked warily.

"You," he answered curtly. He moved her not so gently out of his way, stepped inside, and locked the door behind him before she could recover sufficiently to speak.

Brynna stared up at him with mingled trepidation and excitement. "I thought we'd already settled this issue," she said huskily.

"You've fed me a bunch of nonsense about not knowing your own mind and needing to get your life in order, but we haven't settled anything," he contradicted her.

"It wasn't nonsense, Dan. Everything I said to you was the truth."

"It's also true that you want me just as much as I want you." He moved swiftly and she was in his arms before she could step away. One large hand cupped her cheek as he turned her face to his. "And neither of us is going to get over it until we do something about it."

She'd fought it, she told herself. She really had. And yet she'd known from the beginning that the battle would be lost.

If she'd only been fighting Dan, she'd have won. But she'd been trying to fight herself, too, and she hadn't stood a chance.

For twenty-seven years she'd lived a safe, circumspect life, doing what was expected of her, rarely taking risks or acting without first considering the consequences. Despite her former caution, she'd made mistakes, such as marrying the wrong man.

So now she found herself faced with another choice—one that could well prove devastating.

And for the first time she admitted that her decision had been made the day Dan Westbrook stumbled into her life.

She raised her arms to his shoulders and lifted her face to his. After twenty-seven years, it was time to take a chance.

## Chapter Eight

Sensing the surrender in her actions, Dan groaned and lowered his head to Brynna's. His mouth took hers with the confident aggressiveness he'd shown before in his kisses, but this time she didn't flinch, didn't even try to resist. Her mouth opened to his.

He kissed her slowly, thoroughly. His lips slanted over hers, hard, then soft, then wet and hungry. Only when he'd taken her lips in every way imaginable did he slide his tongue between them to explore the inside of her mouth with equally painstaking care. Brynna thought she was going to lose her mind.

So lost was she in his kiss that she barely noticed when he reached between them to untie the sash of her robe. She gasped when he reached beneath the robe to cup one breast through her thin nightgown. Her nipple hardened instantly against his palm. His fingers flexed and she arched against him, aching for more. "Oh, Dan."

"I want to make love to you, Brynna," he ground out, sliding one hand down her back to hold her more closely against his straining arousal. "I want to learn every inch of your beautiful body, touch you and kiss you until you're wild with desire for me. And then I want to bury myself deep inside you and love you until you know without doubt how foolish you've been to try to deny the chemistry between us."

Her knees went weak. She clung to him with trembling hands. "Yes, Dan. Make love to me," she whispered. "Now."

"Yes. Now." He turned her in his arm and walked beside her as she led him to her bedroom.

She hadn't turned on the light in her bedroom when he'd awakened her, nor did they bother to do so now. Moonlight streamed through the window, giving just enough light to make their bodies glisten as they stood beside the bed. Dan slipped her robe off her shoulders and it fell to the floor, forgotten. She pulled at his sweatshirt until he removed it, slinging it aside.

She hadn't forgotten what a beautiful chest he had. This was the way she'd first seen him that day in the park, strong and virile and beautiful. She'd touched him that day, but only in an impersonal nurturing way. Now she touched him as she'd wanted to then, her hands gliding through the pelt of curls covering his well-developed chest and following the narrowing line of hair down toward his flat, quivering stomach. He bit back a groan as she hesitated and then boldly slipped one hand lower, brushing the straining front of his jeans.

Even as he caught her into his arms and rewarded her with a ravenous kiss, she wondered at her own lack of inhibition with him. She'd pushed away logic and prudence, refused to worry about consequences or risks. She wanted

Dan, wanted him to make love with her, and she intended to show him so. If only she knew what to do to please him.

Releasing her only long enough to kick off his shoes and step out of his jeans and briefs, Dan caught her back into his arms and lifted her high against his chest. He buried his face in her throat. "You're so beautiful," he muttered into her skin. "So soft." Moving sideways, he lifted one knee to the bed and shifted until they were both kneeling in the center of the mattress.

Brynna rested her hands on his chest, her eyes meeting his in the moon-silvered shadows. "I want to please you," she whispered, "but I don't—"

"Ssh," he interrupted gently, covering her mouth with his fingertips. "You please me, Brynna. Just by being you. Now relax and let me make you feel good."

Relax? She was melting into the sheets. He cupped her breasts in his hands and lowered his head to nuzzle them through her nightgown. Impatient with the fabric between them, Brynna reached for the hem of the garment which was tangled around her knees. Dan caught her wrist to stop her. "No. Don't take it off yet. I'm barely holding on to my control now."

He muffled her instinctive protest with his mouth.

Opening her mouth to his, Brynna arched helplessly when his fingers gripped her buttocks. He pulled her snugly against his thighs, his throbbing hardness pressing into the softer flesh of her abdomen. Awed that he could want her so much, Brynna rubbed against him like a sleek, affectionate cat, making him shudder and tighten his grip on her rounded hips. He dipped his tongue into her mouth, withdrew and thrust inside again, mimicking the action of his hips as he rocked against her.

Her fingers clenched in his hair. "I can't take much more of this," she moaned when he finally released her mouth.

"Sweetheart, we haven't even begun," he returned with a wicked, flashing grin before lowering his head again to her straining breasts. At the same time he slipped one hand beneath her gown, shaping the curve of her buttock in his palm before sliding the hand around to cup her feminine mound. Brynna jerked in pleasure when his fingertips parted the silky curls there to explore more intimately.

Dan made soothing, crooning noises against the breast he was suckling as one long, blunt finger penetrated to discover her damp, hot secrets. Her own fingers still tangled in his dark hair, Brynna arched against his hand, her head falling back weakly. "Dan. Dan, please," she whispered, uncertain, herself, what she was begging him to do.

Dan seemed to know just what she wanted—what she needed. His fingers twisted, his thumb pressed harder and she went rigid, crying out raggedly as waves of sensation swept through her. Sensations she'd never experienced before, never even imagined. When the last trembling convulsion had faded, Dan swept her gown over her head and tumbled her backward into the pillows.

Then he began to slowly, so slowly drive her wild again, with leisurely strokes and feverishly scattered, open-mouthed kisses. By the time he settled between her parted thighs, Brynna was writhing mindlessly beneath him, incoherently pleading with him to put an end to the delirious torment. "Yes, sweetheart. Burn for me. Take me inside and let me burn with you," he muttered hoarsely, surging forward.

Again she cried out as she was stretched and filled, her fingernails digging into the sweat-dewed skin of his shoulders. He set a hard, ceaseless rhythm, driving her inexorably to an even higher peak of ecstasy than he'd shown her before. And this time he was with her when she topped that peak, holding her tightly as she sobbed her fulfillment, his own body shuddering with his powerful release. Her last coherent thought before oblivion overtook her was of the way the spectacular fireworks display she'd seen earlier paled against the even more glorious fireworks Dan had orchestrated for her.

Long minutes afterward, Dan finally gathered enough strength to roll off her, bringing her against him as he settled on his side. He brushed a damp strand of hair off her cheek, his hand still notably unsteady. "Are you all right?" he asked, the words low and husky.

She nestled deeper into his arms, groping for words. "It was—I've never—" Frustrated, she stopped, shaking her head on his shoulder.

Seeming to understand, he chuckled deeply and hugged her. "It was like that for me, too. There aren't any words for it, are there?"

Smiling dreamily, she shook her head again. Her fingers splayed across his chest, measuring his slowing heartbeat. She'd pleased him, she thought in misty satisfaction. And he'd shown her a side of herself that she hadn't known existed. She wondered now why she'd been so afraid of something so spectacular.

"We should have done this weeks ago," Dan murmured, beginning to sound drowsy. "Look at all the time we've wasted. It was silly to be worried about what's going to happen later when we can have this now."

Sighing contentedly, he rested his cheek on her tousled hair and fell asleep.

Perhaps she'd gotten used to him sending her messages in song titles. In her mind she heard the opening bars of the Grass Roots' "Let's Live for Today." That song summed up Dan's philosophy, she thought as she lay awake in his arms. Live for today. Don't worry about tomorrow. Maybe that motto worked for him, but for Brynna things were different. She was the kind who needed to understand her feelings, to analyze her reactions. Still so utterly confused about what lay behind her powerful, unfamiliar emotions where Dan was concerned, she couldn't help but wonder what lay ahead for them.

There was still so much she didn't know about him, so much she didn't understand about herself. And it still frightened her.

Deliberately blocking out her worries, she settled her cheek more comfortably onto his shoulder and finally managed to drift into a restless sleep.

Dan left before it was even light, having slept less than three full hours. Brynna murmured a sleepy protest when he slipped out of her arms. "I'd better go," he murmured, pressing a kiss to her ear. "Don't want your neighbors to start talking about you."

He kissed her lightly on sleep-softened lips. "Go back to sleep. I'll call you later."

Exhausted from the events of the evening, she did go back to sleep. It was almost nine when she woke again to lie staring at her ceiling, lighted this time by the sun, attempting to analyze her feelings about what had happened.

She wasn't sorry, she realized at once. No matter what happened now between her and Dan, she wasn't sorry they'd made love. She was absurdly pleased that he'd wanted her so much he'd shown up in the middle of the night to ask her to make love with him.

Ask? Well, no, he hadn't exactly asked, she admitted. He'd told her he wouldn't accept any further excuses and taken her straight to bed.

And then he'd shown her exactly what had been missing during her two and a half years of marriage to Russ. Passion. Raw desire. Release so intense she'd almost lost consciousness from the sheer power of it. Dan had wanted her with an almost savage hunger—as she had him. Their joining was more basic, more primitive than anything she had ever even imagined before. How could she possibly be sorry? And yet—

She couldn't imagine responding to another man as she had to Dan, couldn't even conceive of making love with another man now. But were her feelings stable and reliable, or were they influenced by her loneliness and vulnerability, as she'd feared all along? Did she want marriage, children with him?

She didn't try to delude herself that there would be a happily-ever-after ending for them. Dan had said nothing about wanting her in his life on a permanent basis. Just the opposite, in fact. He'd made it quite clear he wasn't looking for a commitment, did not hold much faith in the institution of marriage.

His ex-fiancée must have hurt him very badly. Would any woman ever stand a chance of gaining his trust?

And why had he left her so early? She didn't believe a word of his explanation that he was protecting her reputation. Dan wasn't the type of man to worry about what the neighbors thought.

Sighing at the impossibility of answering any of the questions he'd left her with, she tossed the tangled sheet away and rolled to sit on the edge of the bed. The sensation of waking nude was unfamiliar, as was the dull ache of the muscles in her upper thighs. Dan had been a very demanding lover and once he'd pushed her past her fears and inhibitions she had been just as aggressive in satisfying her own needs, she remembered, her cheeks flaming.

Pushing her hands through her hair, she stood and walked into the bathroom for a warm shower before church. Forty-five minutes later she was ready, wryly aware that she'd chosen the most prim, modest dress in her wardrobe. Now if only the gleam in her eyes and the flush on her cheeks didn't immediately label her a fallen woman to the rest of the congregation, she thought with an unrepentant giggle.

Brynna ate lunch after church with Mitzi and her children. To Mitzi's undisguised annoyance, Perry had gone straight from church to his office where he claimed he had a great deal to do. Brynna couldn't help remembering Sunday afternoons at her own home when she'd been growing up. Nothing short of a major emergency would have kept her father from Sunday dinner with his family.

"I don't know how much longer I can take it," Mitzi told Brynna when lunch was finished and the children were all occupied elsewhere. "We hardly see each other anymore and when we do, we fight. It's hard on the children and it's hard on me."

"Oh, Mitzi, I'm so sorry. Do you want me to try to talk to Perry again?" Brynna offered, though she hadn't made any progress the last time.

Mitzi shook her head dispiritedly. "It wouldn't do any good. He's completely withdrawn, Brynna. Ever since your father died, he's been driving himself mercilessly. I don't think he even cares about anything but that business anymore."

"He's under so much pressure. It can't be easy trying to compete with Dad. He had so many more years of experience than Perry does now."

"I know that. But it's not that he's trying to do an equal job to your father. He wants to be better. And he's killing himself trying to do it."

"Have you talked to him about counseling?"

Mitzi laughed without humor. "He'd be furious if I even suggested such a thing. In Perry's opinion, our problems are all my fault. I'm too busy with the Festival and the hospital, he says. I'm not sympathetic enough about his problems. Well, what does he want me to do? Sit at home alone every day and most evenings, waiting for him to tell me all about his troubles just so I can sympathize with him? I have a life to lead, too."

"Mitzi, I—"

Mitzi sighed and held up one hand, palm outward. "I'm sorry. I really shouldn't be dumping all this on you. I just needed to talk, you know?"

"Of course I do. Didn't I talk to you for hours before I made the decision to ask Russ for a divorce?"

"Yeah, I guess you did. But enough of me for now. I need to talk about something else for a while. Let's talk about you."

"What about me?" Brynna asked warily.

"You have an awfully suspicious sparkle in your eyes today. Was your date with Bill really so wonderful?"

"I—uh—had a nice time with Bill," Brynna lied lamely, her cheeks going scarlet, to her annoyance.

Mitzi frowned suspiciously at the look on Brynna's face. "Going to be seeing him again soon?"

"I doubt it," Brynna replied, more honestly this time.

"Dan Westbrook watched you all evening, you know. His date was drop-dead gorgeous and he hardly noticed her. I don't think he liked it that you were there with someone else."

"He wasn't exactly pleased," Brynna agreed reluctantly.

"Did he call you this morning? Is that why your eyes have been shining all day?"

Brynna moaned silently and bit her lip, uncertain how to answer Mitzi's questions. She didn't want to lie. She wouldn't even have minded talking out some of her confusion with her closest friend. But how could she possibly talk about what had happened last night? "He came by the house late last night, after the dance," she compromised finally.

Mitzi's green eyes widened dramatically. "He did? When?"

"Late," Brynna answered evasively.

"Oh, ho. *Now* I understand the suspicious glow. He stayed the night, didn't he?" Mitzi couldn't have looked more delighted.

"Most of it. But don't look so thrilled, Mitz. Nothing has really changed between us. He's still not interested in anything more than a brief affair and I still don't know exactly what I'm feeling about him."

Mitzi cocked her head skeptically. "Don't you?"

Brynna squirmed in her chair. "Okay, I—well, I'm pretty deeply infatuated with him. *But*," she added as Mitzi grinned broadly, "it still doesn't change anything. I don't foresee wedding bells in my future with Dan. For one thing, there is something disturbing about Dan that bothers me. A barrier, I suppose, between him and everyone else. A deliberate barrier on his part, beyond which no one else can go. It makes me realize how little I actually know about him. When it comes right down to it, Dan and I are little more than strangers. He knows something about my past, but he's allowed me almost no glimpse of his."

Mitzi frowned. "You think he's hiding something about his past?"

"I have no idea," Brynna replied honestly. "And I guess that sums up my confusion about him. I react to him strongly, physically, but mentally I just don't know. I'm confused."

"What are you going to do?" Mitzi asked sympathetically. "We both know you're not the type to be happy with an affair."

Brynna inhaled and shrugged. "I wish I knew. I just can't seem to stay away from him, though I know it may be a mistake. I've never known anyone else like him, never felt quite this way about another man."

"Oh, Brynna. I hope you're not going to be hurt. I couldn't stand to see you hurt again."

"I'll survive." Brynna tried to sound more confident than she was feeling. "Now we've both unloaded our problems. Let's talk about something more cheerful, shall we?"

Looking reluctant to change the subject, Mitzi still complied. "What about your work? How's the new book coming?"

Brynna smiled in relief. "Very well. I've fallen completely in love with the new characters. I only hope my publishers feel the same about them."

"Oh, they will. I just know it. I can't wait until it's finished so Margie can read it. It's so hard to find quality books for girls that age and you know what a voracious reader she is."

Brynna and Mitzi spent the next hour in carefully cheerful conversation and then Brynna said she had to go. After hugging all her young cousins, she put her arms around Mitzi. "Everything's going to work out for you and Perry, Mitzi. I know you still love each other and somehow you'll find a way to get past this."

She wondered if she should try to approach Perry again, despite Mitzi's pessimism about the results of such interference. She felt as if she really should do something.

The first song she heard when she started her car was "Too Late to Turn Back Now." She reached out and turned off the radio. Dan hadn't sent that particular message, she told herself, since he wasn't on the air just then. Still something about the song made her decidedly nervous.

Dan waited until early evening before picking up the phone to dial Brynna's number. He'd been wanting to call her all day, though he'd cursed himself a number of times for missing her when they'd only been apart for a few hours. When he'd awakened in the early morning and looked down at her sleeping on his shoulder his first impulse had been to run. Making love with her had been like nothing he'd ever known before. Ever. He was letting Brynna Haskell get too close, something he'd sworn he wouldn't do.

And yet, here he was, dialing her number and waiting impatiently for the sound of her voice.

*Sex,* he tried to tell himself once more, but that rationalization was becoming weaker each time. Even he didn't believe it anymore.

"Hello?"

Hell, even her voice made him hard. "Hi. It's Dan."

"Oh. Hi." She sounded suddenly breathless. He wondered if she was embarrassed. Or if—his stomach twisted with the unwelcome thought—she regretted what had happened between them.

"How are you?" he asked a bit more gruffly than he'd intended.

"I'm—fine."

This was getting ridiculous. They both sounded like robots. "Brynna, I just wanted to tell you that last night was spectacular," he said impulsively.

She sounded shyly pleased when she replied. "I thought it was pretty wonderful, myself."

"You were incredible."

"Did you really think so? I was a little nervous."

"Nervous? Why?"

"Well, I'm not—I've never been a particularly sensual woman. I thought maybe there was something lacking in me," she admitted, the words so soft he could hardly hear them.

"You've got to be kidding," he told her incredulously. "Brynna, you're the most sensual woman I've ever known. And believe me, sweetheart, there is nothing lacking in you. Nothing at all."

"Thank you," she told him, making him smile at her prim politeness. He wished he could see her, feel the warmth of the blush that was undoubtedly staining her porcelain-pale cheeks, prove without any further doubt that she was a warmly passionate, fully responsive woman. What an idiot that husband of hers must have been, he thought in disgust.

"Have dinner with me tomorrow night," he said, a gentle command underlying the invitation. "I'll cook for us here."

"All right. What time?"

"Seven. And Brynna?"

"Yes, Dan?"

"Wear your sexiest dress, okay?" By the end of tomorrow evening, Brynna would no longer have cause to believe she wasn't every man's dream of a lover, he decided.

She laughed self-consciously. "Whatever you say."

He liked the sound of that. He brought the call to an end, reminding her to set her alarm for her special song the next morning. She tried to protest, but he hung up, grinning, his entire body already tingling in anticipation of the following evening.

Brynna groaned in embarrassment and hid her face in the pillow when Dan's wake-up song the next morning turned out to be Rod Stewart's "Tonight's the Night." She was going to strangle him, she thought in exasperation, smiling despite herself. There was nothing subtle about Dan Westbrook. She was hardly the innocent virgin ol' Rod was seducing in his song, but Dan certainly had her blushing like one.

She snapped off the radio and hopped out of bed. It was time to do some shopping.

It took her three hours to find exactly the right dress. By that time she'd exhausted nearly every dress shop in the Haskellville area and was beginning to believe she would have to drive into Springfield.

At one of the last shops she found it. The color was innocent enough. A delectable shade of rose that brought out the pink in her fair cheeks, the dress was made of moiré silk. The surplice-cut bodice fell from narrow shoulder straps into a wide, deep vee, coming together only an inch or so above the matching belt. Below the tiny waist, the skirt draped into a tulip hemline, hugging her slender hips and baring her knees.

"You look gorgeous," the wide-eyed teenage salesclerk enthused, a touch of envy on her rather plain young face.

Brynna turned slowly in front of the full-length mirror, wondering if she could possibly find the nerve to wear the dress. And then she pictured Dan's reaction. "I'll take it."

She started getting ready a full hour and a half before she was supposed to leave for Dan's apartment. Following a leisurely soak in a jasmine-scented tub, she worked on her hair and makeup. She twisted her hair into a loose knot on top of her head, held by only a few pins. Her makeup was dramatic but not overdone, highlighting her eyes and finely carved cheekbones. She painted her nails a rose color that closely matched her dress, slid her glittering diamond earrings into her ears, and carefully pulled on new underthings that would have normally made her blush just to look at them. The open front of the dress would not allow for a bra. She refused to dwell on that as she slipped into the enticing garment, adding a frivolously tiny pair of heeled black sandals.

The woman looking back at her from the mirror was a stranger; sultry, bold, slightly wicked. Brynna was stunned. What had gotten into her? She looked as if she had every intention of engaging in an evening of passion. What was worse, that was exactly what she had in mind. She thought briefly of her mother and smiled nostalgically. Alice would have loved the ensemble, cheering her daughter on in her discovery of the sensual, daring part of herself that she'd hidden for so long.

How Brynna wished she could talk to her mother about Dan.

Taking a deep, unsteady breath, she threw one last, almost timid look at the deceptively confident-looking woman in the mirror and headed for her car before she could change her mind and put on her prim and proper Sunday dress.

Her palms were clammy and damp when she knocked on Dan's door. She shouldn't have worn this dress, she thought in despair. Not for a simple dinner at his apartment. She looked like a trollop. An expensive call girl. She looked—

"Beautiful," Dan murmured in heartfelt approval the moment he opened his door, wearing a beautifully tailored dark suit that made her catch her breath in appreciation. His eyes traveled slowly from the top of her head to her sandal-bared, silk-covered toes. "You're the most beautiful woman I've ever seen."

The look in his eyes removed any doubt that she should have worn something else. Suddenly as confident as the woman she'd seen in her mirror, Brynna smiled and stepped past him into his apartment.

He'd set the mood in the apartment with as much care as Brynna had taken choosing her dress. Flowers and candles were everywhere. Soulful, sultry music played from an expensive-looking stereo system. Heavenly smells drifted from the kitchen, making her moisten her carefully painted lips in anticipation of dinner.

She turned to tell him how nicely he'd prepared for her, only to find herself caught in his arms and thoroughly, hungrily kissed. "I don't know if I'm going to last through dinner," Dan muttered into her mouth. "You deliberately set out to make me lose my mind, didn't you?"

She laughed softly, winding her bare arms around his neck. "You told me to wear my sexiest dress," she reminded him.

"I had no idea your wardrobe included anything like *this*," he replied frankly.

She laughed again. "It didn't. I bought it today," she admitted.

He grinned wolfishly. "I'm glad. I hate the thought of anyone else ever seeing you in this dress."

The blatant possessiveness of his words gave Brynna an odd little thrill of pleasure. Like his jealousy of Bill, they gave her hope that she meant something to him, whether he'd admit it or not.

"Dinner's ready," Dan announced, stepping back with a show of reluctance. "And I suddenly have a ravenous appetite."

*But not for food,* he added with his expressive navy eyes.

Brynna didn't even blush as she silently seconded the sentiment, allowing him to lead her to the beautifully set dining table at the far side of the large combination living and dining room.

## Chapter Nine

I didn't realize you were a gourmet chef as well as a dee-jay," Brynna teased, pushing her empty plate away and reaching for the last of her wine.

Dan lifted his own glass in a whimsical toast. "I'm a man of many talents, Ms. Haskell."

She was very glad she was sitting down. His smile went straight to her knees. "I'm well aware of that, Mr. West-brook," she murmured.

His eyes darkened and he stood, reaching for her. She placed her hand in his, rising to meet him. Dan brushed his lips over hers, then led her to the sofa across the room. "I'll take care of that later," he told her firmly when she glanced back at the dishes. "For now I want to concentrate only on you."

"Is this when the seduction starts?" she asked, her look turning coy.

He grinned. "Sweetheart, the seduction started the minute I opened the door and saw you in that dress."

"So who's seducing whom?"

"Good question." He strolled across the candlelit room, turning off the brighter lamps as he went, pausing in front of the stereo. "We need the proper music for this."

Leaning back against the sofa, Brynna slipped out of her shoes and crossed her legs. "I'd better warn you that 'Bolero' always gives me the giggles."

He chuckled. "I think we can find a sexy song that's a bit more modern than Ravel." He set the needle on an album and, shrugging out of his suit jacket, walked back to where she sat as the heartbeat drum opening of "When Doves Cry" filled the room.

She should have known. Dan had chosen a very sexy song, indeed, she observed, and then lost all ability to think clearly as he took her into his arms and covered her mouth with his. Unabashedly sensual lyrics swirled in her head along with the driving, pounding rhythm set by both the song and Dan's hands. Acting out the seductive words, Dan placed her hand on his stomach, his eyes meeting hers. Just as the song said, she could feel him tremble beneath her touch. She leaned forward and rubbed sinuously against his cheek, her mouth seeking and finding his.

Dan reached into the gaping front of her dress, groaning when he found her unbound, swelling breasts. "This dress should be against the law," he muttered, his fingers teasing one pouting nipple. "But I love it."

Urging him gently backward, Brynna pressed a line of kisses along his corded throat, nibbling at the pounding pulse there. Moments later, Dan was lying against the arm of the sofa, Brynna draped over his chest as she loosened his tie and began to work on the buttons of his shirt. His own hands caressed her silk-covered curves as she spread his shirt and lowered her mouth to the tiny points of his nipples. Licking and nibbling at those aroused brown circles, she slid her hand lower, tugging at the buckle of his thin leather belt.

Dan inhaled sharply when her fingers slipped inside the loosened front of his slacks. "Ah, Brynna, you don't know what you're doing to me," he moaned hoarsely.

She slowly measured the throbbing, satiny, hard length of him. "I think I have an idea," she murmured, trailing the very tip of her tongue across his flat stomach, feeling the hard muscles there jerk spasmodically in response.

Pressing another kiss to his mouth, she stood, indicating with one hand that she wanted him to lie still. Taking a deep breath for courage, she reached up to her hair, pulling out the pins and shaking her head to loosen the white-blond curls that tumbled to her shoulders. He watched avidly, his visible pleasure in her actions spurring her to greater daring. Her hands fell to her belt. The belt fell to the floor at her feet and her fingers loosened the one large button holding the dress closed. Dan's breath grew audibly ragged as she shrugged the slinky garment off her shoulders and let it fall, leaving her clad only in a lacy pink garter belt, sheer silk stocking and sinfully tiny pink bikini panties. Candlelight flickered across her hard-tipped bare breasts, reflecting from his avid dark eyes as he stared at her.

His throat worked with his hard swallow. "Oh, God, Brynna."

Smiling, she reached for the clasp of one garter. He stopped her, sitting up to catch her wrists in his hands. "No. Let me."

Her hands fell to her sides.

She was secretly pleased when Dan fumbled a bit at releasing the clasp. And then the stocking was loose and his

mouth moved wetly against the inside of her thigh as his
unsteady hands carefully rolled the sheer silk down her leg.
Dizzy with arousal, Brynna gripped his shoulders to steady
herself as he went to work on the other stocking.

The garter belt and panties joined her other garments at
her feet. His hands sliding behind her thighs, Dan nuzzled
his face against the satiny skin of her stomach, tantalizing
her with quick, scattered flicks of his tongue. And then he
nuzzled lower, nipping at her thighs, moving inward to kiss
her more intimately. Brynna cried out, her fingers clenching into his shoulders, her body arching involuntarily.

Growing impatient, Dan stood and stripped off his
clothes. He lay back on the sofa, pulling her down on top
of him. Bringing her mouth to his, he kissed her deeply, his
hands guiding her hips as he led her to him. Without waiting for further encouragement, Brynna parted her legs and
slid downward, taking him deep inside her. Their gasps
were simultaneous, hoarse. Dan bucked upward, all control gone as Brynna moved against him.

She felt a fierce satisfaction when he shuddered uncon-
trollably beneath her, unable to wait any longer before giving in to his body's violent demand for release. And then
she closed her eyes and cried out his name as her own climax swept through her.

His chest heaving beneath her, Dan held her close,
soothingly stroking her tangled hair. Brynna snuggled
deeper, lost in a haze of contentment. The music had ended
long before but neither had noticed. Their uneven breathing was the only sound left in the room. Until Dan stirred
and sighed. "Well, hell."

Giggling at the wry disgusted tone, Brynna lifted her
head to look questioningly down at him. "Problem?"

"I was going to seduce you," he told her in woeful accusation, his eyes reflecting the smile he was repressing. "I

was going to charm you out of all inhibitions, leaving you convinced you're the sexiest, most responsive woman in the world. But damn if you didn't sweep in here tonight and seduce me, instead. And, I might add, it was the most exciting thing that has ever happened to me."

Pleased, she dropped a butterfly kiss on his mock-stern mouth. "You can seduce me next time," she promised solemnly.

"I'll keep that in mind," he vowed, slipping his hands into her hair to hold her still for his kiss.

Later Dan introduced her to the pleasures of a shared shower, after which he took her to the bedroom and made love to her again. As he'd promised, he took full control of the seduction that time, leaving Brynna limp and somewhat shell-shocked. She dozed for a while in his arms, then reluctantly dressed to leave. Dan didn't ask her to stay the night, saying only that he had to be at the station very early the next morning. He kissed her over and over before she left with swollen, kiss-darkened lips. He also made her promise to call the moment she reached home, just to let him know she'd made it okay. Feeling rather foolish, she complied, mostly because his concern touched her.

She didn't know exactly what it was she felt for Dan Westbrook, but she didn't hesitate to admit to herself that he was a very special man. She was suddenly very glad she'd met him.

She didn't set her alarm that night, so she didn't hear the somewhat smug, feel-good songs Dan played the next morning. Nor did she know that he spent the day alternating between bursts of lightheaded happiness and grave warnings to himself not to get too serious about Brynna.

As if it weren't already too late, he thought with grim resignation.

* * *

Brynna and Mitzi set out cups, saucers, pastries and an enormous pot of coffee on a long table in the conference room. Six comfortable chairs were arranged in a horseshoe around a large-screen television. On the seat of each chair was a clipboard holding score sheets with space for comments, several sharpened pencils and, as a joke, a sample package of aspirin. The Show-Down committee was about to start selecting the twenty-four acts to compete in Show-Down, and the process would take hours on this Saturday three weeks before the Summer Festival.

Because they both knew how grueling the next hours would be, and maybe also because they both needed release from the confusion of their everyday lives, Brynna and Mitzi indulged in lighthearted silliness as they set up the conference room in the Chamber of Commerce building. They giggled helplessly as they took turns mocking the truly awful tapes they knew would be included in the daunting pile of submissions.

"We have to stop this," Brynna gasped at one point, wiping her tear-streaked cheeks. "The others will be here in just a few minutes. They'll think we've lost our minds."

"Maybe we have," Mitzi suggested giddily, impulsively hugging Brynna. "But it's been fun."

"Mmm," Brynna agreed with another choked giggle, warmly returning the hug.

Growing a bit more serious, Mitzi said, "It's good to have you back, Bryn."

Brynna didn't have to ask what she meant. She knew she'd made great progress during the past few weeks in getting back to the usually happy, mostly contented person she'd once been. The events of the past year had knocked her to her knees for a time, but she hadn't stayed down long, she thought with a ripple of pride. She was working again, she was laughing again, and she was involved in an affair that was more passionate, more satisfying than she could ever have imagined before. At the moment, that was enough. "It's good to be back, Mitzi," she said softly, giving her friend one more hug.

"Hey, if you're passing those out, I'm next," a wonderfully familiar voice said from behind her.

Laughing, Brynna turned to find Dan and Chet watching them with broad grins. "Get in line," she answered Dan cockily.

His grin widening, he caught her in his arms and lifted her off her feet. "The line ends right here," he informed her, before giving her a thorough kiss of greeting. "Hi," he said when he finally pulled back for air.

Flushed with pleasure and embarrassment, Brynna slipped out of his arms, carefully avoiding Mitzi's avidly interested eyes. "Hi." She'd seen him only once in the four days since he'd cooked for her, and that had been for lunch on Thursday. It seemed like forever since they'd made love. Already she was aching to be alone with him again. She was still amazed at the ardent, sensual side of herself that Dan had set free.

Something in his eyes told her that Dan was as eager as she to have time alone. "We still on for dinner tonight?" he asked, more as a tantalizing reminder than for confirmation.

"Oh, yes," she murmured before turning to welcome the other two committee members who were just arriving.

Dan couldn't stop watching her as she efficiently organized the committee, inviting them all to help themselves to coffee and pastries before the auditions began, quickly outlining the selection process. She was comfortable with her position as chairman, he realized; relaxed and experienced, confident in her own talents. He admired that in her.

She hadn't stopped smiling since he'd entered the room. Her beautiful blue eyes were larger and more luminous than ever. All trace of the sadness he'd first seen in her was gone. He wondered if he'd played a part in putting the smile back into her eyes. He wanted to believe that he had.

The past four nights had been endless. How could he have gotten so quickly addicted to having her in his arms when he'd made love with her only twice? he wondered over and over. He'd never even spent an entire night with her, and yet his bed seemed so empty now. He'd even found himself reaching for her in the night.

This wouldn't do, he told himself, still watching her as she waved them to their seats. He had to regain control of this affair, keep in mind that she was just another woman. A beautiful, charming, generous, sweet, enchanting, desirable woman, but nothing special, right? He snorted at his own idiocy, making Brynna look at him questioningly as she took her seat beside him, next to the VCR. Shaking his head to indicate that nothing was wrong, he squirmed into a more comfortable position, the clipboard settled firmly on his knee. What he had to do was concentrate on the tapes and stop anticipating the evening before he made a complete fool of himself.

It wasn't easy. He and Brynna had become so attuned that he couldn't help meeting her eyes each time something amused him, only to find that she was already grinning in appreciation. They agreed on almost every detail during the long day, finding the same acts impressively good or painfully bad. They communicated in murmured conversation and shared smiles, or sometimes in lingering, expressive looks. He was still having fun long after they'd broken for a quick lunch of delivered burgers and fries and settled back down to work. But he couldn't help wonder-

ing how much of his pleasure had to do with the fact that
Brynna sat right at his side all day.

Had he ever been this comfortable with a woman? Even
with Melanie, he couldn't remember feeling so—so connected. Actually, he and Melanie hadn't talked all that
much, he remembered. He'd been young, impetuous and
infatuated, convinced that a powerful sexual attraction and
enthusiastic, energetic lovemaking was all there was to love.
He'd wanted to hold on to that excitement, believing that
he could make it last a lifetime. He'd been wrong.

Thinking back to those traumatic days, he tried to remember exactly what it had been like to make love with
Melanie. At the time he'd considered it the ultimate in
pleasure. He was older now, of course, and considerably
more experienced. There'd been many sexual liaisons since.
Good ones.

But when he'd met Brynna he'd learned that there was
much more to making love than he'd even suspected before. Making love with Brynna terrified him, and yet already he was impatient to do it again. What was happening
to him?

The twenty-four entries were selected at last and the
weary committee packed up to leave. It would be up to the
judges to select the winners of this year's Show-Down from
the live performances. Dan stayed behind with Brynna as
she thanked the others for their help and saw them off, then
helped her load her car with the items she was taking home.

"I'm going to run home for a quick shower, then I'll pick
you up for dinner, okay?"

"Fine. I'd like to freshen up, too. I feel a bit wrinkled."

He lifted a hand to her cheek. "It's been a long day.
Tired?"

She shook her head against his palm. "Nothing a shower
and a good dinner won't cure."

He stroked his thumb across her full lower lip. "I give a mean massage."

"Do you?" she murmured, then caught his roving thumb between even white teeth for a playful nip. "Maybe I should test the validity of that claim."

"After dinner?"

"You're on." She stood on her tiptoes to press a quick kiss on his smiling mouth. "See you later."

"Mmm." Brynna stretched like a contented cat, her smile correspondingly feline. "You were absolutely right. You *do* give a mean massage."

Settling her more snugly into his shoulder, Dan tightened his arms around her. "Didn't I tell you? Now be still for a minute, will you? I need some recovery time."

Brynna laughed softly and subsided meekly against his damp, nude body, pulling the sheet over her own bare shoulders. "I'm sure you're exhausted," she sympathized gravely. "You do put a great deal of energy into your massages, don't you?"

"Stop sounding so smug, woman, and rest for a while. You should be tired yourself."

"I am," she admitted, "but I'm not really sleepy, are you?"

He made a sound deep in his throat that could have meant anything. Brynna decided to take it as a negative. Though they'd been together all day, had shared a wonderful dinner at her favorite restaurant and then returned to her house for more of the incredible lovemaking she was rapidly becoming addicted to, she still wasn't tired of Dan's company. She didn't think she could ever be bored with him. She wanted to talk some more. "What's your favorite song?"

He looked into her expectantly upturned face with a quizzical expression. "You're asking that of a deejay? I have dozens of favorite songs."

"Yeah, but isn't there one that's really special? One that gets to you every time you hear it?" she persisted.

He exhaled thoughtfully. "I guess it would be 'Desperado' by the Eagles. There's always been something about that song that stays with me."

Brynna thought about his answer. That particular song had always been one of her favorites as well. She wondered just how closely Dan identified with the life-scarred loner in the lyrics.

"Tell me more about your childhood, Dan. What was your mother like?" she asked somewhat recklessly, telling herself that if she and Dan were to have even a chance of building a serious relationship, they had to get to know more about each other.

He refused to answer. "My turn to ask the questions. What's your favorite song?" he demanded.

"Anything by Elton John," she confessed reluctantly, growing more and more frustrated with that invisible barrier he seemed so determined to keep between them. "I'm a real fan of his—have been since high school. What's your favorite movie?"

*"Butch Cassidy and the Sundance Kid,"* he answered without hesitation.

"But, Dan, they *die* at the end!"

"Not on-screen. It's really a very funny movie. Besides," he added devilishly, "Katherine Ross makes my teeth sweat."

She giggled. "Go for dark-eyed brunettes, do you?"

He sobered abruptly, his fingers toying with a strand of her hair. "Lately I seem to have a serious weakness for blue-eyed blondes."

Taking a deep breath for courage, Brynna propped herself on one elbow and asked, "What did the woman you were engaged to look like?" She really was feeling brave tonight, she thought wonderingly. She hoped she knew what she was doing, pushing him this way. And yet, she didn't really seem to have a choice.

Dan went very still. "How did you know about that?"

"Delia mentioned it in passing. She wasn't really gossiping. She probably thought I already knew."

"I don't want to talk about my ex-fiancée," he told her flatly.

Annoyed, Brynna scooted away from him. "Fine."

In a more conciliatory tone he said, "Brynna, it's old news."

"So was my marriage, but that didn't stop you from asking for the most intimate details of why I married Russ and why the marriage broke up."

He was quiet for several minutes while he considered her accusations. "What do you want to know?" he asked finally, though his tone wasn't particularly encouraging.

"What was her name?"

"Melanie McAdams."

"How old were you?"

"Young. Twenty-two," he clarified. "It was my senior year in college, not long after my father died. She was a couple of years younger, fun to be with, and I guess I needed that then."

"Did you love her?" she asked daringly.

Dan exhaled slowly. "I don't know. I wanted her. At the time, I thought that was love."

"She hurt you, didn't she?"

"Brynna—"

"Dan," she mimicked. "When I protested that the questions you asked about my marriage were too personal, you said you wanted to get to know me and that my marriage seemed to be an important part of my past. Well, that's the way I feel about your engagement.''

"All right, dammit, she hurt me. A friend told me she was sleeping around on me. I didn't believe it until I caught her at it.''

"Oh, Dan, I'm sorry. You must have been devastated,'' Brynna whispered, remembering the careful way he'd once asked her if Russ had been unfaithful to her.

"I was humiliated,'' he bit out roughly, refusing her sympathy. "She made a complete fool of me. Everyone knew what was going on. Everyone but me.''

"What did you do?''

"I walked away. From her, from school. I was six weeks away from earning my degree, but I just wanted out.''

"Did you ever go back for your degree?''

"No. I've gotten along just fine without it.''

"And without a woman to share your life,'' Brynna hazarded, beginning to understand him.

"I'm not interested in permanent ties,'' he agreed. "As you said, I discovered I could get along just fine on my own.''

"But what about marriage? And children. Don't you ever want a family, Dan?''

"Not particularly. I can do without the hassle of custody fights and weekend visitations, not to mention alimony and child support.''

Brynna was appalled by his cynical bitterness. "You're automatically assuming that a marriage would fail.''

"Most do,'' he answered matter-of-factly.

"Half.''

"Okay, half. Not exactly great odds. I wouldn't want a kid of mine to go through what I did when my folks split.''

Another shred of information, given so unwillingly. "How old were you?"

"Ten. Look, it's getting late. I'd better go." He sat up, reaching for his clothes.

Clutching the sheet to her breasts, Brynna struggled upright. "Dan, wait. Let's talk about this some more. I hate to see you missing out on so much of life just because you've had a few bad experiences. You—"

"You're hardly one to lecture me on the joys of marriage," he interrupted, his voice deadly quiet. "Your own lasted less than three years. Town gossip has it that your cousin's marriage is all but over. Why don't you face facts, Brynna?"

She felt the blood drain from her face. She hadn't expected him to throw her own failure at her so cruelly. It hurt. Badly.

Dan threw on his clothes while she sat in unmoving silence. "I'll call you, okay?"

She nodded.

He hesitated for a moment, clearly frustrated, before he turned and walked out. She heard her front door close behind him, then the sound of his car fading into the night. And still she sat, staring at the spot where he'd stood, her heart aching.

She'd told herself all along that she had no future with Dan. She'd considered herself prepared. And yet it seemed she'd harbored some faint hope that they were discovering something special together, that what they had was more than an affair. She supposed she was finding out now how very foolish she'd been.

She knew he hadn't told her everything. She'd learned about his engagement, but there was still something about his parents' marriage that Dan wouldn't share with her. Something that had made him decide he didn't want marriage, a belief sustained by his failed engagement. And now no woman was going to change his mind, especially one who'd already tried marriage once and failed dismally.

It wasn't fair, dammit, she thought with a surge of anger, slamming her fists into her pillow in helpless rage. It wasn't fair that just when she'd gotten her life back together she had to brace herself for another blow. What the hell was she supposed to do?

She didn't hear from Dan on Sunday, but then she really hadn't expected to. Either he was still angry with her for prying out details of his past that he hadn't wanted exposed, or he was giving her time to decide if she wanted to continue seeing him knowing that there was no future in it. She still didn't know. She honestly couldn't see herself sending Dan away voluntarily, no matter how wise it might be to do so. She'd tried that before, and failed. She didn't expect her willpower to be any stronger now, particularly since they'd become lovers.

Staring sightlessly into her mirror as she dressed for church, she formed a new determination. Okay, fine, she thought belligerently. If Dan could get along with a live-for-today philosophy, then so could she. He'd never make her believe he didn't care for her, that there wasn't something real behind their lovemaking, deny it as much as he wanted. She'd just see if he really had the strength to walk away.

If he did, she'd survive. She was a survivor. It was time she did something to prove it.

## Chapter Ten

Early Tuesday morning, Brynna placed a call to her cousin's house, smiling when Mitzi answered. "Hi. I called to sing Happy Birthday to my cuz. I hope he hasn't already left for work."

Mitzi's dispirited sigh carried clearly over the phone lines. "He's not here, Brynna."

"I can't believe he left for the office this early. Why, it's barely—"

"He's not staying here, at all," Mitzi broke in. "He's been living at the corporate apartment since Saturday evening."

"He's—what? But why?"

"I guess you could say we're separated," Mitzi explained dully. "Perry moved out."

Brynna sank bonelessly into a chair. Separated? Mitzi and Perry? It couldn't be. She felt almost more devastated over this news than she had at the end of her own unfortunate marriage. "Mitzi, I'm sorry. What are you going to do?"

"I don't know yet."

Resisting the urge to ask Mitzi why she hadn't told her sooner, Brynna asked only, "What about the children? Do they know?"

"Margie's figured it out. The boys think their father is away on business."

"How's Margie?"

"Not very well. She's sullen and tearful and—" Mitzi's voice broke. "I really hate this for their sakes. They shouldn't have to go through this. You were lucky that you and Russ didn't have children, Brynna."

"Your marriage hasn't ended yet, Mitzi. There's still hope that you can work out your problems."

"I guess." But Mitzi didn't sound nearly as confident as Brynna.

"If you need me—" Brynna said, her voice trailing off with a sense of the inadequacy of words at such a time.

"I know. Thanks, Bryn. I'll talk to you later, okay?"

Brynna replaced the receiver. Maybe Dan was right, she thought dispiritedly. If even Mitzi and Perry were unable to make marriage work, then maybe the odds against success were simply too great in modern times. She knew he would only use Mitzi and Perry as further evidence of his cynical viewpoint.

And then she thought of her own parents, whose love had never wavered until the day they died. That was what Brynna wanted for herself. If only she were sure Dan was the man to trust with the love trapped inside her.

She tried to work, but it was hard to concentrate on the book. Her thoughts kept turning to her cousin's shaky marriage and her own complex affair. By midmorning, she acknowledged that she was wasting her time. Making a sudden decision, she snatched up a gaily wrapped package and left the house.

She found Perry in his office, looking tired and grim and harried. He greeted her with a wariness that he didn't normally display toward her. She suspected he knew that she was about to interfere in his personal life. "What can I do for you, Bryn?" he asked.

"I brought you your birthday present," she replied, holding out the gift. "I called your house early this morning, but Mitzi told me you're not staying there these days."

He took the gift without smiling. "Thanks for the present, Brynna. It was sweet of you to—"

"Darn it, Perry, talk to me!" she interrupted heatedly, sitting on the edge of his desk and forcing him to look at her. "You can't just sit there as if nothing has happened between you and Mitzi. We need to discuss it."

"Brynna, really, I'm very busy. I have a meeting with the department heads in a few minutes. There's hardly time to begin a serious conversation about something like this. Mitzi and I will work out our problems, eventually. We just need a little time."

"You need more than time," Brynna replied bluntly. "You look awful, Perry. When's the last time you got a full night's sleep?"

He shrugged and avoided her eyes. "I'm okay. It's just a particularly busy period here at work. Once I've got everything squared away, I'll get everything worked out at home. I promise."

"Perry, you may not have a home to go back to if you don't do something now," Brynna argued. "You can't just put your life on hold until you feel things are settled here at the office. Are you really going to let a wonderful marriage go down the tubes simply because you're having a busy period at the office, as you put it?"

"Dammit, Brynna—"

Perry's impulsive speech was interrupted by the intercom on his desk. "The department heads are waiting for you, Mr. Haskell," the disembodied voice of his secretary announced. "Shall I tell them that you'll be a few minutes late?"

"No. Tell them I'm on my way," Perry answered, standing and reaching for the jacket to his dark suit. He looked at Brynna with a weak attempt at a smile. "Look, we'll discuss this more later, okay, honey? I really am very busy just now."

"Perry, don't talk to me as though I were a nosy child," Brynna warned. "This is important."

"I know. But I have to go now. Thanks for the birthday present. I'll open it just as soon as I have a few minutes free, I promise."

He left her fuming in his office, utterly frustrated by his refusal to talk. She was getting tired of the men she cared for shutting her out of important parts of their lives, she decided, staring grimly at the incongruously cheerful package sitting unopened on her cousin's desk.


She tried to work again after her unproductive talk with Perry. Her doorbell drew her away from her computer just after noon. She guessed the caller would be Mitzi needing to talk.

She hadn't expected Dan.

It was the first time she'd seen him since he'd left her on Saturday. He hadn't even telephoned since then.

One hand propped on the doorjamb, he looked at her without smiling. "Should I have called before stopping by?" he asked.

She shook her head, holding the door wider. "No, of course not. Come on in."

He stepped around her into the foyer, barely waiting until she'd closed the door before framing her face in his large hands. "I don't know where this relationship of ours is headed," he told her gruffly, staring down into her startled eyes. "I don't know exactly what it is I feel for you. But I've spent the past three days missing you, aching for you, and knowing you're the only woman I want to be with. I don't know if I'll ever be able to promise forever, but I'm yours for now, if you want me."

"I want you," she answered without hesitation, stepping fully into his arms and hugging as much of him as she could reach. "Oh, Dan, I want you so much."

Maybe no one could promise forever, she thought as she turned her face up for his hungry, spine-melting kiss. She would learn to be content with knowing he was hers now. She'd have to.

Brynna captured a pile of scented bubbles in her palm, pursed her lips and blew, giggling when the fluffy ball landed on the end of Dan's nose. Lazily wiping it away, he shifted in the tub, sending water splashing over the sides. "You put in too much water," he rebuked her mildly.

"I'm not used to sharing my bath," she replied, wriggling her toes underwater where they rested on his thigh.

He grunted an unintelligible response, though a fierce surge of jealousy shot through him at the thought of any other man seeing her the way he was seeing her now. Her scrubbed face flushed from the steam rising around her, her pinned-up silvery hair escaping in damp little tendrils on her neck and forehead, her eyes soft and dreamy in the aftermath of the loving they'd shared. Bubble-frosted water lapped at the tops of her creamy breasts, breasts that had filled his hands and mouth so perfectly. *Mine,* he thought, refusing to dwell on the emotions behind the possessiveness.

He'd left the station and headed for her house the minute his morning program ended, though at the time he hadn't known what he was going to say when he arrived. He only knew that he couldn't stay away from her any longer. He couldn't even remember exactly what he *had* said, but whatever it was, Brynna seemed to have been satisfied. At least for now. As always, he pulled his thoughts away from the future.

Brynna's toes wriggled again, moving inward, and he caught her ankle in his hand with a sharp intake of breath, amazed that his body could react so instantaneously after their recent, energetic lovemaking. He narrowed his eyes at her husky, knowing laugh. "Shouldn't you be working?" he asked.

Her smile widened. "I *was* working until some gorgeous hunk came by and distracted me."

He had to grin at that. He rather liked her description. "I suppose you'd rather be sitting at your computer?"

She shook her head. "There's no place I'd rather be than right here."

His grin fading, Dan leaned forward and grasped her wrists, tugging her toward him. "Congratulations, Ms. Haskell. That was exactly the right answer to my question," he drawled in his best radio announcer voice.

"Umm—Dan?" she asked as water sloshed onto the bathroom floor. "Can this be done in a bathtub?"

"Trust me," he assured her, pulling her thighs over his as he demonstrated just how much was possible within the wet intimacy of a bathtub. Brynna cooperated fully, her approval of the demonstration evident in the strangled cries of encouragement she gave him.

Closing his eyes, Dan held her tightly and lost himself in the joy of just being with her. *Mine,* he thought again, his last coherent observation. *Mine.*

"Mitzi and Perry are separated," Brynna said much later, her cheek cradled on Dan's shoulder as they recuperated together in her bed. Though she knew she was only giving him more ammunition in his campaign against marriage, she wanted and needed to talk to him about her feelings.

"I'm sorry to hear that," he replied, and he sounded unexpectedly sincere. "How's Mitzi taking it?"

"Not well. She's devastated. And Perry—well, he's withdrawn. I tried to speak to him but I couldn't even reach him. He promised he'd talk with me sometime, but he wouldn't say when. I think he wants to avoid me."

"I know you're worried about them, but you have to remember that it's their life. Try not to let it upset you too much."

Touched by his concern for her, she snuggled deeper into his shoulder. "I know. But it's hard to watch my only remaining family breaking up. I just hope they can work out their problems. They always had such a good marriage, until my parents died. Perry's never recovered from Dad's death; it's as if he feels compelled to prove himself equal to or even better than Dad was as a CEO."

"Is that the whole problem?"

Brynna sighed. "No. Mitzi's being just as difficult. She's trying to be my mother—socialite, volunteer, organizer. She doesn't seem to understand that my mother didn't try to take on all those things until I was old enough to pretty much take care of myself. When I started developing my own life, Mother needed something to fill hers, so she volunteered for all kinds of community projects. Mitzi has three children still small enough to need her most of the time. By the time she fulfills all her social obligations and gives what time she can to her children, there's no time left for Perry. He resents that, even though he can't seem to see that he's doing the same thing to her over the business.''

"Tough situation.''

"I know. I'd like to just pick them both up and shake some sense into them.''

"It's always tough on the kids,'' Dan mused, old memories deepening his voice.

"You were only ten when your family broke up?'' she asked, wondering if he would be willing now to talk about that time.

"Mmm,'' he murmured.

"Was it a bitter divorce?''

"Yeah. My mother left my father for someone else.'' The bitterness was still there in his voice, sharp and painful. Brynna ached for him, wishing she could reach out the way she really wanted to, knowing he wouldn't let her.

"Did you live with your mother or your father after the divorce?'' she asked instead.

"I lived with my dad.''

Shifting until she was resting her chin on her hand, looking up at him, Brynna studied the hard set to his mouth. He'd never forgiven his mother, she realized. No wonder it had been so horrible for him to discover that his fiancée had also been the unfaithful type. No wonder he had such a problem with trust. Would she ever convince him that some women, herself, for example, could be trusted completely?

She wanted to continue talking about his past while he seemed willing, needing to know as much as possible in order to understand him. "Where did you stay when your father was away?''

"We always had excellent housekeepers, even before my mother left. She never cared much for housekeeping. Dad made sure I was well taken care of when he wasn't around. He cared for me a great deal. God knows why."

Something twisted inside her at the break in Dan's voice even as she frowned in puzzlement at his final words. "Why shouldn't he have cared for you? You were his son and you obviously adored him. It's not surprising that he returned the affection."

Dan sighed deeply. "You wouldn't understand," he muttered, toying absently with a lock of her hair as it lay against her bare shoulder.

"Try me."

He stared at the ceiling, his expression unreadable, for a long time before answering. Finally, with an unconvincing smile, he shook his head. "Maybe some other time."

Before she could say anything else—probably in order to prevent her doing so—he tugged her head to his and kissed her. By the time he released her mouth, he seemed to consider the conversation closed. "I'm starving," he said. "I skipped lunch and now it's almost dinnertime. Why don't we go out for something?"

"Sounds good," she agreed, reluctantly following his lead. "I'll get dressed."

"I suppose you'd better," he concurred, exaggerating his regret. "I'm not about to allow any other man to see you in all your natural beauty."

Sliding from the bed with a chiding groan, Brynna wondered if she'd imagined the edge of possessiveness behind his teasing words.

Dan spent the night with her, no longer seeming to care whether her neighbors noticed. He left early the next morning, in time to make it to the station for his airtime, telling her he'd see her later that day. Though he never really said so, his words and attitude implied that their time from then on would be spent together as much as possible. They were a couple now, and he made no effort to deny the fact, though he made no promises about how long the relationship would continue.

Deciding that it was impossible to sort out her own feelings for now, Brynna made an effort to adopt his one-day-at-a-time philosophy. It seemed to work for him, though she had serious doubts about whether she was capable of being content that way for long.

She spent a long time that day wondering if she should continue to allow herself to grow close to a man who wouldn't share himself fully, a man who could walk away at any time.

As the Summer Festival approached, Brynna's days grew more and more hectic. She worked, conducting several long, satisfactory conversations with her editor and watching with pleasure as the story took shape. Her telephone rang constantly with questions about the festival, arrangements for Show-Down, talks with contestants and judges. Dan teased her about being so much in demand that he had to make appointments to kiss her. He made her laugh when he woke her one morning with the song "Precious and Few," his way of describing the few moments he was able to spend with her during those two weeks.

How she loved those daily messages, she thought contentedly as yet another sweetly romantic song woke her on Friday morning just one week before the festival. It was as if Dan used those songs to express all the feelings he was unable to verbalize when they were together. She treasured each one, even though she had to call and scold him for the teasing innuendo he slipped into his introduction of Three Dog Night's "Easy to Be Hard." He made her laugh; he made her happy, even though she still worried about her continuing family problems.

Dan had been booked as deejay for a local teen dance that Friday evening, so she contented herself with talking to him three times on the telephone during the day. She took advantage of the evening alone to catch up on several tasks she'd allowed to slide the past busy weeks, though she would gladly have ignored them longer for the chance to spend that time with Dan.

When the doorbell rang at nearly midnight, she sprang happily from her chair, tightening the sash of her long, blue silk robe, certain that Dan had been unable to stay away when the dance ended. She almost ran to answer the door.

The caller wasn't Dan.

"Russ!" she said with a gasp, staring at her ex-husband, whom she hadn't seen since some six weeks after their divorce. "What are you doing here?"

"I know it's late," Russ apologized with a somewhat uncertain smile. "But when I drove by and saw the lights on, I thought it would be okay if I stopped. I can come back tomorrow, if you'd rather."

"No, of course not. Come in." She led him into the den, noting that his terribly attractive face was deeply tanned. "You look good, Russ."

"Thanks. So do you," he returned, eyeing her closely, as if sensing a change in her since he'd seen her last. "In fact, you look great. I like the way you're wearing your hair now."

She nodded an acknowledgement before waving him to a chair. "Sit down. Can I get you anything?"

"A cold drink would be nice. I came here straight from the airport in Springfield."

"Where were you before that?" she asked, dropping ice cubes into a glass at the wet bar in one corner of the large room and pouring Russ's favorite Scotch over the ice.

"Thanks," he said, accepting the drink before answering her question. "I flew to Springfield from New York. Before that, the Malay Peninsula."

"You're happy," Brynna observed, curling into a deep armchair and noting the contentment in Russ's brown eyes where there had once been dissatisfaction and restlessness.

He hesitated briefly. "Yes. I love working on the digs, Brynna. I'm sorry things didn't work out between us, but this is the life I was meant to live."

"I know," she answered sincerely. "You were denying everything that made you what you are by trying to settle down here and teach. No one can truly be happy living that way."

Russ smiled at her, the smile that had once warmed her all the way through. Now she could look at his attractive face and feel nothing more than deep affection. "You always did understand me, Bryn."

"Not always," she corrected him quietly. "If I had, we would never have married."

"Maybe it was what we both needed at the time," he suggested, holding his Scotch loosely in his callused hands as he leaned back into the couch and studied her. "Maybe we had to see firsthand what we *didn't* want before we could understand what we really needed."

She shrugged, not wanting to get that philosophical. "Maybe."

Russ's voice deepened. "Brynna, since this is my first chance to get back to the States in so long—well, I just want to tell you how sorry I was about your parents. I didn't get the word for quite some time after the accident and when I heard it devastated me," he said simply. "I was so sorry I couldn't be here for you then."

Her throat tightening, Brynna nodded. "It was hard," she understated drastically. "But I got through it. I appreciate your concern, though."

"It's more than concern," he chided her gently. "I love you, Brynna. I always will."

Reflecting on the maturity that had taught her the many different types of love, she smiled somewhat shakily. "I love you, too, Russ. I'll always value your friendship."

Russ finished his Scotch and set the empty glass on the coffee table. He looked tired, she thought, noting the purple shadows under his eyes. She wondered how long he'd traveled that day. His gaze met hers and again, the look was searching. "Something's different about you," he observed. "What's going on?"

"What do you mean?" she prevaricated.

"Are you seeing someone new?"

"Yes," she admitted. "His name is Dan Westbrook. He's the owner of KHVL now."

"Is it serious?"

"I—don't know yet," she answered cautiously. "It's still new and very tentative."

"Are you happy, Brynna?"

She brushed at a nonexistent speck of lint on the sleeve of her robe. Was she happy? She missed her parents deeply, she worried about the impasse Mitzi and Perry had reached in their marriage, she was still uncertain about the new directions she'd taken in her writing career, and she couldn't help but wonder what would happen between her and Dan. And yet—

"Yes," she said finally. "I am happy."

"I'm glad," he replied and his tone was genuinely pleased. He ran a hand through his longish brown hair and stretched. "Guess I'd better go. I'm crashing at Aunt Nina and Uncle Ned's house tonight. I'll be in town for a couple of weeks visiting family and friends and taking care of some personal business. I'd like to see you again while I'm here. Maybe you'll introduce me to Dan?"

"Maybe," she returned cautiously, wondering if that was such a good idea. Dan was so elusive about their relationship. How would he react to meeting her ex-husband?

Just then her doorbell rang and she realized that she might be finding out sooner than she'd expected.

Dan had been home from the dance less than an hour when the telephone rang. Just after midnight, he noted as he lifted the receiver. His first thought was for Brynna. Was something wrong? he worried. "Yeah?"

"Dan, it's Chet. I'm at the hospital."

"Delia?" Dan surmised, noting the anxiety in his friend's voice. "Is it the baby?" He knew the baby wasn't due for another month.

"Something's wrong. She woke up bleeding heavily. I brought her in and they rushed her into an emergency room and I haven't heard anything since. I'm really scared, Dan."

"I'll be right there," Dan promised, knowing Chet needed someone with him. "I'm sure everything will be all right, Chet."

"God, I hope so," he answered, his voice choked. "If anything happens to Dee—" The words trailed off, too horrible to continue.

"Hold on, Chet. I'm on my way," Dan promised, hanging up the phone and snatching up his car keys.

*Brynna,* he thought, realizing he'd pass her house on the way to the hospital. He needed Brynna with him. She'd know what to do if something terrible happened. He wasn't

sure he'd know what to do, what to say, if the worst occurred, but he had full confidence in Brynna's strength at
such a time.

He pulled into her driveway without even questioning his
instinctive decision to do so.

The lights were still on inside. He was glad she wasn't already in bed. He leaned against the doorbell, then pounded
the door with his fist.

The lace curtain twitched, and then the door flew open,
revealing Brynna standing just inside the foyer, a tempt-
ingly slinky blue robe belted at her waist. "Dan, what's
wrong?" she asked huskily.

She looked so beautiful he wanted to pull her into his
arms, but he couldn't forget his reason for being there, or
the need for haste. "Delia's in the hospital. Something's
wrong—either with her or the baby, or both. I'm not sure.
Chet wasn't exactly coherent. I'm on my way there and I
was hoping—"

"Of course I'll go with you," she assured him immediately, moving aside to let him in. "Just let me throw on
some clothes. I'll only be a minute."

Dan nodded and leaned over to kiss her swiftly.
"Thanks, sweetheart. I knew you—"

He froze as a movement behind her caught his eye. He
looked up sharply to find a handsome young man standing in the doorway of the den, looking quite comfortable
in tan chinos and a white shirt with the sleeves rolled up on
his forearms.

He felt as if he'd been kicked hard in the stomach.

## *Chapter Eleven*

Torn between the look on Dan's face at Russ's sudden appearance and her compulsion to hurry and dress, Brynna shifted restlessly on her bare feet. Seeing Russ there would be disconcerting for any man, but for Dan— She burst into speech. "Dan, this is Russ Gray. He just arrived in town tonight and stopped by to say hello. He—uh—he was just leaving."

Russ smiled pleasantly and extended a hand to Dan, who didn't return the smile, though he did shake the extended hand with reluctant civility. Russ didn't linger, but threw Brynna a quick, almost apologetic smile and hurried out to the car he'd parked at the curb. Dan had missed seeing the car in his anxiety about Delia.

"I'll get dressed now. I'll just be a minute," Brynna promised, pulling her eyes away from Dan's grim expression and hurrying toward her room.

Barely five minutes had passed when she returned, clad in jeans and a pullover top, wearing slip-on canvas shoes on otherwise bare feet, her purse clutched in her hand. "I'm ready."

He held the door for her, his face impassive. "We'd better go, then."

"Yes," Brynna whispered, picturing the bubbly, always laughing Delia with a pang of fear.

Dan didn't speak as he guided the car toward the hospital at reckless speed. Brynna chewed her lower lip, uncomfortably aware of the stiffness in Dan's silence. "He's my ex-husband," she said finally.

"I know," Dan answered, his voice clipped.

"And you also know that there was nothing going on between Russ and me tonight, that we were doing nothing more than talking," she added firmly, turning to face his hard profile. "Don't you?"

He shrugged. "If you say so."

"I say so. It's his first time back in the country since my parents died and he came by tonight to tell me how sorry he was."

"Brynna, you don't owe me explanations."

"Yes, Dan. I do. We have a relationship, however vague you want to keep it, and I believe that I have an obligation to that relationship. As long as you and I are together, you'll never have to worry about me being unfaithful to you. I won't be."

He threw her a guarded look as he pulled into the hospital parking lot. "Finding him there like that threw me," he said carefully, turning his eyes away as he maneuvered the car into a parking space.

"I know. I'm sorry. But you do believe my explanation, don't you?"

His hands gripping the wheel, he stared straight ahead for a long moment. Finally he took a deep breath and released it. "Yes, I believe you."

Her eyes stung with a prickling of tears and her shoulders relaxed for the first time since Dan had spotted Russ. Dan trusted her, she thought, reaching for her door handle as he opened his own door. True, his trust was still tentative, still fragile, but he did trust her in this case. Did that mean there was hope that he'd learned to trust her with his past?

They found Chet pacing blindly in the waiting room. "They still haven't told me anything," he said hoarsely on spotting Dan. "All I know is that they're having to take the baby by cesarean section. Delia's not doing well."

Dan draped a supportive arm around his friend's shoulders, not knowing what to say. He looked at Brynna helplessly. Responding, she stepped forward, touching Chet's arm with a gentle hand. "The doctors at this hospital are excellent," she told him. "I can assure you that Delia's getting the best of care."

Chet nodded. "Yeah. I just wish I knew what was going on."

"The doctors know you're worried," Dan offered. "I'm sure someone will be out just as soon as possible." He nodded toward a vending machine. "Want a cup of coffee?"

"No," Chet answered automatically, then changed his mind. "Yeah, I think I do. Thanks."

"Brynna?" Dan inquired, moving toward the machine.

"Yes, please," she answered gratefully. "I could use a cup. Black."

Pressing the appropriate buttons on the machine, Dan watched out of the corner of his eye as Brynna led Chet to a vinyl bench, urging him to sit down and rest, her low voice carrying to where Dan stood, though he couldn't make out the soothing words. He'd been right to bring her, he thought. Chet was relaxing visibly under Brynna's calming influence.

Damn, he'd hated finding her ex-husband with her so late at night, Brynna looking so relaxed and sexy in her silk robe. When he'd first seen the man, he'd thought, well, better not go into that. But then Brynna had looked at him with stricken eyes asking—no, demanding—his understanding and he'd believed without question that the two of them had been doing no more than talking. He didn't quite understand his own acceptance, nor could he imagine believing any other woman in the same circumstances. But, well, he just couldn't believe Brynna could look at him like that and lie. Every instinct told him she simply wasn't capable of such duplicity.

Carefully carrying three cups of coffee to the bench where Brynna sat comforting his best friend, Dan was aware of a surge of pride in her. She was something, this woman of his, he thought in a moment of chauvinistic pride. A woman to be counted on when he needed her. A woman who wouldn't lie to him, or at least hadn't lied to him so far, he corrected himself, trying to hold on to his carefully cultivated objectivity.

He distributed the coffee, seeing the anguish in Chet's eyes when they met his. The thought of losing Delia was more than Chet could handle. Dan wondered how his friend would survive if the worst happened. What was it like to love that way? he asked himself. To know that depth of love was returned in full? Delia was Chet's center, almost a part of him. Maybe there *were* some women who were worth the risks, Dan reflected, his gaze turning once more to Brynna.

"Mr. Traylor?" The green-clad doctor, his scrubs wrinkled and spotted in places with dark red stains, stopped before the bench on which Chet sat, his lined face creased with a reassuring smile. "Your wife is going to be fine. And so is your daughter."

Chet closed his eyes and slumped on the bench. "Delia's okay?" he repeated, needing confirmation.

"Yes. She's in recovery now, but you'll be able to see her soon."

Dan watched with a grin of relief as Chet's eyes suddenly flew back open. "You said my—my daughter?" he choked.

The doctor chuckled. "That's right. You've got yourself a little girl—and little is quite appropriate, in this case. Five pounds, but perfectly healthy. We have her in the preemie nursery now, where we'll keep an eye on her for a few days, but I didn't see anything to worry about." Sitting down beside Chet, he began to explain exactly what had gone wrong to cause Delia to start hemorrhaging and make the cesarean delivery necessary.

Leaving doctor and new father in privacy, Brynna and Dan retreated to one corner of the waiting room. Brynna hugged Dan tightly. "Thank God they're all right," she murmured.

Holding her warmly against him, Dan nodded against her hair. "Yeah. Chet was about to lose it. Thanks again for coming with me, Brynna."

"I'm just glad you stopped for me," she answered, looking up at him with moist blue eyes. "It meant a lot to me that you wanted me with you."

His hand tangling in her hair, Dan took her lips in a bruising kiss that held all his tangled emotions of the past hour; worry over Delia, his need to have Brynna with him in the crisis, his dismay at finding Russ at her house, his realization that he trusted her as he trusted no other woman. Rather than protesting the roughness of the embrace, Brynna opened her lips to his, welcoming the kiss and returning it in full measure.

The kiss went on until a loudly cleared throat interrupted them. "Hey, you two. You can finish that later, in a more private location," Chet teased, his usual exuberance back in his voice. "I want to introduce you to my daughter. Dr. Mitchell says we can see her through the window of the preemie nursery."

Dan pulled back reluctantly, telling Brynna with his eyes that they would, indeed, finish later what they'd started. Then, smiling, he turned, catching her hand in his and following Chet down the antiseptic hallway.

"That couldn't be your baby," he protested moments later, staring through the glass at the tiny form in the odd-looking, clear-sided bed. "She's much too pretty."

Beaming proudly, Chet threw out his chest. "Was there any question that she would be?"

"Well, Delia's pretty enough, but I was afraid your kid would get some of your ugly genes. Looks like she lucked out."

Chet laughed and playfully punched his friend's arm. "Jerk."

"She's beautiful," Brynna breathed in awe, gazing with misty eyes at the minute, perfect pink body. "Have you and Delia chosen a name yet?"

"Her name is Joy."

Dan lifted an eyebrow. "I thought you'd chosen Amy for a girl."

"We had. But I just changed it," Chet murmured, his eyes focused on his daughter. "Her name is Joy."

Feeling somewhat bemused as he watched his friend, Dan slipped an arm around Brynna's shoulders. He was

exhausted and wanted nothing more now than to go to bed
with Brynna in his arms.

Dan spent the rest of the night with Brynna, just as he'd
fantasized doing. Since it was Saturday, he didn't have to
hurry away the next morning, so Brynna made breakfast
for him—after he'd satisfied his other appetites. "You must
be hungry," she observed, leading him to the kitchen.

"Starved," he answered.

She waved him to a chair at the kitchen table, poured him
a cup of coffee to sip while she prepared his eggs. Feeling
Dan's eyes on her, she turned to smile at him as she worked.
"Chet was walking on air when we left the hospital, wasn't
he?"

"Yeah. Once he saw Delia and Joy and knew they were
going to be all right, he felt great."

"It was such a terrible experience. I can imagine how
frightened he must have been." Brynna kept busy as she
talked, breaking eggs, slipping them into a skillet. "It's not
common for problems like that to occur in childbirth anymore, but it's still so awful when something goes wrong.
Thank God for modern medicine." She knew she was
chattering, but Dan's silence was making her a bit nervous
as he continued to watch her steadily.

"You wanted children, didn't you?" he asked unexpectedly.

She moistened her lips, her eyes fixed on the bubbling
eggs. "Yes. But it's just as well Russ and I didn't have any,
the way things worked out."

"Do you still want children?"

"I'd love to have children," she answered honestly. "I
can't imagine anything more fulfilling than carrying a child,
giving birth to it, then watching it grow. I know there are a
lot of factors to be considered in making the decision to

have a child. There are risks, as we saw today. But, yes, I still hope that maybe someday—'' Her voice trailed off as she deftly lifted the eggs onto a plate, still avoiding Dan's eyes, not sure she wanted to see his reaction to her admission.

Dan changed the subject and left soon after breakfast, claiming he had things to do. She'd hoped he would stay around for a while, but she didn't try to detain him. At least, she thought, he seemed to be in a fairly good mood after the satisfying breakfast she'd made for him.

He kissed her quite thoroughly before he left, pulling back only to ask, ''Brynna?''

Still dazed from the kiss, she murmured, ''Yes?''

He paused for a long time, looking as if there were something he wanted to say but then he seemed to change his mind and kissed her again before she could speak. He left her staring perplexedly after him, wondering if she would ever understand him.

''You couldn't possibly eat anything else,'' Brynna exclaimed in mock horror as Dan eyed the sinful looking pastries displayed at the Greek Orthodox booth.

''Maybe just one small piece of baklava,'' he replied with a grin, pulling her by the wrist through the crowd milling around them until he stood in the pastry line. ''Lord, that looks good.''

''Don't you dare get sick before Show-Down tonight,'' she warned ominously. ''I swear if you do, I'll never forgive you.''

His grin broadened. ''Can I help it if everyone in Haskellville is trying to tempt me with delicious food?'' he protested innocently. ''Besides, I haven't eaten that much today.''

"Not that much? You had barbecued chicken at the Optimist Club booth, smoked knackwurst from the German-American Club, fresh fried pork skins from the Jaycees, fudge brownies from the Baptist women's organization, a snow cone from the Girl Scouts, and now baklava? And we haven't even seen all the booths yet!"

Dan laughed. "I don't suppose you'd believe I'm a growing boy?"

"Depends on which direction you claim to be growing," she retorted, meaningfully eyeing his flat stomach beneath the belt of his snug-fitting khaki shorts.

He only laughed again and defiantly ordered his pastry. Distracted from her teasing nagging, Brynna's nose twitched at a warm, sugary smell drifting from nearby. Turning her head, she saw an eager line of children at the next booth and groaned. Cotton candy. She could never resist cotton candy.

By the time Dan rejoined her, she was happily munching on the fluffy pink stuff—which almost exactly matched the color of the crisp cotton camp shirt she wore with white shorts. "That looks disgusting," he proclaimed, curling his lip at the sweet confection.

"So's your Aunt Mabel," she muttered, allowing another huge bite to dissolve in her mouth.

Grinning at her inane retort, Dan leaned over and kissed her, sticky mouths clinging for a satisfying moment before he pulled away. "Want to go see the magic show?"

Turning into the circle of his arm, she strolled with him down Main Street, which had been closed to traffic for the duration of the day-long Summer Festival. Crowded with attendees, some of whom Brynna knew, many who looked to be visiting from surrounding towns, the street was dressed in festive attire. Balloons, streamers, and banners waved in the welcome breeze that gave some slight relief from the July temperature.

The Summer Festival was running beautifully. Everything was set up for Show-Down. Dan was at Brynna's side. It was a great day, she reflected happily.

"Brynna! Hey, Brynna!" a young voice hailed.

Turning her head, Brynna spotted her young cousin Margie surrounded by a group of colorfully clad adolescents. "Hi, Margie. Having a good time?"

"Uh-huh," Margie returned with an affirmative bob of her red head, her eyes lingering on the man at her cousin's side. "Hi, Dan," she sounded clearly, glowing with pride that she could claim an actual acquaintance with the handsome deejay who had all her friends reduced to giggling speechlessness.

Having met Margie several times through Brynna, Dan smiled at her and leaned over to kiss her cheek, making her flush scarlet with delight. "Hi, beautiful. Whatcha' doing?"

"Just hanging out," Margie returned nonchalantly. "These are my friends. Karen, Valerie, Becky and Lisa."

Dan greeted each infatuated preteen-ager with grave dignity. Brynna had to work very hard to suppress a smile.

"I listen to your show every day," one brown-eyed future beauty told him in a rush of courage. "I think you're really cool."

"Thank you, Valerie," he answered simply. Brynna was impressed that he'd remembered the name. She could never have repeated them all in order.

"Could I have your autograph," the girl asked boldly.

"Sure. Got something to write on?"

Valerie pulled a paper napkin out of the deep pocket of her tropical-print shorts. "Will this do?"

"You bet. Who's got a pen?"

One of the girls produced a fat, hot-pink pen that she wore on a ribbon around her neck, handing it to him along with her own napkin. The others rushed to the closest food booth to grab napkins for signatures, all except Margie who casually mentioned that she could get Dan's autograph anytime she liked since he was dating *her* cousin.

Dan cheerfully signed personalized messages to each of the four girls and a few others who, attracted by the action, wanted to be included. Then, assuring them all he'd see them that evening at Show-Down, he and Brynna managed to escape.

"That," Brynna told him primly, "was very cute. You do know, of course, that I'm the envy of every twelve-year-old in town." And not a few of the older females, she added silently, noting an approvingly assessing look Dan received from a plump blonde of about Brynna's own age.

Dan growled dismissively. "Kids think anyone on the air is a celebrity," he explained self-deprecatingly. "Did you hear that one girl tell me that she always listens to my show just before turning to the Top Forty station she *really* likes? I think she considered it a compliment."

Brynna giggled. "I'm sure she did. At least your station's getting the younger audiences in the mornings. And besides, you're after the more adult audiences, remember? The ones with the buying power for your advertisers."

"Never underestimate the money available for twelve-year-olds to spend." Dan walked in silence for a moment, then spoke again. "How's Margie doing? She looked happy enough just now."

Brynna sighed. "She's fine when she's out with her friends. You know how kids that age are. But at home, she's still withdrawn and sullen. Mitzi can't get through to her lately."

"Poor kid. She just doesn't understand what's going on."

"I know."

"What about the boys?"

"Mitzi's tried to explain to them. Bryan's old enough to be upset; Nathan's still just confused."

"Any progress between Mitzi and Perry?"

Brynna shook her head. "None. I hadn't realized how ridiculously stubborn the two of them could be. Neither one will give an inch. Perry's finally agreed to talk to me; we're going to have lunch together on Wednesday. If he cancels again, I swear I'm going to kidnap him and tie him to a chair until I've had my say, whether he listens or not."

"The prerogative of family," Dan commented. "Give me a call if you need help handling the body."

She smiled and leaned against his shoulder. "Thanks. I just might do that."

Dan glanced at his watch. "We have to keep an eye on the time. Don't want to be late getting changed for your big show tonight."

"Right." She tilted her head back, her hair tumbling over the shoulders of her pink blouse. "Are you at all nervous about being in front of all those people tonight? I would be catatonic, but I guess it's all routine for you."

He chuckled. "Don't believe it. I have this terrible feeling that I'm going to lay a major egg. A performer's worst nightmare is getting up onstage and telling a string of jokes that no one laughs at. Why do you think I insisted on having Chet up there with me? At least this way I can blame it all on him if we bomb."

Brynna laughed and hugged him. "As if that were likely. Poor Delia. She wanted so much to be there tonight."

"Well, at least she's out of the hospital. But I agree with Chet—I think four hours of an amateur talent show would be too much for her just yet."

"I think so, too. At least she'll have someone staying with her this evening to help out with the baby."

"Yeah, Chet said their neighbor volunteered, even though Delia's sure she'd do just fine alone. It'll make Chet feel better, though. He's been very protective of Delia during the past week since he came so close to losing her."

"Mmm. Oh, look, the magic show's starting. Let's find a seat," Brynna urged, tugging at Dan's hand.

Smiling, he allowed himself to be pulled along by her childlike enthusiasm, though their conversation had set him wondering again how he would feel if Brynna's life were in danger. As he had each of the other times the question had occurred to him, he pushed it deliberately away. The possibility was simply too painful to consider.

A roar of laughter from the crowd made Brynna smile as she stood backstage, the clipboard in her hand letting her know which hopeful contestant to motion into place for the next act. Dan needn't have worried about being a success as emcee of the talent show, she reflected rather smugly. He and Chet were in top form that evening and the crowd adored them. Brynna couldn't remember ever being prouder of anyone than she was of her handsome, talented, oh-so-charming lover.

Her lover, she thought again, savoring the words. Dan had made no effort to downplay their relationship before their neighbors in Haskellville. He'd rarely left her side at the festival, having his arm around her or her hand clutched in his more often than not. He was a demonstrative man, and milling crowds had not stopped him from kissing her or hugging her whenever he felt like it—which had been quite often. Rather than being embarrassed by the attention they'd drawn as a couple, Brynna had gloried in Dan's affection, and the look in his eyes when they'd turned so often to hers. The warmth in those looks had ignited an answering flame deep inside her.

Yet no matter how much time they spent together, she was still having no success at all in penetrating the reserve of Dan Westbrook, she thought, her smile dimming. She still didn't quite know what he wanted from her, other than the affair they were having. Nor did she know enough about him to really trust herself to love him. How could she, when she still didn't know what motivated him? And how could he claim to care for her if he wouldn't share with her the real man behind the charming public facade?

The next contestant stepped onstage to the sound of encouragingly welcoming applause and Dan and Chet came behind the curtain to wait with Brynna until their next cue. "It's going well," Dan commented, pulling at his neatly looped bow tie. He and Chet had chosen to wear black tuxedos, giving an air of refinement to the program which pleased the standing-room-only audience.

"It's going beautifully," Brynna corrected, smiling up at him.

He ran warm navy eyes over her soft gray dress with its femininely full skirt that emphasized the shape of her legs. "Speaking of beautiful," he murmured. He hadn't stopped telling her how beautiful she looked all evening. Brynna wasn't at all willing for him to stop doing so.

She ran a hand up his elegant lapel. "Have I mentioned that you should be declared lethal in a tux? You're certainly doing dangerous things to my blood pressure," she murmured flirtatiously.

He lowered his head to lightly brush her pink-tinted lips. "How many more hours until we can be alone at your place?" he asked for her ears alone.

"Too many," she whispered fervently, knowing it would be well after midnight. Already her hands were trembling in anticipation of taking that elegant tux slowly off of him.

"Excuse me, you two, but we have to go onstage now," Chet reminded them tugging at Dan's arm. "Come on, Romeo, save some of that deadly charm for the ladies in the audience."

"I was so proud of you tonight," Dan murmured much, much later, his arms around Brynna as they stood beside her bed.

Her fingers paused where they were loosening his bow tie. "Proud of me? I was proud of you! You were the one onstage, the hit of the evening."

He shook his head firmly, his own hands discovering the long zipper at the back of her dress. "You were the one responsible for the entire evening, the one who made it such a success with your hard work and careful planning. That takes a lot of talent, to organize something like that."

Pleased with the compliment, Brynna stood on stockinged tiptoes to brush his mouth with hers. "Thank you."

"You're welcome." He slipped her dress down over her shoulders, his eyes darkening as the soft light from the bedside lamp glowed against the skin revealed by her lacy bra. "Lord, you're beautiful."

"You're going to make me conceited with all these compliments," she warned him, dropping his tie to the floor and going to work on the studs of his pleated white shirt.

"I can't help it. Every time I look at you I'm stunned again at how beautiful you are."

"Oh, Dan." Her hands slid slowly over his bared chest, fingers brushing through the crisp, swirling dark hair. Her dress fell to a pool around her ankles, followed closely by the rest of their clothing.

Laying her tenderly on the bed, Dan draped himself over her, his hands clenched tightly in her hair. His eyes searched her face hungrily, exciting her as powerfully as a dozen hard kisses. Brynna's eyelids grew heavy and her skin tingled hotly. But her lashes flew up at his next words. "You scare the hell out of me," he said and no smile softened the roughness of his voice.

"Why?" she whispered, studying him with a slight, puzzled frown.

"You make me—feel things," he answered awkwardly. "Things I haven't wanted to feel. Things I've never felt before. Not for anyone. And it scares me, because you're becoming too damned important to me."

Her hand lifted to cup his hard cheek, her heart clenching with fearful hope. "Is that so bad?"

He exhaled slowly. "I don't know," he admitted. "It's not easy learning to trust again. I've protected myself for so long that it's become a habit."

"Trust me, Dan," she said in a sudden, fierce rush. "Please trust me. Don't you know that I would never, never hurt you, never betray your trust? I—" she hesitated. She what? She couldn't make promises, couldn't declare feelings when there were still so many doubts remaining inside her. "You can trust me," she repeated again.

"I can't get enough of you," he muttered, staring down at her with a hunger that seemed to go soul deep. "Every time I'm away from you, I count the minutes until we're together again. I'm not used to feeling that way."

She didn't know what to say. She wanted to ask him to talk to her more, to tell her everything she needed to know

about his past, to help her understand her own compli-
cated emotions by talking about his. But she couldn't.

"I want you," he pleaded, drawing her more fully beneath his throbbingly aroused body. "Now."

"Yes," she moaned, arching to his fevered caresses. In
this way, at least, they communicated fully. "Now, Dan.
Please."

His lovemaking was wild, almost savage, an expression
of the vulnerable confusion he'd just confessed. She didn't
mind. She was feeling decidedly primitive, herself. Later
she would be rather shocked at the near-violence of their
coupling, but for now she threw herself wholeheartedly into
the madness. Her hands and mouth were as demanding as
his and her legs clenched his driving hips in a possessive grip
that urged him on. The sharp cry that left her lips in the
moment of ultimate insanity was unrestrained, incoherent. Dan's harsh, muffled shout followed immediately, the
sounds echoing in the shadowed corners of the room as the
lovers subsided into damp, panting oblivion, locked together, wondering if true sanity would ever return.

With Dan lying heavily on top of her, their sweat-slick
bodies still joined, Brynna drifted into a deep, exhausted
sleep. Her last conscious thought was the realization that
the physical sharing wouldn't always be enough. There
would come a time in their relationship when she'd have to
have more, when they'd have to move forward or end it.
The thought made her shiver with dread.

## Chapter Twelve

Brynna stirred and stretched as Dan woke her with a gentle kiss. "I've got to go now," he murmured. "I've set your alarm for eight."

"All right." Blinking in the early-morning light, she smiled as he leaned over her, fully dressed. It was Wednesday, three days after Show-Down, and he'd spent every night with her since then, leaving early for his morning radio program. At her request, he woke her each morning before he left. She hated waking to an empty bed after spending the night in his arms. She always went back to sleep with the memory of his morning kiss fresh on her lips.

"Today's your lunch with Perry?"

"Mmm-hmm," she murmured, stretching again.

"Let me know how it goes, okay?"

"I'll call you when I get back," she promised.

"Good. See you tonight." He kissed her once more before leaving.

Snuggling into her pillow, Brynna listened to the sounds of his departure. He'd all but moved in with her during the past few days. Neither of them was ready for him to take that serious step. There had been no further talk of their relationship, or of their future, from either of them, but something had changed since the night of Show-Down. Dan seemed more relaxed, more accepting of the ties between them, his smiles less wary, no longer tempered with the distance he'd tried to maintain at the beginning. It was a beginning, she told herself over and over during those days. A very good beginning, indeed.

Showered and dressed in a no-nonsense navy blouse and white linen skirt, her hair in a businesslike twist, she left the house later that morning with determined steps. Perry wasn't weaseling out of their talk today, she told herself resolutely. She was family, she loved him, and she intended to find out just what he intended to do to get his life back in order. He'd been there for her when her parents died, cajoling and bullying her out of the depression that had threatened to overwhelm her, and now it was Brynna's turn to return the favor. He needed her, whether he'd admit it or not, and she would try to help him even if, as she'd half seriously told Dan, she had to tie him to a chair to make him listen.

Perry had been avoiding her for the past week, so she was genuinely appalled when she saw how terrible he looked. The lines around his eyes and mouth had deepened dramatically, his eyes were sunken and shadowed, his skin pale. Concern made her furious that he'd been neglecting himself so badly. "I'm here for our lunch," she announced, her voice brooking no argument.

Perry tried, anyway. "Bryn, honey, I'm really swamped here. Why don't we make it another day?"

She slapped her palms flat on his desk and leaned on her arms, glaring straight into his unhappy, stress-dulled eyes. "Perry Haskell, we are going to lunch *now* and we're going to talk. No, scratch that. *I'm* going to talk; *you're* going to listen."

"Brynna—"

"Perry," she interrupted. "I own enough stock in this company to swing quite a bit of weight with the board, as you well know. Since Dad died, I've allowed you to make all the decisions around here without my interference because I thought you were totally qualified to do so. Well, now I'm not so sure. You have lunch with me now or I swear I'll be at the next board meeting demanding a full physical for you and an investigation into your competence to continue as chief executive officer. I'm not bluffing, Perry," she added as he flushed with temper at her tone.

"Dammit, Brynna, you know full well I'm qualified to run this company! I resent your implication that I'm not."

"Take me to lunch and convince me," she returned without softening. "You certainly haven't shown any evidence of ordinary common sense in the past few months. I want proof that you know exactly what you're doing."

Perry shoved his chair away from the desk and reached for his suit jacket. "Fine. Let's go." His clipped words indicated his anger with her, but Brynna was unrelenting. He was angry, but at least he was listening to her, she thought with grim satisfaction. He wouldn't listen to pleas from family, but he would damned well listen to the demands of an irate major stockholder. Perry had allowed the company to become his only reason for living during the past nine months and it was time to shake him out of his single-minded rut. She acknowledged the encouraging smile she received from Perry's secretary on their way out. His staff had been every bit as concerned about him as his family.

"I'll drive," Perry commanded when Brynna headed automatically toward her car in the parking lot.

She adjusted her course toward his plush Lincoln. "Fine." She could concede this point in order to win a few of her own.

"Where do you want to eat?" Perry asked when they'd buckled themselves into the big car, his tone still annoyingly martyred.

"I don't care. Somewhere quiet where we can talk."

"Ellie's?"

"Fine."

He'd been driving only a few minutes when he burst into speech again. "I'm furious with you, you know."

"Yes, I know," she acknowledged evenly. "I'm pretty mad at you right now, as well."

"You've never interfered in my life before. I don't like being blackmailed into meeting with you like this."

"Then what would you suggest I do, Perry? I asked, I practically begged. I tried everything I knew and you continued to put me off. This is too important for me to let you get away with that."

"My marital problems are private, Brynna. I didn't interfere when you and Russ broke up. The least you can do is grant me the same courtesy."

"I had my parents to talk to when my marriage ended," she returned steadily. "You've got me."

His hands tightened on the steering wheel until his knuckles were white. "I don't need to talk, dammit! If I did, I would have called you. There's nothing you and I can accomplish by discussing my personal life over lunch."

"Maybe not. But we're going to try it, anyway." Brynna finally lost the temper she'd been holding on to so precariously. "God, Perry, have you even looked in a mirror lately? You look like a corpse. You've added ten years to your face in less than nine months. You who've always taken such good care of yourself because you said you didn't want to die early, as your father did. Have you changed your mind, Perry? Do you *want* to kill yourself? If so, why not use a gun? It would be a hell of lot quicker!"

"I'm not trying to kill myself!" Perry shouted back. "All I'm trying to do is—is—" His words ended on a gasp.

Her eyes widening in horror, Brynna watched as his face went white, tinged in the hollows with an alarming shade of blue. "Perry, are you—*Perry!*" she screamed as the car veered out of control, her cousin slumped over the wheel.

She didn't now what they hit. She was reaching for Perry when the impact occurred. Her seat belt stretched with her when she leaned toward Perry, so there was nothing to prevent her head from hitting the dashboard.

Dan had just turned the console over to the midday announcer when Stan, the station news director, rushed in. "Dan! A friend of mine, who's an emergency ambulance dispatcher, just gave me a call with a news tip. Perry Haskell had a heart attack or something while driving and he's crashed his car."

Dan went cold. "Brynna was having lunch with him today."

Stan nodded sympathetically, aware, as was most of Haskellville, that Dan and Brynna had been seeing each other. "She was in the car with him. We don't have the details about either of them, but we were told they've both been taken to the hospital."

"Oh, God," Dan muttered, his voice strangled with fear unlike anything he'd ever known.

As he bolted for his car, he remembered wondering how Chet had felt at the threat of losing the woman he loved. Now he knew.

The first familiar faces Dan saw when he dashed into the emergency waiting room were Mitzi and her three children, huddled together, the youngest boy crying as they waited for news. Dan's gaze focused on Mitzi's haggard, wild-eyed face. He paid little attention to the others in the room as he headed toward her, intent on finding out about Brynna.

Brynna's voice stopped him. "Dan! I was just about to call you."

His heart leaping into his throat, Dan whirled to find her standing beside him, pale and a bit tousled, a darkening bruise on her right cheek and a neat white bandage on her right temple, but otherwise intact. His entire body went limp with relief. "You're all right," he said hoarsely.

"I'm fine," she assured him, taking in the expression on his face, which was undoubtedly almost as pale as her own. Dan made no effort to conceal his emotions. He caught her in his arms, holding her so tightly she wriggled a bit in reaction.

"Oh, God, I thought—" His voice broke, then steadied. "I was afraid I'd lost you."

"Don't you know you couldn't get rid of me even if you tried?" she asked with an attempt at humor, her arms around his waist.

Taking a deep, noticeably unsteady breath, he hugged her once more then drew back. "How's Perry?"

"We don't know, exactly. He wasn't really hurt in the accident, but they're running tests to see whether he suffered a heart attack and, if so, how much damage was done."

Dan turned with her to Perry's family. Nathan was still crying noisily while Bryan asked question after question of his harried mother and Margie sat much too quietly staring at nothing. Mitzi looked ready to burst into tears along with her youngest son. Dan helped in the only way he knew how, by taking charge of the children while Brynna soothed Mitzi.

"C'mere, buddy," he said to Nathan, swinging the sobbing five-year-old into his arms and motioning for Bryan to join them. "Margie, come on. Let's go to the cafeteria for ice cream, okay?"

"I don't really want any ice cream," Margie argued, lower lip quivering.

"Then go with me to help with the boys, okay?" Dan cajoled shamelessly, giving her his best celebrity-type smile.

Weakening, Margie agreed, throwing a questioning look at her mother, who managed a grateful nod for Dan. Nathan had stopped crying at the magic words "ice cream" and even Bryan looked willing to be distracted from his perplexed questions.

Mitzi breathed a sigh of relief when Dan disappeared with the children. "That's one nice man," she murmured, her hands clasped in Brynna's as they sat side by side on the vinyl bench.

"Yes, he is."

"He was frantic when he arrived, you know. I saw his face. He was terrified for you. He's got it bad for you, Bryn."

Brynna swallowed and crossed her arms tightly at her waist. "We haven't talked about our feeling for each other. Not really. How can we when he still won't share his feelings about anything of any importance?"

"Maybe the accident shook him into realizing how much you mean to him. I know what it did for me," Mitzi whispered, looking in the direction of the room where Perry was being cared for.

Though she was glad Mitzi was finally admitting how deeply she loved Perry, Brynna wasn't so sure she wanted a frightening incident to prompt an impetuous response from Dan. There was still too much that Dan had to face from his past for Brynna to believe he was ready to fully commit himself. Too many unresolved fears.

Before she could put her thoughts into words, they were interrupted by Dr. Samuels, who'd been taking care of the Haskell family since Brynna was born. "Perry's being taken to a private room," he told them kindly. "You can both see him soon."

"His heart?" Mitzi asked fearfully.

Dr. Samuels scowled, his bald forehead wrinkling fiercely. "No damage. This was just a warning. His body was telling him that he can't go on without enough rest, proper diet and exercise. I'm ordering him away from the office for a few weeks. I think a family vacation would be in order. Maybe a few days at your cabin in the Ozarks, once we've got him back on his feet," he advised with the confidence of a longtime friend of the family.

Mitzi twisted her hands together. "Oh, but I don't know if we can get away."

"The hell you can't!" Brynna interjected, now almost as angry with Mitzi as she'd been with Perry earlier.

Mitzi looked properly chastened. "Yes, of course we can," she agreed sheepishly. "Perry needs the rest and the children need to be with their parents again. Nothing else matters."

Only slightly appeased, Brynna turned to Dr. Samuels. "Is Perry awake?"

"Oh, yes. I've already had a long, stern talk with him," the physician answered, his chocolate eyes sparkling at Brynna's militant stance.

"Is he up to one more brief lecture?"

Samuels grinned. "Well, keep it short, but, yeah. Go ahead. Wring him out good. It's what your daddy would have done."

Brynna kept that in mind as she faced her cousin shortly afterward. Perry lay in the bed, still looking pale but no longer blue, his hand clutched tightly in his wife's. "I had threatened to tie you to a chair to have my say," she told him curtly. "This is a bit more drastic than I had in mind, but it'll do just as well. And don't interrupt me, Mitzi," she added when her friend showed signs of defending her ailing husband. "I've got a few things to say to both of you."

She planted her feet firmly on the floor, her fists on her hips, chin and shoulders squared. "My parents are dead," she said bluntly, making both Perry and Mitzi look at her in astonishment. "Bryan and Alice Haskell were killed in a car accident nine months ago. I'd give anything in the world if it hadn't happened, but it did, and I've finally let them go. Now why can't the two of you do the same?"

"I'm not quite sure what you mean, Brynna," Mitzi offered warily.

Brynna threw up her hands in disgusted exasperation. "It's so clear! The two of you are trying to be the reincarnation of my parents—only more so! Perry, my father ran Haskell Manufacturing quite adequately, wouldn't you say?"

"Of course he did! He taught me everything I know, saved the company more than once during hard economic times, earned the respect of his employees and peers." Perry's voice was somewhat weak, but undeniably sincere.

"Exactly. And during all those years of leading that company, he never once neglected his wife or child. He was always there for us, always available when we needed him. He would have walked away from the business without a backward look if it came to a choice between that or his loved ones. Yet you've got three children crying in the waiting room because they're afraid of losing the father who has so mysteriously pulled away from them lately."

Perry swallowed audibly. "I never meant to neglect the children," he muttered, stricken. "It's just that I didn't seem to have enough to give. The company, and the kids, and Mitzi—it just seemed too much all of a sudden."

"You *allowed* it to become too much," Brynna insisted. "You didn't trust the excellent staff my father worked so hard to recruit and train. You had to try to do it all yourself. Well, Perry, Haskell Manufacturing survived the death of my father, just as it would have survived your death had your body fully rebelled today instead of simply giving you fair warning."

Ignoring Mitzi's gasp of protest, she met her cousin's eyes steadily. "You are an excellent CEO, Perry, and I'm so very proud of you. But you have to let your associates do their jobs from now on. You have to stop trying to be Superman. If you don't, you're going to lose everything.

"And you, Mitzi," she went on without pausing, swinging her eyes to her cousin's indignant wife. "Your family needs you more right now than all the charities you've become so obsessed with. No one, least of all me, expects you to completely deny your own identity and become no more than an extension of your husband or a slave to your kids. If you want to go to work, if you want to continue with your volunteer service, fine. There's plenty of time for either, if you set some priorities and get your time organized. But you chose to be a wife and mother and you owe those roles every bit as much loyalty as you do the other parts of your life. You seem to have forgotten that lately."

Mitzi looked less defiant. "I—I guess you're right. Maybe I *was* trying to take on too much."

"Maybe you had too many lonely hours you were trying to fill," Perry suggested soberly. "I'm really sorry, Mitzi. I've been a self-centered jerk."

Mitzi caught her breath on a sob and shook her head. "I should have seen what we were doing to each other. We needed to talk, to work out our grief and our insecurities together, but instead we each tried to handle it all alone. We should have known better."

Feeling she'd made her point, Brynna slipped from the room, her eyes misting. They were going to be all right, she thought, almost sagging with relief. Mitzi and Perry had a lot of talking to do, a great deal of reorganizing in their daily lives, but they were going to be all right in the long run. Thank God.

"Everything okay?" Dan asked her when she joined him and the children.

"Everything's fine," Brynna answered, her smile including them all in her answer. She hugged Margie. "Your daddy's going to be just fine."

Dan took Brynna home soon afterward, where he made it a point to personally reassure himself that she was healthy and whole. His lips brushed with exquisite gentleness over the bruise on her cheek, his fingers lightly touching the bandage that covered the cut on her forehead. "You scared the hell out of me," he growled, hugging her again.

"I'm sorry you were frightened," she murmured, burrowing wearily into his arms. "I was pretty shaken up, myself, when Perry grabbed his chest and fell over the wheel. I was sure he was—well, I'm just glad everything's okay."

"You could have both been killed if he'd been driving faster. As it was, the car just glanced off the tree and wedged itself in the drainage ditch. The witnesses to the accident were able to get to you immediately."

"Is that what we hit? A tree? I wasn't really sure, since I only came to in the ambulance on the way to the hospital. And then I was so worried about Perry that I forgot to ask for details of the accident."

"I heard all the details while you were with Mitzi and Perry. You missed a head-on collision with another car by inches."

"Thank God no one else was hurt."

"Don't you ever, ever do anything like that to me again. You hear?" he demanded, holding her closer as they sat side by side on her couch.

She smiled reassuringly. "It's not as if I did it on purpose, you know."

"I'm not so sure," he answered sternly, though his eyes returned her smile. "You've seemed bound and determined to shake me up ever since we met. I haven't been the same since I hit the dirt at your feet."

"And that wasn't my fault, either. You weren't watching where you were going. You should have seen that little dog."

"I was too busy watching a beautiful blonde with big, sad blue eyes," he returned warmly. "Did you know I was on my way over to talk to you? I was trying to decide on exactly the right opening line to really impress you."

She giggled softly. "You found it."

"Hell, if I'd known that was all it took, I'd have fallen over the dog on purpose."

She laughed again, as he'd meant for her to do. A rush of emotion poured through her and with it came the threat of tears. She blinked them back, knowing they were a reaction to all that had happened that day, and not wanting to distress Dan with a fit of hysteria.

Pulling back, her smile rather tremulous, she pushed her hair out of her face. "I'm hungry. I never did have a chance to eat lunch today."

"Come to think about it, neither did I. What would you like?"

"I'll make something for us."

"No way," he insisted. "After all you've been through today, you don't need to be cooking. And I'm not in the mood to cook right now, either. I'll go get us something. What sounds good to you?"

*You,* she wanted to say. But, darn it, she really was hungry, she thought as her stomach growled softly to remind her. "Chinese," she decided on an impulse. "I'll call in an order."

"Sounds good. I'll have one of everything."

She laughed. "You and your appetite."

His eyes glinted devilishly. "Food's not all I've got an appetite for right now. Just wait until we've eaten."

She was looking forward to it.

They ate sitting on the floor beside the coffee table in her den, sharing the numerous delectable dishes straight out of the little white cartons. Brynna had intended to eat hers with a fork, but Dan, acting thoroughly scandalized, had insisted on chopsticks. He was much more skillful with the foreign implement than she. She discovered this to her laughing dismay as a plump, sauce-covered shrimp fell into the lap of her worn, comfortable jeans.

Dan clicked his tongue and shook his head. "No coordination."

Growling, she lunged for him. "I'll show you coordination."

He laughed as he tumbled to the floor beneath her assault, still clutching his chopsticks. "Hey, be careful! You almost impaled yourself. And I thought you said your head hurt."

"The pain reliever's doing its trick. I feel well enough to inform you that you have laughed at me all the way through this meal and I think it's time you stopped," she told him ferociously, draping herself over his prone body.

"Make me," he dared her, grin fading into challenge.

She lowered her head to his. "Exactly what I had in mind."

Dan didn't leave Brynna's side again that day. They made love, shared a soothingly warm bubble bath, watched television as he massaged her sore neck, then made love again with such tenderness that Brynna couldn't stop the tears. Dan seemed compelled to touch her, to make sure that she was all right. He didn't even appear to mind when Russ stopped by for a few minutes to see for himself that Brynna was okay. The two men were carefully polite, for Brynna's sake.

Late that night, holding her tightly in his arms as they lay in her bed, Dan nuzzled his face in her hair and murmured, "I love you, Brynna."

Her heart turned over in her chest, even as her throat tightened in near anguish. This is what she'd been afraid of, she thought sadly. Still shaken by her narrow escape from serious injury, Dan was reacting without thought, telling himself that his panicked response must be due to love. She wanted so badly to believe that he loved her, but she couldn't allow herself to put much faith in this impulsive declaration. There was still too much between them—barriers he'd deliberately maintained.

Not knowing what to say, she said nothing.

After a moment, Dan drew back. "Brynna, did you hear me? I said I love you."

"I heard you, Dan."

"Well?"

She moistened her lips. "Well, what?"

"Dammit, Brynna!" He lifted himself to one elbow and glared down at her. "What's the matter? I said I love you! You could at least show some reaction—it's not as if this was an easy thing for me to say, you know."

Sighing, she cupped her hand against his cheek. "Oh, Dan, I know it wasn't easy for you. And I'm touched by your words, I really am."

"You're touched," he repeated, very still.

"Yes, of course. But we're both very tired tonight and it was a rather traumatic afternoon, to say the least. I—"

"You don't believe me." He sounded stunned as he voiced the realization.

She hesitated.

"Brynna?"

"I believe—you care for me," she said carefully. "I know you were upset when you thought I'd been hurt today."

"You don't believe me." He fell heavily to his back, staring up at the ceiling. "After all we've been through, after I've finally found the guts to admit the way I feel about you, you don't believe me."

"I believe that you believe it right now. I just want to make sure that you're not reacting solely to the shock you received earlier."

Dan laughed, but the sound was without humor. "Hell. Not only don't you trust your own emotions, now you don't trust mine. I'm not confusing friendship with love, Brynna. I'm not your ex-husband. Dammit, I've fought this thing long enough to know what it is I've been up against. I lost the war. I fell in love before I even had a chance to defend myself. Maybe it took your accident to make me admit it, to myself as well as to you, but it's not something I didn't already know, deep inside.''

''All right, so you love me,'' she said as calmly as was possible with her heart pounding so hard it threatened to shake the bed beneath them. ''So now what?''

He turned his head to look at her, his attention arrested. ''What do you mean?''

''Just what I said. Now what? What changes can I expect in our relationship now that you've lost the war, as you put it?''

''I—uh—''

''Do you want to move in with me, live with me here full-time? Do you want marriage? Children? What, Dan?''

''I—uh—''

''You don't even know.'' Pushing her hair back with one hand, she rolled until she was sitting on the side of the bed, her back to him as she fought for control of the crushing disappointment. ''There's still too much you're holding back, Dan. You say you love me, but you're still unwilling to really share with me, to talk to me about your mother, your father, Melanie—all those hurts you still carry around inside you.''

He stirred behind her. She could almost feel his fiery gaze burning into her shoulders. ''Why are you so obsessed with the past?'' he demanded irritably. ''None of that has any-thing to do with you and me.''

''Doesn't it?'' she asked quietly, still without looking at him. ''How am I supposed to understand my feelings for you when I don't really even know you? You won't allow me to know you. You know I like to be very certain of my emotions before I allow myself to be influenced by them. I've told you my reasons, shared my past with you. And yet you're still concealing so much of yourself from me. You're right, Dan. I don't trust my emotions where you're concerned. I never have. And I don't trust yours just now. I can't. You've given me no reason to do so.''

"Okay, so now what?" he demanded, throwing her words back at her. "What do I have to do to prove that I know what I want, what I feel? You want to get married? Fine. We'll get the blood tests tomorrow. We'll be married by next week. Will that convince you?"

She swallowed a sob, determined not to cry. "Don't, Dan. Please. You know that's exactly what I *don't* want. Not just to prove something. Let's just go on the way we have been, can't we? When you're really ready to take the next step in our relationship, you'll know it. We both will."

Her breath left her lungs in a whoosh as she found herself suddenly flat on her back, wrists shackled by his hands as he loomed threatening over her. "You're a coward, Brynna Haskell. Scared to take what I'm offering in case it's not what you hoped for. Well, tough. You've got it, anyway. I love you. And, no, we can't go on as we have been. Everything's different now. *Everything*. Whatever I have to do to prove it, I'll do."

"Dan, I—"

"Just shut up, will you?" he growled, deliberately lowering himself until his bare chest erotically crushed her breasts. "I've heard enough of your careful little speeches tonight. The only thing I want to hear from you now are those little sounds you make when I love you, when I bury myself deep inside you and drive you so wild that you can't say anything but my name, can't see anything but me, can't think of anything but the way I make you feel."

Her moan was half protest, half arousal. His mouth covered hers before she could say anything more.

He made love to her with a fierceness just barely tempered with tenderness, and soon had her reacting exactly as he'd said she would. Arching beneath him, hands clawing and clenching, mouth searching. He heard the ragged sounds torn from her throat and knew she was capable of saying nothing but his name. "Dan! *Dan!*"

"Brynna!" he cried in return, his own voice raw with passion and frustrated emotion. "Oh, God, Brynna. Hold me. Love me, dammit. I love you."

And then he, too, was beyond speech.

Exhausted, Brynna slept heavily, waking only long enough to register that he was leaving the next morning. "I love you," he murmured into her ear, his voice so very gentle this time. "I'll find a way to make you believe me. I swear it."

## Chapter Thirteen

*This Guy's in Love with You.*
*Best of My Love.*
*Silly Love Songs.*
*When a Man Loves a Woman.*
*You're the Best Thing That Ever Happened to Me.*
*Benny and the Jets*

Benny and the Jets'?'' Brynna asked aloud, staring at the radio beside her desk. Dan had been playing one love song after another that morning, all a very blatant campaign to convince her of his feelings. But ''Benny and the Jets''?

''Well, I told him I like anything by Elton John,'' she murmured, a reluctant smile playing on her unpainted lips as the computer monitor glowed unnoticed before her. Still, of all the beautiful, romantic Elton John songs he could have played—

"That one was just to make you smile," Dan's voice announced as the song ended and, as she had all morning, Brynna had the distinct impression he was talking directly to her. "Now for another, very different tune from the same artist, here's my favorite, 'Blue Eyes.' "

"Oooh, that's not playing fair at all," Brynna moaned, burying her face in her hands as the crooning voice washed over her, leaving her feeling decidedly damp and weak. She was tempted to turn the radio off, but ever since she'd realized his entire programming was aimed at her, she'd been afraid of what he might say, too wary not to listen.

She'd challenged him, she realized belatedly, as the song continued to play. She'd handled the night before all wrong. It had just been so painful to hear words of love from him and have to wonder if he really meant them. And so difficult to understand her own reaction to those words.

Was she in love with Dan? she asked herself for the thousandth time. Everything was so different than it had been with Russ, but was this love? How was she supposed to know? Where was she supposed to find the courage to take the risk that their emotions would last?

The telephone rang. Dan was speaking on the radio as she answered the phone, so she knew he wasn't the caller. "Hello?"

"Hi, Bryn."

"Mitzi! Hi. How are you? How's Perry feeling?" Brynna greeted her with a rush of words.

"I'm fine and Perry's feeling much better after a good night's rest. Dr. Samuels says he may let him come home in a couple of days. Perry has agreed to go to the cabin for a week or two. We'll probably leave late next week and come back just in time to get the kids in school."

"That's good. You both need to get away for a few days and the cabin's the perfect place. Take lots of lunch meat

for sandwiches. You don't need to spend all your time pre-
paring meals.''

"You got it. That's exactly what I was going to take—
lunch meat and canned soups. My kids think that's the best
kind of meal, anyway.''

"Did you and Perry have a chance to talk last night?''

"Yes. I left the kids with our neighbor, and Perry and I
spent hours talking. I really hadn't realized how pressured
he felt to prove himself worthy of filling your father's
shoes. Nor how driven I had become to replace Alice in the
community,'' Mitzi admitted. "We were both so foolish.''

"Not foolish, Mitzi,'' Brynna correctly gently. "You just
got carried away. I understand. You know what a hard time
I had adjusting to losing my parents.''

"And yet you dealt with it better than Perry and I did in
the long run. We loved them very deeply, Brynna.''

"So did I. It was hard on all of us. But we made it.''

"Yes, we made it. Thank God.'' Mitzi paused to clear her
throat, then continued. "How's your head?''

"A little sore, but not too bad.''

"That's good. By the way, do you happen to be listening to your boyfriend's radio show this morning?''

Brynna groaned expressively.

Mitzi laughed. "I thought so. Not exactly being subtle,
is he?''

"No, not exactly,'' Brynna agreed wryly.

"I told you he was in love with you.''

"Oh, Mitzi. Everything's so confusing. I didn't want him
to be influenced by the accident, but I think he was. It
shook him up, made him say things I'm not so sure he
means. If he's really in love with me, why did he wait until
after the accident to tell me? Why didn't he say something
before?''

"Well, well. Brynna Haskell is scared witless, isn't she?" Mitzi asked with gentle mockery, unknowingly repeating the same accusation Dan had made the night before. "Terrified of risking another mistake."

"Mitzi, please."

"So how *do* you feel about Dan Westbrook, Bryn?"

The blunt question made Brynna break out in a cold sweat. "I—I don't know."

"You're afraid to admit it, you mean."

"It's just—well, it's all still so confusing. And I guess you're right. I *am* afraid of making another mistake."

"Now it's my turn to give a lecture," Mitzi announced with discernible relish. "Wise up, Brynna. Stop comparing you and Dan to you and Russ. If you can't tell that what you have with Dan is a damned sight more powerful than anything you ever had with Russ, then you're being deliberately dense. You and Russ had a warm, but basically unexciting relationship. You and Dan generate enough electricity to make my hair stand on end every time I'm in the same room with you. That's too rare to lose, kid. Fight for it."

Brynna twisted a lock of hair around one finger. "But how do I know that this 'electric' affair with Dan won't burn itself out even faster than the 'warm, unexciting relationship' I had with Russ?"

"I don't suppose you do know for sure. But, then, how do you know it won't last for the rest of your lives? Believe me, I never thought that Perry and I would ever come as close to splitting up as we have lately. I thought we had the perfect marriage, a love that would last through anything. I was naive. Nothing's perfect and even the strongest, truest love needs nurturing to survive the roughest times. Don't be afraid to try, honey."

"You're enjoying this, aren't you?" Brynna asked accusingly.

Mitzi laughed softly. "After the way you tore into me and Perry yesterday? You bet I am."

Brynna chewed her lower lip, wondering for the first time if she'd overstepped the prerogative of family by interfering in her cousin's marital problems. "Umm, Mitzi," she offered tentatively, "I'm sorry if I said anything to offend either you or Perry yesterday. I was just—"

"Hey, don't go apologizing now! Your scolding was exactly what we both needed to make us stop and look at what we were doing. You were an objective—well, relatively objective observer, which meant that you saw our mistakes more clearly than we did. We both appreciate the fact that you were so concerned about us. We love you, Brynna."

"And I love you both," Brynna returned, relieved. "I'm glad you called."

"I'll talk to you later, okay? In the meantime, listen to your deejay fella. And give yourself a chance to believe him, will you?"

"I'll work on it," Brynna promised.

"Do that," Mitzi advised before hanging up.

Dan called as soon as his program ended. "Have you been listening?" he demanded, laughter in his voice.

"Yes, I've been listening," she answered, trying to sound cross and failing miserably. "You're insane."

"Yes. People in love often are, I'm told," he returned solemnly. "I love you, Brynna Haskell."

Brynna sighed. "Dan, please. Give me a little time, will you? Please don't push this right now."

He grunted a frustrated, incoherent response. "All right," he said finally, reluctantly, "I won't push. But that doesn't change the way I feel."

She was silent, her eyes closing as her head began a dull, weary throb.

"Brynna, I—we have to talk. About a lot of things."

"I know," she said again.

"I've got a couple of meetings with staff here this afternoon, and I'd like to change after work. Why don't you meet me at my apartment, say about five, and I'll grill us some steaks."

"All right."

"If I'm not home when you get there, just use the key I gave you and go on in, okay?"

"Yes." He'd given her the key only the week before, in case of emergency, he'd said offhandedly, not wanting her to read too much into the gesture. She'd never used it.

"I've got to go. Is your head okay? Not too sore?"

"Not too bad," she answered, as she had with Mitzi.

"Good. Call me here if you need anything today, okay?"

"Dan, I'm okay, really. It's just a bump—no concussion, no lasting damage."

"I know. But in case you haven't realized it yet, you're pretty special to me. Take care of yourself for me."

"I will. I'll see you this afternoon, Dan."

"All right. See you then."

She sat for a long time staring at the telephone after she'd recradled it, then headed into the bathroom for a strong, nonprescription pain reliever. The headache she was developing had nothing at all to do with her accident.

Dan wasn't home when she reached his apartment just before five. Aware of the intimacy of doing so, she used the key. She smiled at the condition of his apartment—clean but definitely cluttered. Picking up a shirt he'd thrown over the back of a chair, she hugged it against herself for a moment, drawing in the lingering scent of the crisp after-shave he always wore. Her body reacted with a startling surge of desire. How she'd changed since meeting Dan Westbrook, she thought, amazed at the difference in herself.

She had just replaced the shirt where she'd found it when the telephone rang. She hesitated to answer his phone until it occurred to her that it could be Dan, calling to tell her he'd be later than expected. She lifted the receiver to her ear. "Hello?"

A pause, and then a woman's voice asked, "Is this the number for Dan Westbrook?"

A woman. Brynna swallowed hard, trying and failing to ignore a sudden ripple of primitive jealousy. "Yes, it is. Dan's not in right now, but I'm expecting him at any time. May I take a message?"

"This is his mother," the woman answered, her voice sounding wistful. "I guess there's no need for me to leave a number."

Brynna almost gasped at the words. Dan's *mother*? But it couldn't be! Dan's mother was dead—wasn't she? She remembered asking him if his mother was still alive, the night he'd found her looking at his billboard. "I lost my mother when I was twenty-three," he'd answered, his face hard and emotionless. And he'd spoken of his mother in the past tense on the few occasions when he'd referred to her since.

"If you'd like to leave your number, I'll be sure that he gets it," Brynna promised, groping quickly for a memo pad and pen from her purse.

"He won't return the call," the other woman answered dejectedly. "I only wanted to know if he's all right? Is he happy with his new job and his new home there?"

Something in the woman's voice twisted Brynna's heart. Perhaps it was just empathy, knowing what it was like to love Dan. "Dan is fine, Mrs.—?"

"Flora."

"Flora," Brynna repeated. "My name is Brynna Haskell. Dan's doing very well with his radio station; he's quite popular with the listeners in this area. He's in very good health, so you needn't worry about him."

"Thank you for telling me," Flora whispered, suppressing tears. "You're very kind, Brynna. Are you and Dan—?" She paused delicately.

"Dan and I have been dating for several months," Brynna answered, not knowing how else to explain their relationship. Why hadn't Dan told her his mother was still alive? she wondered again. And why did Flora act as if she should apologize for asking about her son?

"He'll be furious that I called, perhaps even annoyed that you talked to me. You needn't tell him, if you'd rather not. I just had to know that he—" The voice broke pitiably.

"Of course I'll tell him you called. Please, why don't you let me take your number. I'm sure Dan—"

"Thank you, dear, but he won't want to speak with me. There are things he probably hasn't told you about me, mistakes I made in the past that he simply can't forgive. I don't blame him, really, but as I grow older I find myself just needing to hear his voice at times, even though I know he doesn't like me to call. If he really wants to talk to me, he has my number. I've insisted that he keep it, for emergencies."

Brynna held the receiver tighter, her heart aching for the other woman. What could she have done that was so terrible that her only child would treat her this way? "I don't know what to say," she admitted finally.

"I know. Just make my son happy, Brynna, if you can. I can tell by your voice that you care for him a great deal. I'm glad."

Not knowing what to say, Brynna bit her lower lip and remained silent.

The woman who'd identified herself as Dan's mother hung up before Brynna could say anything to prevent it. Brynna was still holding the receiver when the door opened behind her.

"Hi, sweetheart," Dan's voice greeted her, his arms sliding around her waist from behind. "Was that a call for me?"

Brynna replaced the receiver. "Yes," she said, her voice sounding odd even to her. "I thought it might be you calling me, so I answered it."

"Sure. Who was it? Chet?"

Stepping out of his loose embrace, she moved a few feet away, studying his smiling face with troubled eyes. How could she have grown so close to him in so many ways without really knowing him at all? she wondered. "No, it wasn't Chet. It was your mother."

The smile fled instantly from his lips, replaced by a grim, white-edged frown. "What did she want?"

So hostile. "She only wanted to know if you were all right. She was concerned about you."

Dan's snort expressed his feelings quite eloquently. He turned toward the kitchen, brushing a hand through his hair. "I'd better start the steaks. I'm getting hungry, are you?"

She couldn't believe he was planning to drop it with that. "Dan!" she protested, holding out a hand to stop him. "Is that all you intend to say?"

He looked at her without expression. "What else is there to say?"

She had to restrain herself from grinding her teeth. "I didn't even know your mother was still alive! You led me to believe she was dead. I think you did it deliberately."

"As far as I'm concerned, she is," he replied coldly.

Stunned by his heartlessness, she retreated. He must have read her shocked expression all too clearly. "Brynna," he said, reaching for her. "You don't understand."

She flinched, avoiding his touch. "No, I *don't* understand," she agreed heatedly. "You've never made any effort to explain. All I know is that your mother obviously loves you and that you're treating her very badly. Maybe you think you have justification for your actions, but I heard a mother's heartbreak in her voice and it made me hurt for her. All she wanted to know was whether you were well and whether you were happy. That doesn't sound like such a terrible mother."

His hands fell to his side. "You're not going to let this go, are you?"

"How can I?" she demanded. "If this is the way you treat the people who care about you, how do I know I won't be the next one you decide to shove out of your life?"

"Dammit, I didn't shove her out! She walked out!" Dan threw back angrily. "I told you she left my father and me when I was ten."

"Do you really still blame her for divorcing your father when you were just a child, Dan? Other people watch their parents' marriages break up and still manage to salvage their relationships."

"Brynna, you don't—"

"Stop telling me I don't understand!" she almost shouted, whirling in frustration to pace the room. "How *can* I understand? You won't talk to me." She spun back to face him. "Talk to me, dammit! Tell me whatever it is you're hiding from me, whatever it is that makes your eyes so tortured every time you talk about your mother. What did she do when you were twenty-three that was so horrible you considered her dead from then on?''

She pulled in a shaky breath, stepping up to him to cup his set, pale face in her hands. ''Dan, don't you see that I have to know? As long as you're holding whatever this is inside, you can never be free of the past, never be truly free to love me—or anyone else, for that matter.''

He covered her hands with his, gripping her fingers almost painfully. ''Brynna, I love you.''

''That's what you tell me. So help me understand you.''

He closed his eyes. ''All right. I'll try. But you may be sorry you asked.''

''No. I have to know. What happened, Dan? Why did you tell me that you lost your mother at twenty-three?''

''Let's sit down. Do you want anything to drink?''

''No.''

''Well, I do,'' he said, rather grimly, reaching into a cabinet for a bottle and pouring himself a stiff drink. He downed half the contents before returning to sit beside Brynna. She'd never seen him drink before.

Without touching her, he sat on the couch beside her, leaning forward until his forearms rested on his thighs, the glass held loosely between his hands. He stared into it as he started to speak. ''My father met my mother when they were both nineteen. He had just signed up for the Navy and he fell head over heels in love with her. Crazy in love with her. He married her only a few weeks later. She was pretty, spoiled and carefree. Accustomed to being entertained, catered to. She hated being married to a man who was gone for weeks, sometimes months at a time. She wanted glamour, parties, attention. When Dad was gone, she was rarely home. She was usually out with her friends at one popular night spot or another. He knew, and it drove him sick with worry. He hated the fact that she wasn't happy, but he didn't know how to be anything other than what he was— a seaman.''

"There were other men?" Brynna asked, wanting to touch him, but held back by the stern set of his shoulder.

"I wasn't aware of it at the time. I don't know to this day exactly what her entertainment included back then,'' Dan answered bleakly. "She had a lot of single, fast-living women friends. I remember them coming to the house a lot, giggling like kids and drinking quite a bit. She made very sure she didn't have time to sit around missing my dad when he was gone.''

"And you resented her for it. I understand that.''

"Yeah. Yeah, I hated her for playing around like that while my dad was out on a ship somewhere defending his country. And yet, I loved her, too. She was pretty and lavishly affectionate, always laughing and teasing. I understand now what my father saw in her. I didn't see much of her while he was gone. Even then the housekeepers were the ones responsible for me.

"I adored my father,'' he admitted, his voice cracking a bit, bringing a film of tears to Brynna's eyes. "And I saw his face when he'd come home and look at my mother, knowing he'd never be able to make her happy. But still he loved her so much. She was an obsession for him. It almost destroyed him when she announced that she was tired of a part-time marriage and had found someone else, someone wealthier and more socially prominent, who would spoil her thoroughly.''

"And you stayed with your father.''

"I couldn't leave him. I didn't want to leave him. She tried to get me to live with her and her new husband, but I refused and threatened to run away if she insisted. She believed me. My dad needed me. And I needed him. My mother tried to talk me into staying with her just while Dad was gone, but I wouldn't. I resented her too deeply for hurting him.''

Nothing could have kept her from touching him then. Her hand sliding into the crisp dark hair at the back of his bent head, Brynna thought of how devastating it must have been for Dan, loving his father so deeply and watching him suffer. He'd loved his mother despite his resentment toward her and probably felt guilty for loving her when she'd hurt his father so badly. ''Did you see your mother after that?''

''Yeah. She'd visit, call, send presents. We managed to keep a relationship of sorts going, though my first loyalty was always to Dad. He retired from the Navy for health reasons when I was sixteen. From then on, we were inseparable. He went to all my school ball games, took me fishing, entertained my friends. I felt badly about leaving for college. Dad seemed so lost. As long as he lived, he could never mention my mother's name without this wistful look. As I grew older, I told myself that I would never allow myself to love a woman like that. It wasn't natural, wasn't healthy.''

Brynna could accept that. Though she wanted to be loved, she didn't want to become an unhealthy obsession. She wondered if Flora had found herself unable to live up to that kind of compulsive attachment. ''And then your father died when you were twenty-one,'' she prodded gently, remembering what he'd told her earlier.

Dan's nod was barely visible. ''The first semester of my senior year in college. October third. My mother came to the school. She told me he'd died in his sleep. I never knew he had a bad heart; it had been the reason he'd left the Navy, but he hadn't wanted me to know how serious his condition was. He was hoping to live to see me graduate.''

Brynna stroked his hair, biting her lower lip until she tasted blood. She wanted so much to take him into her arms, to tell him he didn't have to say any more. It was so obviously hurting him to have to dredge up the past, but it was so desperately important for her to know everything. "I'm so sorry," she whispered, as much for what she was putting him through as for his loss.

"It hurt," Dan said simply. He threw her a sideways glance before looking back down at his glass. "I guess you know the feeling."

"Yes." She knew all too well.

"Anyway, I threw myself into my school work, determined to graduate for Dad's sake. I met Melanie less than a month after my father died. She had just been dumped by a guy she'd been dating and needed ego-building. I was at loose ends, still hurting, needing someone to be there for me. I thought she was what I needed. She tried hard enough to convince me that she was. By Christmas, we were lovers.

"But Melanie was a butterfly, a party girl. She didn't understand my moods, didn't quite know how to take me during those times when I drew inside myself and gave in to my grief and anger at the way life had treated me. After a few months, she started looking around for someone more fun. She wanted to keep me on the string until she was sure she'd found a replacement. Like my mother, she didn't want to find herself between men for any length of time. I found out the hard way that she was—interviewing prospective replacements. I cut class one morning and dropped in at her apartment. She was entertaining."

Brynna closed her eyes against the incipient tears she refused to shed. Not yet. Not until she'd heard everything. Somehow she knew the worst was yet to come.

Dan drained his glass and set it roughly on the coffee table. "It was too much. I took off, determined I'd never let anyone hurt me again. Loving was too painful, too risky. I had no intention of doing so again."

"So you protected yourself. You didn't allow yourself to love anyone again."

"Not until you," he said, his voice weary, still without looking at her. "I fought it—God, I fought it, but there was no way I could stop myself from loving you."

"Oh, Dan." She leaned against him, resting her cheek against his shoulder. "It must have been hard for you to learn to trust again. But surely you see now that it doesn't always have to be like that. Loving doesn't automatically mean opening yourself to betrayal or rejection. You loved your father and he didn't hurt you."

Dan stiffened, was silent for a tense moment, then spoke too quickly. "No. No, he didn't hurt me."

Frowning, Brynna scrutinized his profile. "Tell me the rest of it, Dan," she prodded gently. "Tell me when you decided to consider your mother dead."

"My father wasn't close to his family. He had some kind of falling out with his own father when he was young. I never knew what it was about, but I always suspected my mother was involved. I met my paternal grandfather several times, but we were never close. Anyway, Granddad died two years after my father, when I was twenty-three. I went to the funeral, learning, much to my surprise, that my grandfather had left me a fairly large sum of money. He'd split everything between his only living offspring, a daughter who'd never married or had children, and me, his only grandchild. My aunt was an ill-tempered, embittered woman who didn't think I should have inherited anything. She'd wanted it all. I was sorry she felt that way and tried to talk to her about it. That's when I found out—when I learned—"

"What, Dan?" Brynna asked softly, holding him more tightly.

Dan took a deep sharp breath. "My 'loving' aunt informed me that I had no right to the money because I wasn't her father's real grandchild. It seems that my father returned from a nine-month tour of sea duty to discover that my mother was four months pregnant. With me."

"Oh, my God."

Ignoring Brynna's choked protest, Dan went on inexorably. "I don't know whether there were other men, or whether the man who fathered me was her only affair. I never wanted to know. My Dad never knew either, I believe. But even that didn't make him leave her. He raised her child as his own, and was the most loving and supportive father I could have ever hoped for. He never let on that I wasn't his. He'd brush aside my questions about my appearance by pointing out members of my mother's family to whom I bore a slight resemblance. I couldn't believe my aunt's story. So I confronted my mother."

"She confirmed it?"

"Yes. Tearfully. Swearing she regretted her weaknesses and that she loved me. She made me sick, telling me how lonely she'd been when Dad was away, how desperately she'd needed to be with someone. She even told me that the main reason she'd left my dad was because she couldn't stand looking into his eyes and knowing how badly she'd hurt him."

"But she let him keep you and never tried to tell you the truth, fearing, perhaps, that the knowledge would drive a wedge between you and your father," Brynna pointed out, her voice sounding strained from the tears now streaming down her face.

"No, they—she never told me," he said, his own voice finally expressing emotion. "They kept it from me until I had to find out on my own, in the hardest way possible."

*They.* Brynna winced, realizing what Dan had not yet admitted even to himself. His anger wasn't solely with his mother. He felt just as betrayed by his father, who'd never told him the truth. She wondered if she had the courage to force him to accept that one final fact. She wondered if it would destroy him—destroy *them*—if she did.

## Chapter Fourteen

Your father loved you, Dan," she began very carefully. "He thought he was protecting you by not telling you, like when he didn't tell you about his heart."

"He should have told me," Dan rasped in little more than a whisper. "About both. He shouldn't have—"

"What?"

He surged to his feet in a rush of emotion, pacing restlessly around the room, finally slamming his fist down on the dining table in the far corner. "Dammit, he shouldn't have lied to me!" he shouted, his eyes anguished. "He was the only person in the world I really believed I could trust, and he lied to me my entire life! Everything was a lie!"

"No! Dan, it wasn't a lie!" Brynna swiped futilely at the fresh tears on her cheeks, coming to her feet to face him squarely. "He loved you. To him, you *were* his son. You must have represented all the dreams, all the hopes he'd had when he was young and in love. He needed you, and you were there for him, just as he was always there for you.''

"Do you know how it made me feel to find out the truth?'' he demanded, a muscle jumping convulsively in his cheek. "To know that everyone but me had known all along?''

"Dan, I'm not saying that what he did was right. But he must have been so afraid of losing you as well as your mother. He needed you too much to risk that. Don't you see?''

He looked down at her for a long time, then pulled her not very gently into his arms, burying his face in her hair. "Ah, hell, Brynna,'' he muttered, sounding suddenly tired. "I just don't know what to think now. About anything. Finding out the truth about my father threw me so hard that I still haven't sorted out all my emotions. I told myself I loved him and hated my mother for all she'd done to him—and to me. But all along I guess I've resented him for not telling me and for dying before I could hash it out with him or find out how he really felt about it all. I managed to put it behind me for the past few years simply by refusing to think about it, but now it's all come back and I—I don't know how I feel.''

"I understand, Dan. I understand,'' she soothed, holding as much of him as she could reach, wanting so desperately to pull him even closer, to shelter him from any more pain.

"Brynna.'' He lifted her face to his, his mouth covering hers in a kiss that seared all the way to her soul, burning with the intensity of his emotions. Wanting nothing but to comfort him, she pressed closer to him, her lips opening to his without reservation. His hands moved over her seeking reassurance that she was there for him. She sensed the exact moment when his need for comfort changed to a desperate craving for more.

His kiss changed, becoming less tentative, more demanding. His hands, no longer so gentle, swept over the pliant curves beneath them, leaving tiny flames in their wake. He needed the mindless pleasure she could give him. Glorying in the knowledge that she could bring him solace, if only briefly, she arched into his touch, welcoming him.

Dan groaned and swiftly tugged her colorful summer sweater over her head, tossing it heedlessly to one side. "I need to see you," he murmured hoarsely, reaching for the clasp of her bra. "Touch you."

"Touch me, then," she urged, helping him with the fastening of her cotton slacks. "As much as you want."

There was no thought of her own needs, her own gratification as she helped him shed his own clothing, her lips scattering arousing, feverish kisses over his skin. This time, her joy was in pleasing him. Falling to her knees, she freed first one foot, then the other from his slacks, then tossed the slacks aside with the briefs she'd brought down at the same time. His hands clenching in her hair, Dan jerked involuntarily when she pressed open, moist lips to the inside of his thigh. "Ah, Brynna," he groaned, his body already filming with perspiration.

Boldly, her mouth moved inward. She was rewarded for her daring by his raw moans of pleasure as she explored him with lips and tongue and the very edge of her teeth. Her hands curled around his strong, hair-roughened thighs, and she treasured the slight trembling in the powerful muscles beneath his tanned skin. He was concentrating on her now, thinking of nothing but her. Which was exactly what she wanted.

When Dan could stand no more, he dropped beside her, pulling her hungrily beneath him. She arched to his thrust, taking him deeply within her, her eyes closed, her hands curling around his heaving shoulders. Her legs tightened around his hips, urging him on when he would have slowed. Ignoring his halfhearted protest, she slipped her hands down his sweat-beaded sides, gripping his buttocks to pull him more tightly inside her, knowing her actions would make it impossible for him to hold back. Groaning harshly, he surrendered, driving himself deeper and faster until he cried out and shuddered in an explosive climax.

Smiling through her tears, Brynna only held him more tightly, kissing his damp hair and temples, stroking him with long, soothing caresses. "It's okay," she reassured him, over and over. "Everything's okay, Dan."

He lay still and silent for so long that she was beginning to wonder if he'd fallen asleep when he finally stirred, and looked up. His expression was regretful. "I'm sorry. I—you didn't—"

She shook her head, smiling tenderly at him. "Please don't apologize. I wanted to please you."

He kissed her. "You did," he assured her, his lips hovering over hers. His hand left the breast it had covered to slide downward. "Let me—"

She caught his wrist in her hand. "No. It's not necessary. Not this time."

He kissed her again, then rolled away from her, one forearm over his eyes. "Damn, but I'm tired," he said.

"You've had a long day."

"Yeah. A hell of a long day." He pushed himself up to a sitting position. "I think I'll take a quick shower. Then you can have one, if you like, while I cook the steaks."

"You don't have to cook tonight. I'd be glad to—"

He shook his head. "No, I'd like to do it. It'll give me something to do to get my mind off everything for a while," he explained with a crooked half smile. Grabbing his clothes as he stood, he looked down at her as she sat up and reached for her own things. "I'll just be a minute."

True to his word, Dan took a very quick shower, emerging to find Brynna wrapped in his robe, waiting. Rubbing his hair with a towel, he smiled at her as he passed on his way to the closet, unself-consciously nude. "Shower's all yours."

She reluctantly pulled her gaze away from his magnificent body. "Thanks. I won't be long."

"Take your time. How do you want your steak?"

"Medium."

"You got it." He touched her cheek as he passed her again, dressed this time in a pair of worn jeans.

Brynna wandered into the bathroom, worrying her lower lip between her teeth. Dan was in an odd mood, she thought. She supposed she should understand, but she wanted so badly to know if he felt that anything had changed between them. She was so terribly insecure when it came to their relationship.

Soaping herself slowly, she stood beneath the deliciously warm shower and thought about what Dan had told her. Brynna had never been betrayed, not like that. And yet Dan had felt betrayed over and over. How must it feel? What kind of scars did such betrayal leave? How much courage must it take to risk such pain again? She wondered if she'd have the strength to try again after so many devastating shocks.

It wasn't over, of course. Knowing what had happened between Dan and his mother didn't solve the problem. Dan would never be free of his defensiveness until he truly put the past behind him, and ignoring his mother wasn't the way to do it. He had to face her, had to try to come to terms with his feelings for both his mother and the man who'd always been his beloved father. And he was going to be upset with Brynna for insisting he do so.

She found herself praying, as she hastily dried off, for wisdom, courage and strength. And for Dan.

"How's your steak?" Dan inquired, the first words he'd spoken since they'd sat down to eat some fifteen minutes earlier.

"Very good. Thank you." Her own voice was just as stilted, just as insincere. Neither of them cared about the steaks.

"Can I get you anything else?"

"No. Thank you." She looked at the piece of meat on her fork, lifted it halfway to her mouth, then listlessly replaced it on her plate. What little appetite she'd had was gone.

Watching her, Dan sighed and pushed his own plate away. "I'm not really hungry, either." He stood and held out his hand to her. "We'll clean this up later. Let's sit on the couch for a little while."

She placed her hand in his and his fingers closed around hers with reassuring warmth. Side by side on the couch, Brynna's cheek on his chest, his arms snugly holding her, they listened to the softly playing stereo, neither of them interested in television or idle chatter. Both knew they had to talk seriously, and soon; neither wanted to start the conversation.

Brynna could finally wait no longer. "What are you going to do?"

"About what?" he asked cautiously.

Swallowing impatience, she answered just as carefully. "About your mother."

He stiffened. "Nothing. She's getting along just fine. Her last husband left her well-off financially, and her health is good. She doesn't need anything."

"She needs her son."

"It's too late for that."

"It's not too late, Dan. It will only be too late when she's gone, and then I'm afraid you'll regret waiting so long."

"Dammit, Brynna." He tangled his fingers in her hair, pulling her face up so that she had to look into his frustrated, unhappy eyes. "Why can't you let it go?"

"Because *you* haven't" she whispered in return. "It's there between us, all the time. Like a—a gauze curtain that I can see through but can't penetrate. I see what we can have together once you let down those defenses of yours, but I don't know how to reach you."

"Brynna, what happened between me and my mother has nothing to do with what you and I have."

"How can you say that? You told me yourself that the reason you haven't allowed anyone to get close to you in the past years is because of your feelings about your parents, reinforced by your broken engagement."

"I also told you that I love you, that I fell in love with you in spite of my past. Doesn't that mean anything to you?" he asked bleakly.

Her hands lifted impulsively to cradle his cheeks. "Oh, Dan, of course it means something to me! But before I can sort out my own feelings and look to a future for us, we have to know that the past is truly behind us. My fears about the mistakes I made with Russ, your confused and bitter feelings toward your mother. I'm scared, Dan. Scared that the past won't ever leave us alone if we don't do something about it."

His fingers tightened almost painfully in the thick curls he held. "I love you," he told her roughly. "God, I love you. How can you even doubt that?"

She looked at him steadily. "I'm—beginning to believe you," she said at last. "But, as I've asked you before, now what?"

He closed his eyes in exasperation. "I don't know," he whispered harshly. "Dammit, I just don't know. I want you with me all the time. I want to share your life and have you share mine. I want to sleep with you every night, to wake with you every morning. I can't imagine ever making love to another woman. But marriage, and children, I don't know if I'm ready."

"And neither am I," Brynna answered, trying to keep her voice steady though her hands trembled at the gravity of their words. "But I have to know that we want the same things, ultimately. I don't want to find out two or three years from now that I've committed myself to another man whose wants and needs are completely different from my own. It's so much more crucial for me to know what I'm doing and what I'm getting into this time. If you and I were together for that long and then didn't make it, I honestly think it would destroy me."

He pulled her into his arms. "I know. I think that's what I'm so afraid of. I've never had the power to hurt anyone else the way I know I could hurt you. I'm not sure I can deal with the responsibility."

"I don't want you to feel responsible for me," she argued. "Not like that. I can take care of myself, but I have to start now. I just need to know all the risks."

"I love you, Brynna. You once said you wanted someday to be married again, to have the chance to raise a child. I believe I want that, too. We're both scared, sweetheart.

Not only of the risks to our own emotions, but of the risks we may be taking with any child we create.''

"Yes," she agreed. "That's exactly what I'm afraid of. Knowing that everything you do has repercussions on that young, vulnerable life—just as *your* parents' actions shaped what you are. I think that's what you're most afraid of. Your parents hurt you so horribly that you're terrified of taking on that kind of responsibility yourself.''

He swallowed visibly and nodded. "Yeah. I guess when it comes down to it, I'm as scared and uncertain as you are.''

"Because you still haven't come to terms with your mother.''

"I don't know. Maybe." He didn't look fully convinced.

Pulling back, Brynna looked up at him. "My parents are dead. There's not a day that goes by that I don't wish I still had them with me. I wish they could have met you and that I had my mother to talk to about the way I feel, the fears I have. And I would have loved to meet your father. He sounds like such a loving, caring man, despite any mistakes he made with you. They're gone, Dan, and we can't bring them back.

"But your mother is still alive. She's human, yes. She has her flaws and weaknesses. I'm not saying you should love her just because she's your mother. Some people just don't deserve love. But from what I sensed when I spoke to her, I don't think she's one of those people. I think she deeply regrets the mistakes she made and wants to try to make amends. And you can't just keep pretending she's dead. She's alive, Dan, and she'll always be there, in the back of your mind until it truly is too late.''

"You're asking me to reconcile with her. I just don't know if I can, Brynna. So much has happened. So many years have passed since we had any kind of relationship at all.''

"I know. And I'm only asking you to try. Because if the day ever comes when we're ready to have that family you just mentioned, I will want our children to know their grandmother, the only grandparent they'll have the opportunity to know. Even if you and I don't make it together, if eventually you have a family with someone else—'' The words were incredibly hard to say despite the doubts that still lingered deep inside her. "I can't bear the thought of that poor woman growing old and being all alone with her regrets and her sad memories, knowing she has a son and maybe grandchildren who won't even allow her in their lives.''

"I'm still so damned angry with her for what she did to my—to my father.'' He suddenly sounded so young and confused that Brynna had to fight tears.

"I know,'' she murmured through a painfully tight throat. "Maybe you should tell her that. And then consider it behind you and see if there's anything salvageable for the future. I don't know, Dan. I'm no expert on human relationships. But I have such a strong, certain feeling that you have to make some effort to settle things with your mother if you and I are ever to have a chance of making a life together.''

Dan stared at her for a very long time. She met his look without blinking. Finally he kissed her, very lightly. "I love you, Brynna,'' he said with renewed determination, "too much to lose you without a fight. But I know now that you're right about us needing time. There's just too much to think about to make any decisions on impulse.''

"Yes,'' she agreed. "You do need time. We both do.''

He kissed her again, longer this time. "Want to help me clean the kitchen?'' he murmured against her lips, his own curving into the first smile he'd given her in what seemed like hours.

"I can't think of anything I'd rather do."

"It takes so little to entertain you," he teased, pulling her to her feet.

"What can I say? I'm easy."

"My kind of woman," he returned. Though his eyes were still too serious, he was obviously making an effort to ease the tension of the evening and Brynna cooperated fully.

He needed time.

So did she. She was gambling her entire future on the outcome of their relationship.

"You're sure you won't stay?" Dan asked later as Brynna prepared to leave.

She touched his cheek, smiling. "No. Not tonight."

"I'll call you," he promised.

"I know. But don't rush it. Take as long as you need to think about what you want to do next. Just know that I—" her voice cracked "—that I'm around if you need to talk."

He caught her in his arms for a rib-compressing hug. "I love you," he muttered into her hair. "More than anything. We'll work it out, sweetheart."

"I hope so," she whispered. Knowing she'd better leave while she still could, Brynna broke away, hurrying off without looking back, though she knew Dan watched her until she was out of sight. She had to wipe tears from her cheeks more than once during the drive home, but she found herself foolishly optimistic that they had paved the way for a new beginning. At least now everything was out in the open, she told herself bracingly.

Dan didn't wake her the next morning. Another deejay, announcing that he was filling for the "vacationing" Dan Westbrook, woke her with a song Dan never would have played at 8:00 a.m.—"their" time. Brynna was concerned, but she made no effort to call Dan. When he was ready, he'd contact her. Truth be told, she had a lot of thinking to do on her own.

She finished her book. It felt good to send it to her editor. She was pleased with her end product. During the next few days she did some shopping, visited with friends, had dinner one evening with Mason and started a new outline for another book.

And she missed Dan every moment. As the days passed and she still didn't hear from him, it began to dawn on her just how deeply he'd worked his way into her life. If this wasn't love, she thought with a tremor of fear, then she no longer knew what love was. Surely there couldn't be any more to it than this.

And now that she was finally beginning to recognize the emotion, to tentatively trust it, she couldn't help but worry that it might be too late.

Flora had aged in the three years since Dan had last seen her. He looked in the doorway and tried to analyze the way he felt. Traces of the laughing, carefree woman he remembered from his earliest childhood lingered in her fading blue eyes. Her glossy dark hair had long since turned gray; her pretty, once proudly maintained face was now lined with time and experience. She was still slim, perhaps too much so. She looked frail and older than her fifty-nine years. She appeared thoroughly stunned to see him.

"Dan," she murmured, her voice choked. "I—wasn't expecting you."

"I know. Is this a bad time? I can come back."

"No!" Her fine-boned hand went to her throat. "No, of course not. Please come in."

The home his mother had shared with her late husband reminded him of Brynna. Very tasteful and expensive, yet still somehow welcoming. He'd never noticed this on his few previous visits. But then, Brynna had changed his view of many things, he thought, taking a seat at his mother's urging.

"Brynna told me you'd called," he began when his mother had also been seated nervously on the very edge of a delicate-looking armchair.

"Yes. I hope you weren't annoyed with me. I was just thinking about you, wondering how you were, and I couldn't resist calling," Flora answered wistfully.

Dan shrugged noncommittally.

"She seemed very nice." Flora offered after a moment. "She has a lovely voice."

"She *is* very nice. I'm in love with her," Dan answered rather bluntly, almost daring his mother to respond. He knew he was acting like a jerk, but, dammit, how was he supposed to act? he wondered irritably. Maybe he should have brought Brynna with him. She'd know what to say, how to act to put everyone at ease. She had a talent for that sort of thing. And yet he knew this was something he had to do alone. For Brynna's sake as much as his own.

Flora caught her breath. "I'm very happy for you."

"We haven't settled anything between us yet. Your felicitations may be a bit premature."

Flora clasped her hands in the lap of her simple gray dress until her knuckles whitened. "I hope things work out for you. I want you to be happy, Dan. If all goes well, I would love to meet her. Will you—will you bring her here sometime?" she asked hesitantly.

"I'm thinking about it," Dan admitted. "Brynna seems to think that you and I have to get some things settled before she and I go any further with our relationship. I don't know if she's right or not, but it's important to her." He left unspoken, but implied, that he was there only because of his love for Brynna.

Flora's throat worked visibly. "What—what sort of things?"

Dan looked away, shoving a hand through his hair, before making himself face her again. "I hated you when I found out what you did to my father—and to me," he said in a rush of words held back too long. "I already resented you for so much, but when you took my dad away from me by admitting that he wasn't really my father, I hated you."

Though she paled dramatically, Flora sat up straight, her chin held high. "I know. I always knew you would. That's why I could never tell you."

Dan's own hands clenched into fists on his knees. "All those years, every time he looked at me, he saw another man's bastard." His voice sounded, and felt, like gravel as it left his throat.

"No!" Flora's voice was stronger now, ringing with conviction. "Every time Leland looked at you, he saw a young man he loved with all his heart. From the day you were born he loved you. You were his son, in every way that mattered at that time. He couldn't have loved you more had he fathered you himself."

"Do you even know who fathered me?" Dan asked bitterly, not wanting her to see how much her answer meant to him.

"Yes," she whispered, flinching at his cruelty but still managing to face him steadily. "I know. Do you want the name?"

He shook his head violently. "No! I don't care about that now. As far as I'm concerned, Dad was my real father, the only one I ever wanted."

"I never tried to take you away from him. I wanted so badly to have you with me as you were growing up. You were my only child, the only one I could ever have, but I wouldn't take you with me when you wanted only to be with him."

He didn't know if she was simply stating facts or trying to make points with him. He didn't care. "I trusted him. I wasn't sure I could trust you."

"I never gave you much reason to trust me, did I?"

"No. Turned out I couldn't completely trust either of you," he muttered.

Again, Flora denied his assertion. "You're wrong about that. Leland wanted to tell you from the beginning. He was concerned that you would find out someday from others, just as you did eventually, and he thought it would be easier for you to know all along. I was the one who didn't want you to know. I couldn't bear for you to know how weak and foolish I'd been. I begged him not to tell you. I promised I'd never be unfaithful again if only he'd allow us to try again to live as a family. He agreed because he could never deny me anything I wanted. Later, well, it was just too late. I think Leland actually forgot that you weren't really his child biologically. Maybe he forgot deliberately, because he wished so very much it were true. He was a man who loved with everything inside him."

"Yes," Dan agreed, his voice hardening again. "He loved you that way. Until the day he died."

Flora swallowed, her lined throat working with the painfulness of the action. "I know. I could never live up to the image he had of me. I knew all along that I didn't deserve to be loved that way. It's not easy to be the object of

another person's obsession, Dan. I don't really expect you
to understand, but your father's love wasn't a natural,
healthy feeling. Perhaps another woman could have received that love without feeling smothered, but I couldn't.
I'm sorry. For Leland and for myself. But mostly for you."

Dan glanced slowly around the room in which they sat,
in the house that Leland never could have afforded. His
eyes fell on a framed photograph on the piano in one corner. "Did you love *him*?" he asked quietly, nodding toward the gray-haired man in the picture. "Were you
faithful to him?"

"Yes. Marshall and I were very happy together. I made
a real effort to be a good wife to him, to learn from the
mistakes I made when I was young and spoiled and too
pretty for my own good. I told Marshall everything before
I married him, so he knew what I'd done. And yet he loved
me—gently, warmly, undemandingly. My only regret is that
you would never allow yourself to get to know him better.
He was quite fond of you, you know."

"He wasn't Dad."

"I know. No one could be. Perhaps," she suggested very
carefully, "perhaps your love for Leland was a bit ex-
treme, just as his was for you. And for me."

Dan squared his jaw in instinctive defiance. "I loved him
the way all boys love their dads. There was nothing unnat-
ural about it. He needed someone to love him uncondi-
tionally."

Flora didn't press. "I won't ask you to forgive the things
I did to Leland, Dan. Those things aren't even yours to
forgive. But I do want you to know that I never meant to
hurt you. I have always loved you and I was the best mother
I knew how to be. I'm sorry I couldn't be the kind of
mother you needed."

Dan consciously relaxed his fist, staring down at his fingers. "That's all in the past now. Maybe we should let it stay there," he murmured, remembering Brynna's words. Closing his eyes, he conjured a vivid image of her face, letting his love for her sweep over him and give him courage to face his mother again. "I'm willing to start over if you are. If Brynna and I do work things out, if she agrees to marry me and start a family, she'll want our kids to know their grandmother."

The hope that flared in Flora's eyes was almost painful to witness. "And what do *you* want, Dan?" she whispered.

He hesitated. "I want Brynna to be happy," he answered at last. "If it hadn't been so important to her, I probably wouldn't have come today. I would have gone on as before pretending you didn't exist. I'm sorry, but this time we have to be honest with each other."

"I don't care why you're here," Flora said. "I only want to know that you'll give me another chance. Try to get to know me all over, the way I am now, not the way I was in the past. I want so much to know my grandchildren," she finished, the tears she'd been holding back spilling onto her cheeks.

"Then we'll try. No guarantees, you understand. But I'll try."

"That's all I can ask. It's so much more than I expected. Thank you, Dan."

"You can thank Brynna."

"I will, when I meet her. Have you asked her to marry you?"

His mouth turned up in a wry half smile. "No, I haven't actually asked her, yet. I had to do this first."

"She'll accept," Flora said with a mother's confidence in her child's desirability. "I can't imagine that she would turn you down."

"Brynna has her own problems to work out," Dan replied with less certainty, trying not to show his dread that Brynna would never learn to trust his feelings for her. He hoped she'd be pleased when he told her about this meeting with his mother. The tension between mother and son was still there, of course. The childhood scars would never completely disappear. But there remained that indefinable blood bond that could never completely be ignored. Maybe it was enough, Dan thought. He didn't know if he was happy, exactly, with this new beginning, but he was aware of an old, constant ache gradually fading away inside him. Like a festering splinter finally extracted, leaving the wound to heal on its own. Maybe it was enough.

"I'd like to stay here for a day or two, if it's okay with you," he requested. "I want to tell you about my life in Haskellville, and especially about Brynna."

Flora rose to her feet, her face glowing with hope and happiness. "You've always been welcome in this house, Dan." Very tentatively, she touched his shoulder. "Thank you."

Somewhat awkwardly, he patted that fragile, hesitant hand. He wasn't quite ready to put his arms around her and consider all forgiven, but it was a start.

Brynna would be pleased, he thought again. And, accepting his mother's invitation to join her for afternoon tea and cakes, he began to tell her all about the woman he loved. The woman who'd given him the courage to start over.

## Chapter Fifteen

Tightening the sash of her robe, Brynna hurried for the front door in answer to the impatient summons of the bell. She knew who was calling in the middle of this Sunday night. It could only be Dan, whom she hadn't seen in almost a week. Even as she nervously released the locks to let him in, she wondered if she was really ready for this meeting.

It took only one look at him, so tall and handsome in the soft porch lighting, looking at her with such cautious vulnerability, for her to realize that she'd been an idiot to deny her feelings for so long. A silly, cowardly idiot. She loved him.

"Dan," she whispered, throwing herself into his arms. "I've missed you so much."

His arms closed around her so tightly it was almost painful, but she never dreamed of protesting. He could never hold her closely enough.

"Brynna, sweetheart." His voice was rough and unsteady. "I've missed you too. God, I've missed you."

Blinking back tears, she pulled him inside. She'd been in bed before his arrival, so the house was dark and quiet. As soon as the door was locked behind him, she stepped back into his open arms, savoring the warm, so very real feel of him. "Are you okay?" she asked.

He smiled gently. "I'm fine. I've got a lot to tell you."

"You do?" She trembled at the thought of what might yet come.

"Yes. But first—" He kissed her, so deeply, so hotly, so hungrily that she all but melted into his chest. He gloried in her fervent response. "Brynna, we need to talk. But, God, I want you so much."

"Oh, Dan, I want you, too. It seems like so long," she murmured, aching with the need to be loved by him.

Losing all patience, he swept her into his arms, turning toward her bedroom. Brynna locked her hands around his neck and snuggled next to him. They'd talk, she promised herself. She'd tell him all she'd decided in his absence and find out if he'd made any progress in his own soul-searching. But later.

Stopping at her invitingly rumpled bed, Dan hastily untied her robe, slipping it off her shoulders and turning immediately to the tiny buttons of her cotton gown. Then he quickly stripped off his own clothes.

When they were both nude, he reached with unsteady hands to cup her breasts, lifting them as he bent to taste first one, then the other. She tasted so sweet, so fresh. He could never get enough of that particular taste. Nor of the way she gasped and arched to him when he opened his mouth wide to take one hardening tip deep inside. No one had ever responded to him so generously and honestly.

Wanting her so badly he ached, he forced himself to concentrate on her pleasure. He hadn't forgotten the last time they'd made love, when she'd so unselfishly given him the mindless, soothing release he'd needed without asking anything for herself. It was going to be different this time, he decided.

His hand trailed downward, fingers sliding into the downy soft, white-blond curls between her legs. Was there anything softer, silkier than the skin he discovered in that hidden juncture? he wondered. His mouth moved upward to her pulsing throat as his fingers slipped into the dampening folds that welcomed him so hotly.

"Dan," she moaned, clinging to him as she trembled against his hand. "Oh, Dan, I want you so much."

"I'm yours, sweetheart. Forever," he promised, knowing he would have no trouble fulfilling the vow. He belonged more to her than to himself now.

He wanted nothing more than to throw himself on her and let loose the passion boiling inside him. But he was rewarded for his self-control by her breathless cries of pleasure.

As if sensing how fragile his control was at that moment, Brynna slipped a hand between them to close her fingers around his hot, painfully swollen member. Dan shuddered, fighting desperately to hold on. "Ah, babe, don't do that," he muttered between clenched teeth. "I want to make this last."

"I want you. I've missed you so much," she whispered, stroking him, moving shamelessly against him. "Please, Dan. Love me."

"I do. I love you." He tumbled her onto the bed, raining feverish kisses over her cheeks, her throat, her breasts, her stomach. "I love you so much."

Her hands pulled impatiently at his shoulders. "Now, Dan. Please. Now."

It was no use trying to wait any longer. Moaning low in his throat, he surged upward, sliding deep, deep inside her. She closed around him in urgent demand, refusing to allow him to savor, drawing him on with rhythmic undulations that drove him out of his mind. "Brynna!" he gasped, his hips catching her rhythm, then setting an even faster one of his own. "Ah, God, Brynna, I—I love you."

They were the last coherent words he spoke for some time.

For her, they were enough.

Nestled warmly in Dan's arms, Brynna finally whispered the truth that had come to her during the time they'd been apart. "I love you, Dan."

He stiffened and turned her face to his with an unsteady hand. "You're—sure?"

She couldn't help but smile, albeit tremulously. "Yes. I'm sure. But I don't blame you for asking, as wishy-washy as I've been with you."

"I understood your reasons for caution," he told her soberly, though his eyes were gleaming with joy. "You knew there was still too much hanging over us from our pasts. You've come to terms with your fears?"

"Yes," she answered without hesitation. "I made a mistake about my feelings for Russ, about my reasons for marrying him, but I'm not mistaken this time. I love you, Dan. For real, forever."

"Ah, Brynna, if you knew how happy it makes me to hear you say that. I love you, too. For real, forever."

She smiled at his repetition of her words, but the smile faded as she asked, "You've been thinking about your mother? Doing something about the anger and bitterness you've been carrying around for so long?''

"I've been in Chicago."

She was surprised. She hadn't known he'd left town. "Chicago?"

He nodded. "I spent the weekend with my mother. She wants very much to meet you."

"You were with your mother?" she repeated, dumb-founded. Her hand tightened on his bare chest. "How did it go?" she asked anxiously.

"My mother and I will never have an ideal, close rela-tionship. The past can't be erased and it won't be forgot-ten, but we've agreed to put it behind us and go on from here. She seemed pleased with that compromise."

Brynna suspected that Flora had been overjoyed, but she only smiled and reached up to kiss his cheek, their skin sliding intimately, warmly together with the movement. "I'm glad. I'm looking forward to meeting her."

"I did something else while I was gone," Dan said, shifting beneath her, his expression the slightest bit sheep-ish.

"What?" she asked encouragingly, her eyes on his face.

"I visited my father's grave. And I—well, I got some things off my chest. I told him how much I'd loved him, and yet how angry I was that he never told me the truth. I guess you think that's kind of strange."

"No, I don't think that at all. You needed to say those things aloud—to him. Did you feel better afterward?"

"Oddly enough, I did," he admitted. "I must've been in that cemetery for a couple of hours, but when I left I felt more at peace than I've felt in years."

"Then you did the right thing."

"Yeah. I guess." Again, he squirmed, looking away from her then quickly back again. "I'm sorry I haven't called you. I know you must have been worried."

"Yes," she answered candidly. "I was. But I understood."

"I'm sorry," he said again. "I thought it was for the best if I had my head straight before I got back in touch with you. I didn't want to hurt either of us again with my insecurity." He tangled one hand in her hair in a sudden, desperate surge of emotion. "I think I loved you from the moment I saw you, but I couldn't believe you were as wonderful as you seemed. I didn't think anyone could be. I kept looking for flaws, for reasons not to get involved with you—and I couldn't find any. The more time I spent with you, the more addicted I became to you, until finally I couldn't bear the thought of being with anyone else. It scared the hell out of me, Brynna. You know why."

"Yes." She'd learned so much about Dan since that day in the park. She knew now the demons that had been driving him then.

"I guess I knew for sure how far gone I was the night Delia had her baby, when I came for you and found another man here. I still don't know why I didn't explode, but for some reason I trusted you. It was a shock to realize exactly how much I did trust you, and what a risk that sort of trust entailed."

"I know."

"You've made me whole again, Brynna, and happier than I've ever been."

"Oh, Dan. I was as frightened as you were," she whispered, clinging to him. "From the moment we met, you overwhelmed me. I was still so confused, so vulnerable from everything that had happened to me in the past year, that I was terrified I'd misinterpret the feelings you brought out in me. And yet I felt so close to you, so connected to you. I turned to you when I was upset and when I was happy and when I needed comfort. Even when I was afraid of what I felt for you, I needed you. And you were there for me. You taught me so much about myself, in so many different ways. I love you, Dan. I was so foolish to try to deny it."

"Never again," he said, his mouth hovering a breath away from hers. "Never deny your feelings again."

"No," she agreed, leaning forward to close the infinitesimal gap between them. "Nor you."

Dan left early the next morning, telling her he had to get back to work. Still sleepy from the passionate demands of their lovemaking only a few hours before, Brynna murmured a protest that he had to go, making him laugh softly and kiss her tenderly. "Listen to my show when you wake up, okay sweetheart?" he asked, stroking her hair from her face. "It's going to be a special one."

"Okay," she mumbled, only half aware of what he was saying. "See you later."

She slipped back into sleep.

Groaning in protest, Brynna burrowed more deeply into the pillows when the telephone's strident summons demanded her attention a couple of hours later. She frowned, looking at the empty, wrinkled pillow beside her. Had Dan really been with her during the night, or had she only dreamed him? she wondered in hazy disorientation, even as she reached for the telephone. The stiffness in her muscles as she stretched provided her answer. She was smiling smugly when she pressed the receiver to her ear. "Hello?" she murmured, noting the time. Eight-thirty. She'd slept later than she'd intended.

"Brynna? Did I wake you?" The voice was Delia's, bright and disgustingly cheerful.

Brynna smiled, only a little disappointed that the caller wasn't Dan. "Well, yes. I—umm—I didn't sleep very well last night."

"Then I take it you're not listening to the radio."

"No. I was just about to turn it on. Is there something I should know?"

"Well, only if you're interested in hearing our dear Danny making a total ass of himself right on the air."

Brynna reached full wakefulness before Delia finished the sentence. "What's he doing?" she asked, struggling upright.

Delia's voice brimmed with laughter. "I think you'd better turn your radio on. You've got to do something about him."

"Why?" Brynna asked again. "What's he doing?"

"Well, so far this morning, he's played 'Chapel of Love', 'Wedding Bell Blues', 'The Wedding Song' and 'We've Only Just Begun.' I don't know about you, but it sounds to me like he's trying to send someone a message. As a matter of fact, he's mentioned your name a time or two."

Her cheeks going hot, Brynna covered her face with her free hand, her heart pounding. "I think you're right. I'd better turn on my radio."

"Don't you dare forget to invite me to the wedding."

"You'll be one of my bridesmaids," Brynna promised recklessly. "Thanks for calling, Dee."

"I wouldn't have missed this for the world. I'm just so happy for you and Danny," Delia returned softly before hanging up.

"I intend to keep playing these love songs until my lady calls to accept my proposal." Dan was announcing cheerfully as the radio came on. "So if you're listening, Brynna, do the rest of the audience a favor and get on the the phone, will you?''

And then his voice was replaced by the opening notes of ''Happy Together'' by the Turtles.

Laughing and crying all at once, Brynna pulled the telephone into her lap, her fingers trembling as she punched the number that would connect her to Dan. ''Are you crazy?'' she demanded the moment he answered, sounding as if he knew in advance who was calling.

Dan laughed. ''Yeah,'' he agreed rashly. ''Crazy about you. So what are you going to do about it?''

''I'm going to marry you, you idiot. If I don't die of embarrassment first.''

His whoop made it necessary for her to hold the phone away from her ear. '''Atta girl!'' he told her in not particularly romantic approval, making her laugh again.

''When will I see you?'' she demanded impatiently.

''I'll be there later this afternoon,'' he promised. ''And I want you wearing a smile when I get there, you hear?''

''Mmm. And what else?''

''Oh, there's no need to overdress. Just a smile will do,'' he teased.

''I love you, Dan.''

His voice was much more serious when he spoke this time. ''I love you, too, Brynna. I'll see you soon.''

''All right. And Dan?''

''Yeah?''

''Try not to embarrass me any further today, will you?''

He only laughed and hung up.

Not quite trusting him, she left the radio on.

''She called!'' Dan announced the moment the song was over. ''I promised I wouldn't say any more about my proposal, but I think the next song will let you know her answer. You've made me very happy, lady.''

And he played Blood, Sweat and Tears' "You've Made Me So Very Happy."

Brynna danced across her bedroom, still laughing, the tears still rolling down her cheeks. Whatever soul-searching Dan had done during the past few days, he must have reached some very satisfying conclusions. There'd been a deep contentment in his voice, a sure certainty in his typically offbeat marriage proposal. He knew what he was doing, and he was holding nothing back now.

Looking heavenward, Brynna pressed her hands tightly together. "Thank you," she murmured, standing very still for a long moment before rushing to shower and prepare for Dan's arrival.

"That's one beautiful smile you're wearing, sweetheart," Dan told her approvingly when she opened the door in answer to his ring. "But, lovely as it is, the rest of it can go." He meaningfully eyed her soft blue dress as he spoke.

Brynna laughed, feeling herself blushing. "I wasn't about to open the door wearing nothing but a smile," she replied sternly. "Do you know how many people have called me or dropped by today? You could have been just anyone!"

"Got some attention, did we?" he inquired without the least trace of shame.

She rolled her eyes expressively. "Yes, I think you could say we got some attention. Everyone in Haskellville knows we're engaged."

"Good. Now you can't back out."

"I have no intention of backing out," she said, her gaze holding his.

He smiled, the love in his eyes weakening her knees. She was distracted by a sound at their feet. Looking down, she choked on a startled laugh. "Where did *that* come from?" she demanded.

Dan lifted one imperious eyebrow. "*That* is a he. I bought him for you—a little souvenir of our first meeting."

Dropping to her knees, Brynna allowed the shaggy little dog to enthusiastically wash her face with his tongue. He seemed to be delighted with his new owners. The dog looked very much like the one that had brought Dan to the ground in front of her on that spring morning some four months earlier.

"I love him," she said, giggling at the puppy's enthusiasm. "What's his name?"

"Elton."

She laughed. "After my favorite singer. You nut."

"We're keeping him, then?"

She looked up to find him grinning at her, that long, sexy dimple deepening. "You bet we're keeping him. And thanks."

"I have another present for you."

Gently urging the dog to sit still, an impossible task, she stood again. "Another present?" she asked warily, looking around and hoping Elton didn't have a brother.

He reached into his pocket. "Yeah. I hope you like this one as well as you did Elton." His eyes were tender, watchful as he extended his hand.

The ring was incredibly beautiful. The round diamond caught the light and threw it joyfully outward, gaily celebrating its purpose. "Oh, Dan," she whispered, hugging the ring to her chest with both hands.

"Do you like it?" he asked with just a hint of uncertainty.

She slipped it onto her left hand, not surprised that it fit perfectly. And then she threw herself into Dan's arms. "I love it. And you."

He caught her eagerly, one hand at the back of her head to hold her face into his shoulder. "I love you, Brynna. I want to marry you more than I've ever wanted anything in my life. Tell me again that you will."

"Yes," she whispered freeing her face so that she could look up at him with adoring eyes. "Yes."

His mouth covered hers.

Much, much later, Brynna drew back. A smile played on her slightly swollen lips as she led him inside, Elton tugging playfully at his leash as he followed. "Is he housebroken?"

Dan shrugged, his smile rueful. "Probably not. He's pretty young. I got him at the animal shelter. He'd been abandoned."

"Then I think we can assume we have training to do." She didn't care. She loved the little dog. And the man who'd brought him for such a blatantly sentimental reason.

Snuggled together on the couch in her den, they repeated the vows of love they'd made the night before, happily making plans for the future. A future that Dan insisted should include children. "I never realized how much I wanted kids," he admitted sheepishly, "until I saw Chet with Joy. All I could think of was how happy it would make me to have a child with you. It scared me silly at first."

"Not any more?"

He smiled down at her. "Not anymore. Guess I've learned a lot about myself since I fell at your feet, sweetheart."

"Guess so." She leaned into his arms, lifting her face invitingly to his.

He caught his breath, and lowered his head towards hers, his dark eyes burning with awakening desire. As her own body flamed in response, Brynna parted her moistened lips for him, already anticipating the lovemaking she craved so wantonly. It had only been a matter of hours since they'd made love, and it seemed like days.

She blinked and fell back against the couch when she found herself suddenly abandoned.

"Dammit, Elton, not on the carpet!" Dan yelled, diving to make a grab for the puppy.

Brynna watched, head spinning, as Dan made a dash for the back door, Elton dangling from his hands.

She started to laugh in sheer, light-headed joy.

"What did you do with Elton?" Brynna asked shortly afterward, when Dan had returned to the den to snatch her unceremoniously into his arms and carry her into her bedroom.

He grinned down at her, aware that she wasn't protesting his actions, simply asking a question. "I closed him in the kitchen with a bowl of water and lots of newspapers. He was playing with a tennis ball when I left him."

"Where'd you find a tennis ball?"

"There was an unopened can of them in the pantry. I won't ask why you keep tennis balls in the kitchen pantry," he added, concentrating on the buttons closing the front of her dress. He caught his breath as he parted the fabric to reveal the sheer, flimsy material she wore beneath. God, she was beautiful, he thought, sliding the garment off her creamy shoulders.

"I—umm—bought them the last time I went shopping. I must have put them away with the groceries I got at the same time," Brynna answered as she went to work on the snap of his jeans.

Dan lowered her to the bed, pausing to lift her left hand and press an almost reverent kiss on the finger that bore his ring.

She pulled him into her arms. "Love me now," she whispered, a challenge to which he responded quite satisfactorily.

Much later, Dan stirred and tightened his arms around the damp, limp body of the woman he loved. "Marry me soon, Brynna. I don't want to wait."

"Yes, Dan. Very soon," she promised, snuggling into his shoulder as she recovered her strength. "I don't want to wait, either."

Laying his cheek against her impossibly soft hair, he closed his eyes in contentment and wondered what he'd ever done to deserve her. He'd been given another chance at love, and this time he would allow nothing to destroy it.

There was one last problem to be ironed out before the wedding, though Brynna was unaware of it until only a few days before the ceremony. They'd been out for dinner, and she'd discovered, to her surprise, that Dan was having a bit of trouble dealing with her money.

"What does *that* have to do with anything?" she asked, genuinely puzzled, as they talked about it in her den shortly afterward.

"I'll never make a lot of money running a small radio station in a small Missouri town," he answered. "I never aspired to wealth or social position. We'll have to decide how to handle it—who pays what, whose salary goes where, that sort of thing."

Brynna took his face between her hands, gave him her most intimidating glare, and spoke very slowly and concisely. "Money is the least important consideration in our relationship, Dan Westbrook, and I refuse to allow you to make an issue of it. Yes, my parents left me quite well off and yes, I make a nice salary of my own. Yes, I like to live well and take advantage of the little extras that money can buy. Now, do you have any objection to that?''

"Well, I—"

"Good," she interrupted before he could go on. "You may as well resign yourself to wealth and social position, because you take on both when we marry. No one thinks you're marrying me for those reasons, and even if anyone did, I wouldn't care. We are equal partners in this union, Dan, and there's no such thing as yours or mine. Only ours. You got that?''

He grinned in amusement at her uncharacteristically stern tone. "Yes, ma'am.''

"Good," she said again, quite smugly, and then she produced her wedding present to him, a thin, gold watch that looked every bit as expensive as it was.

Dan loved the watch. He struggled with his conscience for maybe ten seconds before clasping it around his wrist to admire it. "It's fantastic," he admitted, rather sheepishly.

"I'm glad you like it. I happen to adore the present you gave me," she answered evenly, hugging the squirming little dog she'd lifted into her lap. "Do you understand now that the money doesn't matter?''

He reached gently over to lift Elton out of her lap and set him on the floor, pushing Brynna backward until she lay flat on the couch. "I can get used to it," he muttered just before he covered her mouth with his. "I love you, Brynna.''

"Show me," she challenged in the spirit of a true Missouri native.

He did. Very thoroughly.

\* \* \*

Mitzi served as matron of honor, her eyes glowing with her renewed joy in her own marriage and with happiness for Brynna. Perry proudly gave the bride away, both of them thinking fondly of her father and how pleased he would have been with the man Brynna had chosen for her second and last husband.

As Brynna had promised, Delia was bridesmaid, fully recovered now from the ordeal of Joy's birth. Chet was best man, and the exuberant couple added life and laughter to the solemn proceedings. Brynna knew she and Dan had friends for life in Chet and Delia. Already she loved them as deeply as Dan did.

The church was filled with well-wishers, people who'd known Brynna since childhood, who were delighted to share in her happiness. The general consensus was that Brynna had chosen very well this time. She couldn't have agreed more.

On the pew reserved for the groom's family, Flora sat wiping tears from her glowing eyes, her smile brilliant as she watched Perry escort the bride down the aisle. Brynna returned her smile warmly. She liked what she'd seen of Dan's mother, though she would never quite forget the pain Dan had suffered because of her. Flora, in turn, was almost pathetically grateful to Brynna for reuniting her with her son, though Brynna had assured the woman repeatedly that it had been solely Dan's decision to make that trip to Chicago.

Finally, Brynna turned her eyes to look at the man who would, in only minutes, be her husband. Dan.

As she took those last steps, a dozen images flashed through her head. Dan in the park, virile and tanned and perspiring from his exercise, smiling up at her from where he'd fallen almost at her feet. Walking hand in hand with her through the park after their picnic lunch. Tall and handsome in his tuxedo the night of Show-Down. Hurting and vulnerable in her arms the night he'd told her about his parents.

And now he waited for her at the altar, his face glowing with love and trust. They'd both learned so much about trust during the past few months.

She laid her hand in his, smiling up at him as his fingers closed tightly around hers.

Though she'd been through a similar ceremony before, Brynna felt all new as she repeated the words that would legally join them as husband and wife. This time she knew with every molecule of her being that she was saying the words for the last time, that she and Dan would be together until death alone parted them. This man was her destiny, her future, despite any mistakes she may have made in the past. Despite any he had made.

The kiss he gave her at the end of the brief ceremony told her that he felt exactly the same way.

They'd chosen to honeymoon in an exclusive resort in the Great Smoky Mountains near Gatlinburg, Tennessee, a vacation area that had been a favorite of Brynna's family during her childhood.

"We're going to have to leave this room, eventually," Dan murmured with a show of reluctance, nibbling on Brynna's ear even as he spoke.

"But why?" she asked lazily, eyes closed as she luxuriated in his caresses.

His hand swept slowly down the length of her bare body, almost distracting her from the conversation. "Well, we've used up two full days of our honeymoon and we haven't seen any of the scenery," he pointed out, lowering his mouth to nuzzle her throat. "You said you wanted to take me sightseeing, show me all the beauty of the area."

"Mmm." Her fingers walked slowly across his chest, pausing to circle one brown nipple. "I did say that, didn't I?"

He pressed a moist kiss to the upper curve of one aroused breast. "Yes. You did."

Her arms going around his neck as she arched into his skillful lovemaking, Brynna sighed blissfully and closed her eyes. "Maybe we'll come back for our first anniversary," she suggested, her voice growing husky. "We'll go sightseeing then."

The smile he gave her was nothing short of piratical. "Don't bet on it," he growled meaningfully.

The only words spoken after that were passionate, mutual vows of love. Neither found any fault with the breathless incoherence of that particular conversation.

\* \* \* \* \*

*Silhouette Romance*

## LONG, TALL TEXANS

### Diana Palmer brings you the second Award of Excellence title
### SUTTON'S WAY

In Diana Palmer's bestselling Long, Tall Texans trilogy, you had a mesmerizing glimpse of Quinn Sutton—a mean, lean Wyoming wildcat of a man, with a disposition to match.

Now, in September, Quinn's back with a story of his own. Set in the Wyoming wilderness, he learns a few things about women from snowbound beauty Amanda Callaway—and a lot more about love.

He's a Texan at heart . . . who soon has a Wyoming wedding in mind!

The Award of Excellence is given to one specially selected title per month. Spend September discovering *Sutton's Way* #670 . . . only in Silhouette Romance.

RS670-1R

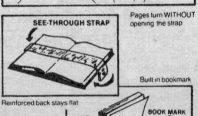

# COMING SOON...

*Indulge a Little*
*Give a Lot*

An irresistible opportunity to pamper
yourself with free* gifts and help a
great cause, Big Brothers/Big Sisters
Programs and Services.

*With proofs-of-purchase plus postage and handling.

## Watch for it in October!

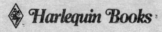 *Harlequin Books*

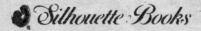 *Silhouette Books*

IND